William Ingraham Kip

The Early Days Of My Episcopate

William Ingraham Kip

The Early Days Of My Episcopate

ISBN/EAN: 9783742813695

Manufactured in Europe, USA, Canada, Australia, Japa

Cover: Foto ©Andreas Hilbeck / pixelio.de

Manufactured and distributed by brebook publishing software
(www.brebook.com)

William Ingraham Kip

The Early Days Of My Episcopate

THE

EARLY DAYS OF MY EPISCOPATE

BY THE

RIGHT REV. WM. INGRAHAM KIP, D.D., LL.D.

BISHOP OF CALIFORNIA

—◁※▷—

NEW YORK
THOMAS WHITTAKER
2 & 3 BIBLE HOUSE
1892

INSCRIBED

BY THE AUTHOR

TO HIS FRIEND AND BROTHER

THE RIGHT REVEREND WILLIAM FORD NICHOLS, D.D.

PREFACE

THIS account of the early days of my episcopate was written in the year 1859–1860, with the intention of bequeathing the manuscript to my family, to be put to press after my life had closed, and when the generation of which it speaks should have passed away.

Thirty-one years have come and gone since then. I live to see the fulfilment of many prophecies it makes the death of many hopes it records.

Beyond the allotted span of years, I meet the new generation that I had made my heirs. With me still are many friends of the olden time, to whose solicitations I yield in sending forth this work unaltered from the shape it took when I sat down to write the story of the early days of the Church in California, to bequeath it—as Lord Bacon, in his will, did his "name and memory" —"to the next ages."

SAN FRANCISCO, *March*, 1891.

CONTENTS.

EARLY DAYS OF MY EPISCOPATE.

I.

THE APPOINTMENT.

My interest in behalf of California had been awakened long before I ever expected to be personally connected with the Church on the Pacific. When I was living in Albany, as Rector of St. Paul's Church, my family physician had a brother-in-law, who was one of the Wardens of Trinity Church, San Francisco. His letters were regularly read to me, until I became acquainted with the history and advancement of the Church in that city.

In 1852, Mr. Mines, the Rector of Trinity Church, died, and the Vestry wrote to friends in the East for a successor. The charge was offered to several persons, and at last to the Rev. Christopher B. Wyatt, Assistant Minister of the Church of the Holy Apostles in New York. About this time, when one day talking with my physician on the subject of California, the question was put to me, I believe by his wife, as if a sudden thought,—" Why would not *you* go ? " The suggestion struck me favorably. I had been fifteen years in Albany,—had built up a large congregation, —and it seemed as if there was no room for progress or enlargement in the future. On the other hand, in San Francisco was a new field,—a rising empire,—and there was a freshness and enterprise in founding the Church in that region which rather fascinated my imagination. I seemed too to be more free from family ties than most clergymen. I had only two children. My eldest son, Lawrence, was a cadet at West Point, so that I had but one living with me, a son not yet fourteen, and if I went, he could accompany us. After discussing the matter, therefore, I almost concluded, that if Mr. Wyatt did not go, I would.

Shortly afterwards, I received a call to St. Peter's Church, Baltimore, vacant by the removal of Dr. (since Bishop) Atkinson, to Grace Church. I determined not to accept it, but having occasion the next week to visit Baltimore, to lecture before some association, I deferred my answer till then. On the afternoon of my arrival, I called on my old friend Bishop Whittingham. As I entered his study, he greeted me with—

" Well, I hope you have not come here to tell me you are not going to St. Peter's ! "

I answered him that such was my decision, and then we talked it over. In the course of our conversation I mentioned, incidentally, that if Mr. Wyatt did not accept the call to San Francisco it would be offered to me, and that I was strongly disposed to go. Bishop Whittingham seemed to catch at this as suggesting new thoughts. He looked down a moment, and then said in his rapid, impressive way:

" I've new light ! I've new light ! You must go to California, but not as a Presbyter. You must go out in another capacity. If you'll go to California, I'll pardon you for not coming to St. Peter's ! "

This was the germ of the California Episcopate. Here was

the first suggestion of what afterwards developed into a plan which has changed my whole life. From this conversation grew up the idea of sending out a Missionary Bishop, and with this, my name, through Bishop Whittingham's suggestions, became necessarily connected. Subsequently, Mr. Wyatt determined to accept the call to San Francisco, and sailed in April, 1853; so that the idea of my going as a Presbyter was abandoned and I had nothing to do but remain quiet and await the leadings of Providence.

In October, 1853, the General Convention met in New York, and the subject of Episcopal supervision for California was a prominent matter before it for discussion. Some time before, the Convocation in California had formed itself into a Diocese, and the question at issue was, whether, as Missionary Bishops, by Canon VIII. of 1844, are elected "to exercise Episcopal functions in States or Territories *not organized into Dioceses*," one could legally be appointed for California. The House of Bishops, after a long debate, determined, as they had not yet received California into union with the Convention or recognized it as a Diocese, to ignore its formation and treat it entirely as Missionary ground.

I was accordingly nominated by my old friend Bishop Wainwright. Bishop Williams told me afterwards that the talk which ensued was exceedingly amusing. My qualifications were freely discussed, then those of my wife; then our parents were talked over, and finally they got back to our grandparents, showing a belief in inherited traits rather unusual in this country. Some of the Bishops who were afraid my Churchmanship was rather too elevated in its character, proposed to Bishop Alonzo Potter (of Pennsylvania) to nominate a distinguished Presbyter of his Diocese. This, though a strong friend of mine, he felt obliged to do, and the vote was taken. It stood twenty for me, and six for the Rev. Dr. ——. Bishop Potter then himself moved that it be unanimous, which was passed. I would here mention, that on my arrival in New York, a few days afterwards, Dr. —— (the other candidate), came to me with his warm congratulations, and assured me that his name was used entirely without his knowledge or consent. He has since been elected to one of our largest eastern Dioceses.

At the same session, the Rev. F. T. Scott, D.D., of Georgia, was nominated as Missionary Bishop of Oregon and Washington Territories.

Both these nominations were at once forwarded to the House of Clerical and Lay Deputies, where they met with some opposition. The point with regard to California was the constitutional difficulty which had already been mooted in the House of Bishops. With regard to Oregon and Washington Territories, it was thought by many that the appointment was premature. Both were, however, confirmed by a large majority.

On the same day I received several telegraphic messages from New York, informing me of the result and urging me to come down at once. The next morning's mail brought a shower of congratulatory letters from my friends among the Bishops, and I accordingly departed for New York.

I confess, this matter came upon me as a surprise. Although it had been so much talked about for the last few months, I had doubted to the last moment whether any decided action would be taken by the House of Bishops.

Before this, too, going to California was a thing to dream about ; now, it became a reality, and for the first time there was forced upon me the consideration of how much I should leave behind. Again, going as a Presbyter was a different matter, as I could at any time resign and return. But, going as a leader in "the consecrated host of God's elect," seemed engaging in a contest from which there could be no retreat. Upon talking to Bishop Whittingham he said:—"You must go. They should have had a Bishop in California three years ago, and if you do not go now, they will not have one for three years to come. The House of Bishops is breaking up, and we cannot elect any one else. The responsibility of this will rest upon you."

This was in fact summing up the matter. There was no room for hesitation or discussion on my part. After twenty-six Bishops had said it was my duty to go, all I could do was to assent.

II.

WHEN I look back to the election and consecration, everything seems to me like a dream. The consecration was over before I had recovered from the first effects of the surprise produced by the election.

When I reached New York, I found the House of Bishops on the point of adjourning. They had been in session about three weeks and each one was impatient to get home to his Diocese. They insisted, therefore, on the consecration at once taking place. In fact, so hurried was this matter, that I never received any official notice of my election nor did I in any way send an acceptance. The Bishops talked to me as if my going were taken for granted, and they acted accordingly.

Our Presiding Bishop,—Brownell of Connecticut,—from his age and growing infirmities, was too much exhausted by the long sitting of the House to officiate at the consecration. As I was to be the first Missionary Bishop sent to the Pacific, he appointed to act as consecrator in his place, Bishop Kemper, the first Missionary Bishop ever elected in our Church. It was an arrangement very agreeable to my

6

own views and feelings, as Bishop Kemper had always been a strong friend of mine; but it was attended with one disadvantage. As the senior Bishop present must consecrate, it prevented all those who were above Bishop Kemper on the list from being present. Bishop Hopkins (Vermont), Doane (New Jersey), and Otey (Tennessee), with a number of others, were obliged to absent themselves, though in the city.

The consecration was appointed to take place in Trinity Church, New York, the next week, on October 28th, the Festival of St. Simon and St. Jude. The Bishops who took part in the services were, Kemper (Wisconsin), A. Lee (Delaware), Boone (Foreign Missionary Bishop to China), Freeman (Arkansas), Burgess (Maine), Upfold (Indiana), Whitehouse (Illinois), and Wainwright (New York). Besides these, two clergymen were present from our mother Church of England, and read the lessons. These were the Venerable Archdeacon Trew, of Nassau, West Indies, and Edmund Hobhouse, Fellow of Merton College, Oxford, since appointed Bishop of Nelson in New Zealand. The presentation of the candidate was to have been made by my old friends, Bishops Whittingham and Wainwright. The former, however, was too ill to leave his room, and Bishop Upfold was substituted. Bishop Brownell appointed, to deliver the sermon, my brother-in-law, Bishop Burgess of Maine. His discourse was from I Thess. i. 5—"For our Gospel came not unto you in word only, but also in power, and in the Holy Ghost, and in much assurance, as ye know what manner of men we were among you for your sake." From this eloquent production I must make two extracts. The first is his description of California:—

"In this foremost temple of the great mart and metropolis of this new western world, we are assembled for a work which cannot be without fruit in distant regions. From this spot, and from the act which we are now to accomplish, the course, if Providence favors it, is straight to the Golden Gate which opens towards eastern Asia. He who shall enter there as the first Protestant Bishop, will see before him the land which is the treasure house of this Republic. Behind it are the vales and rivers and snowy mountains, which are to our far west the farther west, and amidst them lie the seats of that abominable and sensual impiety, the cry of which goes up to heaven, like that of Sodom and Gomorrah, from the valley of the Dead Salt Sea. Still beyond spread the deserts which divide, but will not long divide, the Christians of this continent. Upon the edge of this vast field he will stand when he shall place his foot on the shore of the Pacific. There he is to labor, and there, in the common course of Providence, are to be his life-long abode and his grave. There he is to be occupied in laying the foundations of a Church which must be a pillar and ground of the truth for wide lands and for unborn millions. While it retains and upholds the doctrine and the discipline of the Apostles, it must pre-eminently shine as a city set on an hill, and as a light of the world. Few of the issues can he live to witness. But, in the years to come, if years are given him, he must recall the prospects which opened upon him in this hour, and again when he saw the coast of that Western Ocean."

The other is the conclusion,—the address to the candidate—which draws a picture of the difficulties to be encountered, which each year has since realized:—

"And now, my dear brother, now, more than ever before, this work is to be made yours, with the highest responsibilities, the largest sphere, the most various tasks, and I will not refrain from adding, the most peculiar perils. It is not the Episcopate alone, nor the Missionary Episcopate alone. It is an Episcopate to be exercised where fellow laborers are still to be gathered; where seminaries are yet to be founded; where congregations are mostly to be begun. There is no past on which you can lean; and it is more than possible that around you will be little of that support which we need and find among the incitements and encouragements of well-established Christian communities. The minister of Christ whose charge is remote and lonely, must walk with God, or sink into spiritual slumber; for no mortal aid will fan continually the flame upon his inward altar. You go where thirst for gold, impatience of restraint, the vices of adventurers, and all the ills of unavoidable lawlessness, have been before you; where the softening and instructive influences of old age and of childhood, can, as yet, be little known, and where female piety throws but a small measure of its familiar light over the surface and the heart of society. A lover of the world, a pleaser of men, a reed shaken by the wind, has nowhere his place among the standard bearers of Christ; but least of all, on such an outpost, beleaguered by such temptations. But of the scene of your labors you will soon know much more than any of us now understand from afar. There is one armor, and but one, which will prepare you both to defend your own soul, and to carry forward the banner of Christ and of His Church. Many prayers ascend for you in this house; they can ask for you nothing so needful and so precious as an humble, steadfast, upright heart in every change; for simplicity and godly sincerity will bear you through all safe and successful. Of all things which are at war with these, I say to you, in the name of the Church which sends you, and in the words of the Apostle to an ancient Bishop,—'O man of God, flee these things, and follow after righteousness, godliness, faith, love, patience, meekness. Fight the good fight of faith; lay hold on eternal life whereunto thou art also called, and hast professed a good profession before many witnesses. I give thee charge in the sight of God, and before Jesus Christ, that thou keep this commandment without spot, unrebukable, until the appearing of our Lord Jesus Christ.' We shall part at the table of our Saviour, we who are assembled here from such various and distant portions of His vineyard. My dear brother, when the whole length and breadth of our vast country shall lie between you and some who are nearest to your heart; when it shall seem to you almost as if the grave had separated you from those to whom you have so long ministered; feel that you are beloved; feel that you are remembered in daily and nightly prayers; feel that the whole Church accompanies you with its eager hopes; and be strong and watch over your deeds and words and thoughts; that through the grace of the Holy Spirit, you may be blameless and faithful to the end, and that the word of God may have free course and be glorified. And when all saints shall be gathered at last, to sit down with Apostles and with patriarchs in the Kingdom of Heaven, may we and many for whom we labor, be numbered among those who shall come thither from the east and from the west ! "

The day opened with a driving rain storm, which continued through the morning. At noon, however, it cleared and the sun came out brightly. The *Church Journal* gave the following beautiful account of this change:—

"The weather was exceedingly unpleasant during the early part of the morning, but after the consecration of the Bishop, and as the Communion office was proceeding, the clouds broke away, and a gleam of tinted sunshine fell upon the altar and lighted up the sanctuary. This was beautifully illustrative of the history of the Church in California. The beginnings have long been overcast with storms and clouds, overhung with darkness and gloom. But now that a Bishop has been consecrated for her, and clergy will flock with him to labor in the desolate places of that spiritual wilderness, we doubt not that the clouds will ere long break, and roll away, and the All-glorious Sun of Righteousness will shine cheeringly upon a land abundantly bringing forth her increase."

III.

So anxious were the Bishops for me to reach my field of labor, that they pressed my immediate departure. I found it, however, no easy work to break up all the plans of a lifetime and to prepare to go out to an entirely strange land; yet less than a month was devoted to this. I was obliged to spend the next week in a rapid visit to St. James' College, Maryland, where I had promised to deliver the address before the Literary Societies, the Commencement having been postponed to this late period on account of sickness during the summer. It, however, added much to the pleasure of the journey to have the company of my friend Mr. Hobhouse. Then came two weeks of labor and packing at Albany, with the pain of an auction that dispersed old familiar household treasures which I could not take with me. Then the leave-taking and the farewell sermon, and on Monday I turned my back upon what had been my home for fifteen years. Two days' visit to West Point, to take leave of my son Lawrence,—a few days at New Haven, at Mrs. Hillhouse's, where my wife was enabled to meet with most of her family,—and we went to New York to sail. My last clerical duty was on Sunday morning, the

12

18th, when, in Trinity Church, New York, I preached an ordination sermon for Bishop Wainwright.

Tuesday, Dec. 20th, found me on board the steamer *George Law,* with my wife and my son Willie. Troops of friends were about us to say farewell, and with some it was our last meeting in this world. Before a year had passed, three of them had gone. Among those who stood with me in the cabin, were Bishop Wainwright and the Rev. Charles W. Halsey, Rector of Christ Church, New York, and a member of the Committee for Domestic Missions. In a few months both of these were in their graves, while my old colleague in Albany, Dr. Horatio Potter, who was then with them, was sitting in Bishop Wainwright's seat. Another, too, who was there, the Rev. J. H. Hanson, was also shortly numbered with the dead. He had come on board to hand me his volume of " The Lost Prince " (in defence of the claims of Eleazur Williams to be the Bourbon), which had that day issued from the press. The weather was dark and gloomy,—a few inches of snow had fallen, and was lying half melted on the ground,—no sunshine lighted it up, the air was raw and chilly, with a leaden sky above,—and everything seemed in unison with our feelings.

At two P. M. the steamer fired her gun, and the last cable which bound us to the wharf was thrown off. As we slowly glided out into the stream, and saw sorrowing relatives and friends standing on the wharf and waving their last adieus, we felt that our ties to home were broken and we were fairly under way. It is easy to talk of severing the associations of a lifetime, and going forth to seek a new home, " not knowing the things that shall befall us there"; but when it comes to the actual reality, and we catch our last view of the faces of friends sorrowing because they may see us no more, it becomes something widely different. Yet the die was cast, and we could only look to the shadowy future.

At five P. M. the engine was stopped for a few moments, and a small boat came alongside to take the pilot off to his own little vessel, which was dancing on the waves a short distance from us. Our steamer had previously been searched, and tickets shown to find out those who had smuggled themselves on board. This is a necessary precaution before we get to sea, particularly in these California vessels, as so many, when funds are wanting, are willing to adopt any measures to get to the land of gold. Two or three poor wretches were detected and sent back in the pilot's boat. As they were handed—not in the most gentle manner— over the side of the steamer, we were aroused by terrific shrieks, and found they proceeded from a poor German who was being forced into the boat. He shouted and yelled and clung to the railing, and in all my life I never saw such a picture of agony and despair as was depicted on his ghastly face. "I paid de ship; oh, mine goots, mine goots, I leave mine goots. Mine comrade, mine comrade!" he shrieked. "Put him off," sternly shouted the captain. But just as his last hold was being unclasped by the sailors, there was a rush through the crowd, and another German appeared, holding out a ticket. It was the missing document, just in time to save him. It seemed that both their names had been placed on the same ticket, which was in charge of his comrade, the clerk had not noticed it, and their ignorance of English prevented them from making the proper explanations. No wonder he shrieked, when his " goots " were on board, and he was about to be sent back to New York without friends or means.

The first evening was dreary enough. It was excessively cold, and there was no fire. Upon appealing to one of the black waiters in behalf of the ladies, he gave us the comforting reply—" No fire aboard dis ship, 'cause you be warm in two days." There were about seven hundred passengers, the majority of them a very rough set. In fact it cannot be otherwise, as most of those who flock to California from all parts of the world are mere adventurers. The unavoidable confusion of this crowd contrasts badly with the order and propriety of our vessels to Europe. There are about a hundred and fifty first cabin passengers. As soon as they have finished a meal, the second cabin passengers pour in to get theirs at the same table.

Then, too, there are thieves who go up and down in these steamers for the purpose of stealing. The returning Californians, who are supposed to be well supplied with gold, are their particular victims. There is necessity, therefore, for the most vigilant police. On the second day out, a passenger's trunk was opened and rifled. The key was found in the steerage, and a man whom a waiter had seen at two o'clock in the morning in the first cabin was arrested. He was stripped and examined by the captain and purser, but nothing was found to convict him. The next day, the mate arrested a steerage passenger who was loading his revolver, as he said, to shoot another. The pistol was confiscated and the man informed that if he indulged in amusements of that kind, he should have summary justice executed upon him.

In the first few days we had the most remarkable run I have ever seen at sea. There were scarcely any waves or wind, and everything about us was as calm as it could have been on the Hudson river, presenting no possible inducements to sea-sickness. Our progress has averaged about two hundred and twenty miles a day. On board of a ship " one day telleth another." We lounge in the cabin, try to read, and walk on the deck. A few, who have the *entrée* of Captain McGowan's pleasant stateroom on deck, gather there, and hear from the old Californians wonderful stories of the terrors of crossing the Isthmus. It is strange how soon we get up a home feeling in the vessel and all its associations become familiar. There is, however, an entire monotony. Mrs. Osgood, I believe it is, says, the only two things which vary life at such a time are—

" Sometimes we ship a sea, alas! and sometimes see a ship."

We went, one morning, under the direction of the Captain, on an exploring expedition through the ship. We descended by the narrow iron stairs story after story, until we got below the surface of the water. There were the immense boilers, and all around us the massive machinery working as smoothly and quietly as possible, seeming, in the results they produced, to be the very triumph of human ingenuity. The two engines cost about $80,000. Thence we went down into the crowded steerage. There, open berths are ranged on each side, and they struck us, particularly when we reached the tropics, as decidedly more comfortable than our closed staterooms. Open portholes at the sides and gratings above give air and light, while, owing to the assiduous care of Mr. Howard, the first mate, perfect cleanliness prevails. I noticed life preservers hanging on every side, of which the Captain told me there were eight hundred on board. The whole place, too, seemed vocal with music. There was a German who had several hundred canary birds in small cages, which he was taking out to San Francisco, where they will bring very high prices.

The first cabin presents a curious appearance, of an evening when the sea is quiet and all can be out. Dispersed along the tables, which stretch the whole length of the cabin, are perhaps a hundred men playing cards, though all gambling is strictly forbidden. Many more passengers, male and female, are scattered about, talking or trying to read while a musician who has placed his notes on the table is practising on the violin as coolly as if he were in his own room alone. By ten o'clock, however, all is quiet in the cabin, for no lights are permitted, after that hour, in the staterooms.

Friday noon found us exactly in the latitude of St. Augustine, and the air gave proof that we were rapidly drawing near to the tropics. The little stove in the Captain's room (the only one, by the way, in the ship), has been taken down, and to-day the awnings are to be put up. Overcoats are discarded, and the decks present a summer scene.

The Festival of the Nativity dawned upon us as beautiful a day as the imagination could conceive. There seemed scarcely a ripple on the sea, and not a steamboat on the Hudson, in the month of June, passes over a smoother surface. At 8 o'clock we made our first land, the little Island of Maraguana, exactly as the Captain had predicted. At ten o'clock arrangements were made on the quarter-deck for service, and I read the prayers of the Church and gave them a Christmas sermon. We had a large congregation, though very few Church people. It was pleasant to be able thus, on the wide sea, to observe this Festival, and, while we knew many prayers were offering up for us at home, to send forth ours for the faithful everywhere. In the afternoon I went forward to the steerage, and by means of a colporteur, who was distributing tracts, arranged a service. The passengers crowded around me in a circle, and listened to the prayers I read and the address I made them, which, with many, I fear, is the last they will ever hear on that subject. About a hundred and fifty are going out as laborers on the Panama Railroad, and half of them, before six months have passed, will be in their graves. I pressed on them this contingency as fully as I could, and gave notice if any of them wished to see me during the voyage, either for advice or in sickness, to send for me and I would go to them.

The days now are growing longer. At half-past six the sun had just set, and the west was covered with golden clouds. The air was as warm as June, and in the evening the passengers were all gathered on deck, the brilliant constellations in this southern sky rendering it as bright as moonlight. And thus closed the Festival, as pleasant a day as could be spent, were it not for the consideration of absence from those we hold dear.

Monday, 26th. Hot—hot! We passed the point of Cuba in the night, and are now within sight of the hills of San Domingo. A steamer is seen on the distant horizon, which the Captain decides to be the *Yankee Blade*, that left when we did. Flying fish are rising from the ocean about us, and every one on board is giving evidence of the effects of a tropical atmosphere. Reading is hard work, and writing harder. In the afternoon we made Jamaica, and until dark were running along the coast near enough to see the trees and houses. It is a bold, mountainous region, similar in appearance, we were told, to the Sandwich Islands. The eminences were wreathed at the top with clouds, while a purple light from the setting sun rested on the beautiful slopes. At six P. M. a canoe came off and put on board a half-naked negro pilot. We were then about forty miles from Kingston. At nine o'clock we reached the entrance of the harbor, the remains of the old city of Port Royal, destroyed many years ago by an earthquake. A couple of rockets thrown up brought off the health officer and custom house official to discharge their duties, and then we anchored for the night.

Sunday, 27th. At daylight we had before us the prospect of this beautiful scenery, the high mountains back, and the old city on a plateau at their base. The steamer weighed anchor at six o'clock and went in three miles to the wharf. The groups of cocoanut trees with their tufted tops made picturesque features as they rose out of the gardens of the city. Our first visitors were troops of negroes, who plunged into the water to swim round the ship and dive for coins thrown to them, a performance in which they never failed to be successful, coming up with the money in their mouths. In company with a few friends, I went on shore and took breakfast at the hotel. In that delightful atmosphere, before the coolness of the morning had gone off, the breeze blowing in through the open windows, our breakfast of coffee, rolls, eggs and oranges was a perfect luxury after a week at sea.

Kingston has an antique air, and at the same time marks of a visible decay. The houses are all alike, with large piazzas and every contrivance for avoiding heat. Nothing, however, but the arrival of a steamer infuses any life into the place. The streets are crowded with the most wretched looking negroes to be seen on the face of the earth. Lazy, shiftless, and diseased, the men will not work since the Manumission Act has freed them. Even coaling the steamer is done by women. About a hundred march on board in a line, with tubs on their heads (tub and coal together weighing about ninety pounds), and with a wild song empty them into the hold. The men work a day, and then live for a week on its wage. The depth of degradation to which the negro population has sunk, is, we were told, indescribable. The inhabitants of Sodom were pure compared with them. "Once," said a gentleman to me, "you did not see an untidy negro in the streets. Now, look at them!"—pointing to a group of squalid wretches. This is the unvarying testimony of the residents.

Everything about the streets has a very tropical appearance. Turbaned negro women are everywhere, offering for sale the greatest profusion of fruits. We took a carriage to drive into the country, stopping on our way at the Parish Church, which happened to be open. It is a venerable building in the form of a cross, the walls and pavement covered with monuments of the old aristocracy of the island, or of British officers who had died here. The Rector, the Rev. Dr. Stewart, had not yet arrived for service, but the sexton, having learned my name, in-

formed him of our visit, and, just before we sailed, he came
down to the steamer to see me. It was too late, however,
to go on board, and he was obliged to merely send me his
card.

Just beyond the city is a fair country house, once occupied by Santa Anna during one of his temporary exiles from
Mexico. The barracks, too, where the West India Regiment
is quartered, are near the city. The Regiment is composed
of negroes under the command of British officers. The
privates, with their black faces and crimson uniforms, made
a curious appearance.

We drove out to the residence of the Bishop, Aubrey
George Spencer. He is a grandson of Lord Spencer and
a descendant of the great Duke of Marlborough. Both the
Bishop and his brother, the late Bishop of Madras, had
visited the States, where I had become acquainted with
them. His residence is about four miles from the city, and is
the most beautiful place in the neighborhood. It was purchased by the government for an Episcopal residence, but
has been given up by the Bishop for a college. I regret-
ted to find he was absent for health at his place farther
up the mountains, as it would have afforded me pleasure
to renew our acquaintance. The Rev. W. Hanford, of the
college, was there, who received us with the utmost cordiality, and with whom we spent a pleasant half-hour.

The summer houses differ only in size. They have
broad verandahs, and the luxuriant gardens are often
fenced in with cactus, twelve feet high. The roads were
crowded with negro women on their way to market, their
fruit carried in large baskets on their heads, or on little
donkeys driven before them. On our way through town we

stopped to see our consul, Col. Harrison. The old gentleman, now eighty-four years of age, is, perhaps, the only man
living who had a commission from Washington. He is a
cousin of the late President Harrison, his room-mate at
school, and commissioned with him in the army. When
fifteen years of age, as he told us, being in England, he was
pressed for a sailor, and remained for several years on
British ships of war. At last, in the Mediterranean, there
came an old Admiral, who, before the Revolution, when
stationed on our coast, had been entertained by his family in
Virginia. Young Harrison made himself known to him, and
was at once released and restored to his country. He had
now passed more than half a century in the West Indies.
Last year he visited New York, after an absence of fifty-two
years. What a change must he have witnessed! It was
like dropping down on a new planet.

The *Star of the West*, which left when we did, has just
come in. She goes to San Juan for her passengers to take
the Nicaragua route. I went on board of her, but found no
familiar face. Among her passengers was Thomas Francis
Meagher, one of the expatriated Irish patriots, who, we
heard, was quietly shut up in the Captain's office. Being
on British ground, it was advisable for him not to leave the
protection of our flag. He is to deliver in San Francisco
a course of lectures on the Irish Orators.

We have an accession of passengers. Fifty coolies, imported into Kingston from the East Indies, to work in
place of the negroes, are going to labor on the Panama
Railroad. Poor fellows! they will probably soon find their
graves. At two o'clock the gun again fired, and, as before,
we swept out into a smooth and summer sea.

December 29th.   For two days we have been sailing over the Caribbean Sea. How the very name brings up the stories I read in my boyhood of the exploits of the bold buccaneers in these waters!   The north star, night after night, is sinking in the heavens, while on the edge of the horizon, toward morning, we see the brilliant Southern Cross—that emblem of our salvation—gemmed on the skies, on which the old Spanish Cavaliers gazed with such mysterious awe. To-night we expect (D. V.) to reach Aspinwall.

IV.

PASSAGE OF THE ISTHMUS.

WE entered the harbor of Aspinwall late at night (Dec. 29th), and at sunrise next morning, from the vessel's deck, had the whole landscape before us. It is a beautiful bay, with a little straggling settlement of one street which curves round in a semi-circle parallel to the edge of the water. The steamers formerly landed at Chagres, nine miles distant; but this place has been substituted for it, because at Chagres they were obliged to anchor some distance from the shore, and landing in boats was not only difficult, but also dangerous in stormy weather. Aspinwall has therefore grown up at once, as a depot. It consists merely of a few wooden hotels with imposing names, and residences for those connected in any way with the steamer and railroad companies. Thick forests hem in the line of houses, and cocoanut trees with their high tufts wave over them and grow to the water's edge. It presents a beautiful scene, and no one, in the warm and balmy atmosphere which was so grateful to us that morning—looking forth on the deep green foliage, the golden sunlight bathing everything, and the clear waters rippling to the shore—would imagine that the air is loaded with miasma.

24

Yet so it is, and, for health, it enjoys a reputation equal to that of the coast of Africa. It is impossible, I believe, for any one to reside here even for a few weeks, without being prostrated by the fever, and sometimes a few days' detention, waiting for the steamer, will be sufficient to impart it to the passengers.

When steamers stopped at Chagres, passengers were poled up the river Chagres to Cruces, against a rapid current, often taking three or four days, though they could descend in a few hours. Now, the Panama Railroad, which begins at Aspinwall, has partly obviated this difficulty. It extends about twenty-five miles, and by next autumn is expected to be carried through to Panama. When this is done, one of the greatest inconveniences of a passage to California will be over. The difficulty now is, not only the risk and trouble of getting yourselves over the Isthmus, but also your baggage. The safest plan is to send it from New York by express. This, however, is expensive, costing from forty cents upward a pound, from New York to San Francisco. Then it is necessary that all articles liable to be injured by water, such as silk dresses and papers, should be enclosed in a tin box with the top soldered in and with a light wooden covering; for the mules, in crossing from Cruces to Panama, will sometimes lie down in the water, and before they can be forced up, trunks are saturated. A person named Hinckley had recently established an express from ship to ship, that is, from Aspinwall to Panama. He charged twelve cents a pound, and it was probably the best and safest way for travellers to get their personal effects through. He sold transit tickets for the Isthmus, including railroad, boat and mule tickets, for thirty dollars each. Our whole expenses in crossing the Isthmus, including hotel charges at Cruces, Panama, etc., were about fifty dollars for each individual. This was probably the fair average.

The *El Dorado* from New Orleans and the *Yankee Blade* from New York came in, a few hours after we did. After a bad breakfast on the steamer, we prepared to leave Aspinwall. The train started at nine A.M., and that morning it consisted of eleven passenger cars. The road leads through an unbroken forest, part of it a wet marsh, but everywhere something new to us from the luxuriance of tropical vegetation. The cocoanut, palm, and date trees were about us, while occasionally there was some giant of the forest which looked as if it had been attaining its growth since Columbus discovered the country. Many of them were draped with vines to the top, while the whole formed a dense thicket, which seemed impenetrable. Beautiful flowers occasionally bloomed in the forest; so that there was nothing to remind us that it was the end of December. Every few miles we found ourselves on the banks of the Chagres River, which winds round into all sorts of twistings. Now and then we passed a native hut. It was always thatched with straw, sometimes without any sides, perfectly open, or else with sides of light bamboo only. The natives were lounging about, or reclining in their hammocks, almost naked, fine specimens of the *dolce far niente.* Occasionally, too, we saw groups of the Irish, who were employed as workmen on the railroad. They looked pale and miserable, and reminded me of the wretched peasantry seen in the vicinity of the Pontine Marshes in Italy. It is almost certain death to them to be employed here, and we were told that every foot of the road, so far as it has been finished, has cost the life of a laborer, and yet they are coming out by hundreds to complete it.

At some little hamlet of the natives, between Barbacos and Gorgona, the railroad at present ends. Here passengers were discharged on the top of a high, steep, muddy bank of the Chagres River. This was "confusion worse confounded," and passengers, trunks, express bales and all, were tumbled down to the river in a miscellaneous mass. Here was lying a number of boats and barges of various forms, in which we were to embark. Our own was a broad, flat-bottomed boat, holding about thirty-five persons, with a low, wooden awning over it, so that there was just room to sit upright. On the outside was a broad ledge, on which our six native boatmen walked up and down from the bows to the stern, as, singing a monotonous song, they poled the boat up the river. They were naked, but for a little cotton cloth around the loins. The distance was nine miles, and we were nearly five hours in accomplishing it; for the current was strong, and often we seemed to make scarcely any progress. The scenery, however, was wild and splendid, though the animal life which once abounded has gone. The waters were formerly filled with alligators, that basked in the sun, and the overhanging trees gay with parrots and monkeys, chattering among the branches; but the rush of Americans through this route, with the constant discharge of their revolvers, has frightened them into other retreats.

As on the railroad, we saw nothing but native huts, and frequently passed women washing clothes on the banks. After travelling about three miles, we reached Gorgona.

This is the dividing point from which the other route is made. From Gorgona there is a road to Panama, but at this season it is hardly passable for mud, and travellers are generally obliged to take that by Cruces, which is twenty-three miles long.

Between five and six o'clock we came within sight of Cruces, and were beginning to felicitate ourselves on our journey's end, when the owner of the boat, who is called the *patrone*, discovered that two or three of the passengers had not paid. (They had in fact been directed by Hinckley to take the boat and settle with him afterwards.) He therefore took advantage of this and demanded of them more than double the ordinary fare. This they of course refused to pay, when he quietly stopped his boat on the opposite shore, within a quarter of a mile of the town, and there we lay. No attention was paid to the remonstrances of the thirty passengers who had tickets, and for nearly an hour, with the miasma of the evening gathering around us, we were kept there, jeered at by the other boats as they passed. Had there been a less respectable company on board, he would have been pitched into the river and the boat poled over; but it was filled with ladies and gentlemen, who finally made a contribution and complied with his extortionate demand.

We reached Cruces just at evening, to find that, in addition to our own shipload of several hundreds, the hamlet was crowded with returning Californians on their way over from Panama. Cruces has a population of a few hundred natives and mongrels, all the original houses being the usual thatched bamboo huts. There is an old dilapidated stone Church, built two centuries ago by their Spanish conquerors, now fast falling to decay. At one end of the town a wooden tavern has been hastily run up. It has no glass in the windows, and is about as enticing in appearance as the long shanties erected for Irish laborers. This was our only stopping place. We found it filled with hundreds of ruffians, and with great trouble secured for the ladies a place upstairs containing half a dozen beds. Here, they had at least a partial retirement, though the noise within and without forbade all sleep. The lower story was filled with long tables, which were spread again and again for a succession of dinners, where very many, with oaths and imprecations, as they struggled for their places, got what they could at one dollar each. The only chance for the decent portion was to get together at one end, and procure something to eat, if possible. I have taken my meals in many queer places when travelling, but I confess never before under such repulsive circumstances. The company, the conversation, the dirt, formed a union which, to the ladies particularly, was appalling.

But the worst was to come. At bedtime the gentlemen of the party were shown to a large garret. The walls were covered with wooden bunks three tiers high, two more rows through the centre, and the intervals filled with cots. On each of these cots and bunks was a single sheet, (which looked as if it had been used for a year), no bed, but a pillow without any case. Here we were to sleep with some two hundred others, of the class we saw downstairs. We threw ourselves down in our clothes, but sleep was out of the question. All around us was one wild confusion, kept up through the night. I have heard sailors talk in the forecastle, and prisoners in the galleys, " but never aught like this." There were not only the most awful blasphemies that human ingenuity could devise, but the most foul-mouthed ribaldry that could be conceived by a perverted imagination. They called each other "Texas," and "Red River," etc., showing which parts of the country had the honor of claiming our associates. A party would rise from their beds, and, under the dim lanterns which hung from the beams, produce their brandy-bottles, and with oaths drink until they reeled again to their bunks. Then a man would treat the assembly to a tune on his fiddle, which was followed by a round of applause, including all the low slang calls of the pit and gallery. To make matters worse, next to us was a pen (I can call it nothing else,) of boards about ten feet high, intended to afford a private room for females. This happened to be occupied by some "women of the baser sort," whose loud ribaldry infinitely amused the kindred spirits on our side of the partition, who accordingly replied to them in the same terms. Altogether, I set down that scene as more like Pandemonium than anything I had ever before witnessed. It was enough to convince one of the doctrine of total depravity.

We endured it till about midnight, when my son and I rose and wandered downstairs. Here, every place was full, men sleeping on benches and under tables, till about one o'clock, when a tremendous noise arose out of doors. There was a rush, then were heard shouts and blows, and oaths in Spanish, all ending in a regular fight which drew every one to the doors and windows. It was the arrival of some hundreds of mules, which were to take on the express. It took an hour to load and get them off. At this time, too, in one of the native houses near, a *fandango* was going on, and singing and the music of castinets were united with the other noises that "murdered sleep." We secured some chairs in which to sit, and thus passed the night at Cruces.

At three o'clock in the morning the tables were again spread, and then commenced a succession of breakfasts, lasting till all the assembled company had gone, some to Panama and some to Aspinwall. At daylight we called the ladies and paid our bill,—one dollar apiece lodging for those who had bunks, and two dollars each for the ladies who were in the *private* rooms. The evening before, we had selected one of the most decent native houses, and made a contract for breakfast for five persons for six dollars, stipulating particularly for a clean table cloth. Our host performed his part well, and we felt better prepared for our long ride.

Then came a new scene of confusion, the selection of mules. Hundreds were brought up and we who had Hinckley's tickets selected from them as we could. But not being wise in the subject of mules, it proved to me a matter of chance. Those I received for Mrs. Kip and my son Willie were good; mine was miserable. The express baggage is bound on mules, two trunks on each; six mules are put under the charge of two natives, and so they set off in small parties. The wonder to me is, that half the baggage gets safely to Panama, as it is in the power of these natives at any time to drive their mules to one side in the woods and rifle the trunks. This undoubtedly is sometimes done; for when we left Panama several mules had not yet arrived, and the passengers had to go without their trunks, though the express agent assured them, of course, that the missing baggage would probably soon be in, to be forwarded by next steamer.

In this way, in small parties, the passengers set out from

Cruces, and struggled across the Isthmus for the twenty-three miles, as their mules' speed and bottom allowed. With a first-rate mule, it may be pleasant, and those who had one enjoyed it. The distance is thus passed sometimes in four or five hours; but to whip an obstinate mule, as I did, for eleven hours, is quite a different matter.

As soon as we left Cruces, we plunged into the forest. The road is but a narrow bridle path through the gorges of the mountains, often just wide enough for a single mule to pass, with high rocks rising twenty feet on each side. Trees overhang it, and in some places it is so dark that a Kentuckian present said, " it reminded him of the entrance to the Mammoth Cave." It turns round sharp angles, so that one halting behind, fifty feet, cannot be seen by his party. Now, there is a high shelving rock to scramble up,—then, one equally steep to descend; so that we involuntarily shut our eyes, and do not pretend to guide the mules. In these rocks there are often holes for the mule's feet, into which he invariably puts them, for they have been worn by the use of those who have passed over the road for centuries before him. These deep ravines are sometimes filled up to the mule's knees with mud and water. Into this he dashes, splashing it over his rider, so that when he reaches Panama he is in anything but a presentable state. At times, the road expands into a broader space, where there are a few native huts, or a Spaniard has a place of refreshment for travellers.

There is some historical interest about this road. For centuries it was an Indian path across the Isthmus. Then the Spanish conquerors came, who improved it, paved it in some places with heavy stones, and over this brought on mules' backs all their treasures from Peru to ship them to Spain. Since their day, it has been suffered to go to decay. The heavy upturned stones form the danger of the road, and if a mule loses his footing or goes down, it is at the risk of his rider's limbs. The scenery, however, is magnificent, and now and then we have a wide stretch of landscape as we rise on the side of a mountain.

My party soon outrode me, and in the course of the day I was with four or five companies for a time. Most of the day, however, I was alone. On one occasion I came up with Mrs. Kip and our party, resting at a native hut. Finding they intended to remain some time, I passed on, as my mule went so slowly. I had hired a native to accompany me as guide, to prevent my getting off the path; but after going with me for a couple of miles, he deserted, and went back. Reaching the native hut, he was recognized by Mrs. Kip and questioned as to why he had left me. He stated, in reply, that I had got into a by-path and been murdered. As such things do happen on the Isthmus, and she knew I was alone and unarmed, it can be imagined what an excitement was produced. The Spaniard at whose hut they were stopping, and who, I afterwards learned, was one of the greatest scoundrels on the Isthmus, did all he could to augment her fears, that he might induce her to employ him to send an express on to Panama. Fortunately, just at that time, some returning Californians who were crossing towards Cruces came up. They remembered me by the description my party gave, and having seen me after the native had left, assured them that I must be safe. However, they were left in the greatest uncertainty till they came up with me, two hours later.

In the meanwhile I had gone on alone about six or seven miles, whipping up my lagging mule till he and I were tired out. Now and then some of our own passengers passed me, or two or three almost naked natives, armed with their machettes or long knives, but we only exchanged greetings. Perfectly wearied, I thought I must be near my journey's end, when, riding up to a little romantic river, I found some of our passengers resting there, and learned that I had yet six miles to go. Just then, others, who had passed Mrs. Kip, came up and told us of her fright, and we waited till she arrived.

I subsequently found that this travelling alone was a foolish risk. The natives, once harmless, have become so civilized as every month to be growing more dangerous and untrustworthy. One of our passengers, who was alone, was knocked senseless and stripped. The express party found him in that state and brought him in. A lady who got behind her party was robbed in the same way. My son Willie, when at one time he had loitered out of sight of his friends, met some natives who put their hands on him and demanded brandy, but finding he had none, let him go on. No molestation, however, was offered to me.

A few miles from Panama we leave the mountains and descend into the open country. Just outside of the city we meet with massive ruins—the remains of former generations —now entirely buried in the rank tropical vegetation, everything showing that a greater race formerly held the country.

We straggled in, as our mules were able, at different times. Willie got in with one party at half past three o'clock. Mrs. Kip came in with another at five, having sustained no injuries except from her fright, though her mule had twice rolled with her. I reached Panama alone, at six, perfectly wearied out. It was the hardest day's ride I have ever had, worse even than the ascent of Vesuvius.

V.

VOYAGE UP THE PACIFIC.

My first view of the Pacific was from the high grounds which overlook Panama. It would perhaps have been proper to have got up a sensation on the occasion, but after eleven hours spent on an obstinate mule, I was incapable of any emotions but those of utter weariness. The prospect, however, from that point was a fine one, with the city below partly hemmed in by its old walls, and then the wide-spread bay beyond.

The old city of Panama was some nine miles further south, but after various sieges, and sacking by the buccaneers, it was entirely abandoned, and the present city founded at the head of the bay.

It possesses the advantage of being further from the ocean, and in a place of greater security against attacks from that side, as vessels of any size are obliged to anchor at least two miles off. The old city, we were told, is entirely in ruins. Dense forests have now grown up where it stood, and all that can be seen among the crumbling ruins is the old church tower rising through the foliage. In this climate, when a place is once deserted, nature immediately asserts her claim to it, and in a few seasons the

36

luxuriant tropical vegetation buries it as entirely as if centuries had passed since the occupants were there. Any one
who has read " Stephen's Central America," will remember
this fact. We were told that at a very short distance from the side of our road over the Isthmus, were to
be found ruins of the kind described by him; but now entirely concealed in the depths of the forest.

The present city of Panama, like all these old Spanish
cities in New Grenada, has the appearance of having been
built by an entirely different race from that which now in-
habits it. And such is the case. The old Spaniards who
erected these massive buildings have been succeeded by
degenerate descendants of a mongrel race, without enterprise
or energy. They are contented to live in the residences of
their predecessors till they fall into ruins, but seem to have
not even the skill to repair them. Panama, indeed, before the emigration to California, had sunk down until it
was gradually dying a natural death. The rush of Americans
through it has galvanized it into a temporary animation; but
as soon as the railroad is finished, the depot of which will be
without the city, it will relapse into its former repose. The
walls around it, massive in their day, are now crumbling to
pieces, as is the fine old battery on the point where some
enormous pieces of Spanish brass cannon are still mounted.

The greater part of the city seems at one time to have
been owned by churches or monasteries. Most of these
are in ruins, the wild vines growing over their walls. The
Cathedral of the Grand Plaza is a very large building, with
two high towers, and the front ornamented with statues of
saints in niches. It is built of a rich brown stone, but
the sides and towers have been whitewashed, for want

of energy to clear away the moss and dampness which were gathering on the surface. We stopped for a few minutes to see the interior, and found it wretched and tawdry in the extreme. Mass was celebrating, and we noticed that several of the assistants were natives, or showed very plainly the mixed race to which they belonged.

The Aspinwall House, with its fine large rooms, reminding us by their polished floors of a French or Italian hotel, compensated for the miserable night at Cruces. It is on the foreign plan, affording rooms only, while the lodgers go out to a restaurant for their meals. The native population, as the people in the south of Europe, seem to live in the streets; and the general air of the houses, together with the costumes of the richly dressed women we met, with the black veils thrown over their heads, would have rendered it easy for us to imagine ourselves in a city of old Spain.

It was New Year's Eve when we entered Panama, but the weather was exceedingly hot, and the peculiarly oppressive atmosphere was very exhausting. Fortunately for us, a ship had arrived a few days before, bringing ice from Sitka in Russian America, and we enjoyed what was a rare luxury in Panama. Glasses of ice-water at one dime each were in great demand at that time.

The next day was Sunday, although no one would have suspected it from anything to be seen in the city. The influx of the steamer's passengers was one of the harvests of the shop-keepers of Panama, and every place of business was open to enable them to avail themselves of it. There is a service performed here for the benefit of the few American residents, by a Congregational minister. He called on me immediately after breakfast, and offered the

use of his room, with a request that I would officiate; but
between the ride of the day before and the exhaustion of
the climate, I was in no condition to avail myself of his
offer.

Our steamer, the *Golden Gate*, was to sail in the evening,
and we were directed to be on board by five o'clock. At
four, therefore, we were on the wharf, where we found
some thirty passengers, baggage, etc., crowded into a launch,
under the guidance of a couple of natives, who were to
carry us out to the steamer, nearly three miles off. The
beginning of our voyage was by no means promising. Our
boatmen either did not understand managing the vessel,
or else she was too crowded to allow them to do so. When
about half way over the bay she jibed, the boom swept
across, and all managed to dodge out of the way, except one
lady, sitting next to me on the gunwale, who was
swept into the water. Then, for a few moments, all was
confusion, and the vessel left to herself, while the natives
yelled, the ladies shrieked, and the gentlemen shouted. In
the midst of all, the poor woman would have found her
way to the bottom, or been devoured by the sharks which
abound in the bay, had she not providentially become en-
tangled in some ropes dragging behind our launch. They
were thus able to reach her from the stern, and finally
succeeded in dragging her on deck. Then there was an attempt to get alongside of the steamer which our boatmen
missed, succeeded by sundry other jibings, to the great
terror of the ladies, and then a tack or two more out into
the bay, before they were able to board her.

The *Golden Gate* is probably the most magnificent sea
steamer afloat. Since she came into the Pacific, she has

been arranged in a style which would not have answered on the more stormy Atlantic.   An elegant saloon (one hundred and four feet by twenty-four) has been erected on her upper deck, lined with staterooms which open into a gallery without.   These staterooms are built over the guards of the vessel, and project beyond its deck; an arrangement which, it is obvious, although very pleasant, would not answer in a sea liable to severe storms.

We went to sea at nine o'clock Sunday night, and for the first week there was but little variety.   We soon settled ourselves down to our daily employments of reading and writing, until a home feeling was created.   The principal business of most, however, was to keep themselves cool, for the weather was hot and summer clothes in demand.   We were some distance from the coast, though we occasionally saw some point; the moonlight nights were beautiful, and the Southern Cross just seen on the horizon.

Friday evening, January 6th. We reach the Bay of Acapulco, Mexico.   Here the steamer is obliged to stop, to lay in her supply of coal.   We went in at about nine o'clock.   It was almost as light as day, so that we were able to see the features of this singular harbor.   The channel winds among some islands, turns one or two sharp angles, until we find ourselves opposite the little town, when, looking back, we cannot see the passage by which we have entered.   We are completely hemmed in by high hills and seem to be floating in a little lake.   The town itself is an insignificant place on a narrow plateau at the foot of the mountains, and is said to be the hottest place on the coast. We found the air perfectly stifling, being entirely cut off from the fresh breezes of the ocean.

We have had some cases of Isthmus fever on board, but none so far has ended fatally. Persons crossing the Isthmus are liable to fever if care is not taken, although my wonder is that more are not prostrated by it. Many, just arriving from a cold climate, indulge at once in tropical fruits, eat oranges, pine-apples, bananas, and even cocoanuts which the natives hardly eat, and expose themselves to the sun and the night air. Almost as pernicious as these fruits is the water on the Isthmus, which should not be drunk alone, for it is filled with decayed vegetable matter. The fever is particularly fatal among the steerage passengers (we had at one time twenty ill from this cause), who, in addition to other acts of imprudence, heat their system with brandy.

The weather has been very pleasant, except some little roughness when crossing the Bay of Tehuantepec, and again in passing the three hundred miles at the entrance of the Gulf of California. We were in this situation on Sunday the 8th, yet I was sufficiently free from sea-sickness to have service in the saloon in the morning. Every arrangement was made by Captain Isham to facilitate this object, and we had quite a numerous congregation assembled to unite in the first public worship they had been permitted to enjoy in this year. Thursday morning we made Cape St. Lucas, and had our first view of California. Everything so far has gone on admirably. We have, one day, made as much as three hundred and five miles in twenty-four hours, and our Captain is in high spirits, expecting to make the shortest run ever known. He looks forward to our breakfasting in San Francisco, next Saturday morning.

Wednesday, January 11th (I copy from my journal). Last night came the reverse. At eight o'clock the engine stopped, and on examination it was found that the massive shaft, about twenty inches in diameter, had broken in two. Providentially we were thirty miles from the coast, with the wind setting off shore. Had it been otherwise, with the strong current there is drawing towards the land, we might have shared the fate of the *Independence,* the *America,* and the *Winfield Scott,* which, during the last two years, have been lost upon these shores. As it was, we drifted off during the night to the southwest, at the mercy of the winds and waves; and so we have continued to do through the whole of this day, till we are now very far off our course.

The *Golden Gate* has two engines; and for the last twenty-four hours every effort has been made to remove a portion of the broken shaft, so as to allow her to use the other side, and get under way with one wheel. She has been listed over on one side, as far as possible—to the terror of most of the passengers, who supposed she was going to capsize —to cut away the buckets of the starboard wheel, which otherwise would drag in the water and impede her.

At daylight, the *Uncle Sam,* which left Panama with us, came in sight, and seeing our situation, ran down to within a quarter of a mile of us. She could do nothing, however, to help us, for as the sea was running, it would have been difficult to have taken off our passengers, and she therefore stood off again to the north and left us. It was a beautiful sight to see her pitching about on the waves, plunging her bowsprit under, and then rising so as to show a long line of her keel.

During the morning the sea went down, and we have

done nothing all day, but drift—drift to the west. The Captain estimates that we have drifted about thirty-five miles farther off coast. In the direction we are going, we should bring up one of these days at the Marquesas Islands. We are not by any means in a pleasant situation. If we get under way, with one wheel, we can work our way in slowly, over the nine hundred miles of ocean yet to be traversed. If any accident should happen, and the remaining wheel be disabled, what is to be done? Our sails are too light to produce much effect, and we should have to wait for a favorable breeze and try to get in to shore, to anchor in some place of safety until relieved. Besides, there are between nine hundred and one thousand persons on board, and the steamer has not provisions for a protracted voyage. The Captain has to-day taken measures to guard against this contingency. We have been put upon two meals a day, breakfast and dinner; tea is abolished. Some of the ladies, as usual at twelve o'clock, sent one of the waiters to the pantry for lunch, when he came back with the announcement,—"Lunches *is* stopped."

Thursday, 12th. A quiet, idle day. The engineers are working at the machinery, in the hope of getting under way in a few days. The passengers are yawning, sleeping, playing cards from morning till night, trying to read, or discussing our prospects for the future. The water is as smooth as a mill-pond, and we are slowly going westward with the drift of the ocean, for there is no wind. It seems strange to see this magnificent steamer, that lately dashed so rapidly through the sea, floating along so helpless and disabled. We are now served with salt water for washing. Fresh water is to be used for drinking only, as it may be necessary to husband our resources. We are provisioned, the Captain says, for twelve days, and by putting us on allowance our stores could last much longer.

Dolphins and sharks have been playing about the ship all day. One of the latter was so close to the surface that we could see the pilot fish which always accompanies it, swimming at its side. The sea is alive with shoals of porpoises, while at a distance we saw a number of small grampus whales. During the evening there was a large whale not far from us, as we could hear him blow when he rose to the surface. It was bright moonlight, and we sat in the gallery by our staterooms till a late hour, watching the stars set, one by one, as if their light were quenched in the waste of waters about us.

Friday, 13th. It is rather amusing to hear the opinions of the passengers as to the cause of our accident, and their prophecies of the future. One Spanish gentleman thus agreeably sketched out our programme :—

"Fust, dere will be hungry; den, dere will be no sugar water."

"But"—said some one,—"there's plenty of sugar on board."

"Ah! I mean de water dat is not salt, for de drink and de shave. Den, dere will be no wine. Den, de machinery is fix, an—he no go."

Monday, 16th. We kept on drifting until Saturday evening, when it was announced, to the great joy of all, that the machinery was partially repaired, so that one wheel could be used. Since then we have been heading for San Diego, the most southern point of Northern California, about five

hundred miles distant. It is, however, slow work. In the
last twenty-four hours we have made about one-hundred
and eight miles. Everything now depends upon this one
wheel, and another accident would leave us without resource. We hope (D. V.), to get to San Diego by Wednesday morning, and then the Captain can determine by
the state of the steamer, whether to go on with her or
to wait until another steamer is sent from San Francisco
(four-hundred and fifty miles distant), to bring us up.

In the meanwhile, provisions are growing scarce, and we
have been put on an allowance of water. Part of a tumbler-
full is given to each one at dinner, none of which is to be taken
from the table. Sunday morning a committee from the four-
hundred passengers in the steerage came to the Captain
to demand an increase of food. Upon his refusing to comply, they warned him, that "there were some dangerous
men in the steerage." He thanked them for their information, "as in case of any trouble he should know how to deal
with them." Some of the cabin passengers, however, find
it rather long to go without anything to eat from two P. M.
till eight A. M. the next day, with the keen appetite people
have at sea.

Early this morning we passed within a mile of a whaler,
which sent a boat off to us to procure papers. She was
from New Bedford, and had been out somewhat over two
years, having on board three thousand barrels of oil. The
boat passed under our quarter, and the papers which could
be collected were thrown to it. They will be read and re-
read, advertisements and all. We have again got back to
the coast, having made land in the afternoon, and are now
in the track of the steamers, so that we may meet the

John L. Stephens, which leaves San Francisco this morning.

Tuesday, 17th.   We have been, for the last few days, getting slowly forward.   Providentially the weather has been calm, and we are approaching San Diego, where we can procure provisions to add to our stock.   It is evening, and the headlands show that we are not many miles distant.   The Captain says we shall reach the harbor about midnight, and we seem therefore to have come to the end of another stage in our protracted voyage.

VI.

WRECK OF THE "GOLDEN GATE."

We entered the harbor of San Diego at about one o'clock on Wednesday morning, the 18th. It was a calm and beautiful day, that dawned upon us with the softness of atmosphere characteristic of this climate. The air was as warm as that of June. On coming on deck, at sunrise, we found ourselves in a deep bay, around which we looked in vain for the town of San Diego. The landing, or *Plaza*, opposite to which we had anchored, has only three or four houses, including a drinking-shop and the Custom House. Along shore stand some old hide houses, mentioned by Dana in his "Two Years Before the Mast," which, at that time, were the scene of his labors. On the rising ground behind them are some thirty or forty graves, with a wooden paling to each, most of them being the last resting-places of our countrymen who had died on board the steamships which stop here. The town of San Diego is about four miles distant, at the head of the bay, but almost concealed from view at the Plaza, by the rising ground which intervenes.

The Captain, at daylight, rode up to the town, and succeeded in procuring about fifteen miserable bullocks, for

47

which fifty-five dollars apiece were paid, the proper value being from twenty to twenty-five dollars. They were driven down to the beach, killed, and taken on board, with some other provisions hastily collected; so that by noon we were ready to sail.

At three o'clock they got up steam, and we prepared to leave the harbor. About the same time, a small steamer, the *Goliah*, trading between this place and San Francisco, which also had arrived early in the morning, weighed her anchor and set out on her return. While the *Golden Gate* was swinging around by a hawser from an old hulk anchored near the shore, the cable broke, and we were left in the stream, before she had headed the right way. Down we floated, sometimes sideways, sometimes straight, the single wheel which could be used not having power enough to bring her round. The channel is narrow and winding, with a reef of sand near the entrance of the harbor. Under all these difficulties, the Captain managed the vessel, as all allowed, in a masterly way, availing himself of every eddy to sweep her around, until we were five miles from the landing, and apparently just entering the ocean. Just at this moment, the tide carried her around, and we felt her stern slightly strike the bar. With full power in the engine, she would at once have been freed, but with one wheel this was impossible. The engine could not act upon her with sufficient force; and after striking several times, she grounded firmly, with her bow swinging clear.

The *Goliah* was at this time about a mile from us. Our flag was at once run up with the union down, as a signal of distress, and she came to us. A boat was sent off to her with a heavy hawser, and her engine was put in

motion to drag us off. After straining the hawser to its utmost capacity, without moving us, it suddenly parted. Another was sent off, which also snapped, in a short time,
with the same ill success. The tide at this time was rapidly
falling; and it became evident that it was of no use at present
to repeat the experiment. Captain Haley (of the *Goliah*)
therefore sent word that he would return at evening,
when the tide rose, and could then probably succeed in
bringing us off.

With the close of the day, most unexpectedly came signs
of a change of weather. The sea became very rough, and
the swell of the surf around us gave token of a wild night.
The *Goliah*, however, which was anchored near us, about six
o'clock took another hawser, and for some time renewed the
attempt. But after several efforts, which produced no effect, the cable broke like the others. Seeing it to be a
hopeless case, with the storm every moment increasing, and
the sea then so high that no boat could pass between the
two steamers, the *Goliah* abandoned us, and went up the
harbor, to take refuge for the night at an anchorage pro-
tected from the wind and sea.

Some six months afterwards, I had occasion to go with
Captain Haley in his steamer, from San Francisco, down
the coast to Monterey. I asked him what he thought of us
that evening, when he went off. He said, "that for two
hours he thought of nothing but himself, that he had never
been in such a hurricane, he could not see his course, and
did not know to that day how he found his way up the
harbor. When, however, he had time to think of us, he
gave up all hope of ever seeing us again."

As the hawser parted, the gale struck us with its full vio-

lence. It was utterly unlike anything I had ever experienced. It seemed to grow dark at once. It was indeed
one of those tornadoes which occur but once in twenty
years on the Pacific, but which when they do come are fearful in their strength. As it struck the *Golden Gate,* the steamer swung round, and was dashed broadside upon the reef,
in the very midst of the breakers. We were then about a
mile and a quarter from shore, surrounded on all sides by the
breakers, the night exceedingly dark, and the sea sweeping
over us. The rain, too, was falling in sheets, while the
gale had broken upon us with hurricane violence. I have
been in some of the worst storms of winter, off the coast
of France, and was once in one of those terrible gales,
which briefly, but with such violence, sweep over the Mediterranean, but I never witnessed anything, in its effects,
equal to this. Nor is this opinion the exaggeration of my
own fears, arising from our perilous situation. We were
told afterwards, by those on shore who were residents
here, that they had not for years experienced a storm equal
to it in violence. While at one time the waves swept over
us, at another, as they dashed by us in huge masses, seeth-
ing in foam as far as we could see, the whole surface of the
ocean seemed flattened down by the violence of the wind.

Another difficulty of our situation arose from the fact,
that we had nearly one thousand persons on board. Most
of these, from character and want of self-discipline, could
not exert over themselves the control necessary at a crisis
of danger, when the strict government of a ship-of-war was
requisite. When, therefore, our ship first went upon the
reef, as she keeled over on one side, throwing passengers
and everything movable to the windward, there was such a

scene of terror as I never before had witnessed. The crowd rushed wildly into the great saloon, clinging to everything which could prevent falling, and exhibiting every possible variety of character.

And then, every few moments the sea would raise the immense mass and throw it still farther among the breakers, where it would come down with a crash. This was repeated again and again, and followed by a cracking and straining beneath our feet, which seemed to the uninitiated as if it were parting at midships. Then every one would hold his breath for a minute or two, till he saw whether the ship were going to pieces, and when he found she had survived that shock, would catch it again with a long gasp. Every time, too, that she thus struck on her side, there would be a wreck of everything breakable, the very noise of which added to the confusion and fear. Even the dining tables and settees, which were clamped down with strong iron fastenings, were torn up and hurled to the other end of the saloon.

The question, indeed, on which everything in regard to us rested, was, whether or not the steamer was strong enough to bear all this thumping through the night, without going to pieces. Had it broken up, few of us could have reached the shore, from which we were more than a mile distant, with wild breakers intervening. As it was, providentially for us, our steamer was built with the strength of a frigate. The Captain, next morning, said, that "there was not another steamer on that coast, that could have left at daylight more than a few planks scattered along the shore." A shipmaster, too, who was at the landing, told us he watched us through the early part of the night, by the lights dancing up and down as the vessel struck, and finally went to bed with the feeling that before morning we should be entirely broken up. With those indeed who realized that this was likely, it was a fearful night.

There was another danger, too, even if she held together, which was foreseen and feared by those who were experienced in such matters. The steamer (as I have stated in a previous chaper), has an upper saloon, the staterooms of which are built on the guards, which extend ten feet over the sides, and form, therefore, the floor of those rooms. At one o'clock in the morning, the sea commenced tearing up these guards, as she lay over on the windward side, so that as the waves breached over her, they dashed through the staterooms into the saloons. As she was settling more and more on that side, it was feared that the staterooms and upper works would be entirely carried away, when the sea would necessarily pour down into the lower cabin and fill it. In this case, even if she held together, the thousand persons on board would be driven forward, to take their stand at the bow, a place which afforded hardly foothold for such a crowd.

Attempts were made during the night to right her, by getting up some sails, but they were at once blown to ribbons, and the foremast cracked in such a way as to be useless. The engine was kept going, to avail ourselves of any favorable change in the position of the vessel, until the water rose to the furnace gratings, when the fires were necessarily put out. The passengers were then all summoned to take their stand upon the starboard guards, to try and trim her by the counterbalance of their weight. There they remained for hours, exposed to all the storm, and drenched to the skin.

And thus the night,—to many the most anxious they had ever passed—wore away. Our hope was, that when, towards morning, the tide turned, the gale, as frequently happens, would abate. I confess, I never in my life so often consulted my watch, or looked so earnestly for the dawn of day. About three o'clock, after some thumping and straining, the steamer seemed gradually to right herself, so that one danger was lessened. Why this favorable change occurred, I have never found any one able to give an explanation. Probably, as she was driven further upon the reef, she worked her way down into the sand, and got into a more even position. Happily for us, the reef was entirely of sand, for had there been a single rock beneath her, she would have gone to pieces in two hours. Towards morning, as we had hoped, the gale abated. Looking over our beautiful saloon, more than a hundred feet long, I was struck with its changed and desolate appearance. It was thoroughly drenched, as the sea had swept through it; while tables and settees were torn up and piled against the openings which the waves had made. On the floor, the passengers were lying in every attitude, having sunk into sleep from utter exhaustion.

There is one consideration, however, connected with this night, which we could not but bear in mind. It is admitted by all with whom we have conversed, that our grounding on the Zuninga Shoal was providential for us, and probably saved the lives of hundreds. Had we not done so, we should, in a few minutes more, have passed Point Loma, and been out to sea. It would have been impossible for us to have made offing enough to have been clear of the coast before the gale struck us. With the comparatively little power we possessed, we could not have kept off the land, and would probably have gone ashore some distance farther up the rocky coast. In that case, the immediate destruction of the vessel, and of course of the greater part of the passengers, would have been inevitable.

When the next morning dawned, the wind had abated, and the gale had evidently passed over, though the sea was still exceedingly high. At eight o'clock, the *Goliah* came down to within a mile of us; but after reconnoitering our situation, and seeing that she could be of no use to us, she returned up the harbor. It was evidently impossible for her to hold any communication with us, as we were at least a hundred yards upon the shoal, and entirely surrounded by breakers, among which a boat could not live. Great, therefore, as was naturally the desire of the passengers to get to land, they found they must wait till the sea went down, and probably spend another night on board. The day, however, passed quietly; for the steamer seemed to have become so firmly bedded in the sand, that the return of high tide did not move her, or lift her so as to renew her thumping. It was evident, too, that she had filled with sand and several feet of water, which tended to keep her more steady. She was what sailors call "hogged."

During the next night, which, providentially for us, was perfectly calm, she did not move in her position, except to list over farther on her side. This was probably caused by the shifting of the water in her; and towards morning, the sea having gone down, the guns of the steamer were fired, as a signal to the shore. This brought down the *Goliah,* and the *Southerner* (which had arrived the day before from San Francisco); and, the breakers having subsided, their boats were all put into requisition to remove the passengers. In the course of the morning this was safely effected, and we were all crowded into the other two steamers. We left our noble vessel with deep regret, as we beheld her lying over on her side. It was reported she had five feet of water, and that the pumps were out of order. The general opinion, among those acquainted with such matters, was that she had bilged, and it would probably be impossible to get her off; an opinion, which the result happily did not warrant.

In the afternoon, after taking on the passengers, with a portion of the baggage, the *Goliah* and *Southerner* returned up the bay to their former anchorage, and before night all were safely landed on the Plaza, rejoiced once more to set foot on *terra firma*.

VII.

SAN DIEGO.

WHEN we landed from the *Golden Gate*, the usually quiet shore of San Diego presented an unaccustomed scene. Instead of a solitary individual moving here and there, nearly a thousand people were scattered about the beach. And a most desolate looking and feeling company we were! As many as possible had taken refuge under the few roofs there were, while the rest were in parties on the shore, seated on their trunks and wondering what they should do for the night. The hills back of the Plaza are covered with low straggling bushes, as far as the eye can reach, without a single tree, and therefore furnished no fuel as a means of cooking for the crowd which had been fasting since morning. I afterwards learned there was much suffering through that night. Many had of course to camp out in the open air, while ladies, who were fortunate enough to obtain a shelter, found that this was all they had secured. It was generally an entirely vacant room, with nothing in the shape of bed or bedding. In addition to hunger, we suffered from cold, for though the days at this season are warm, the nights are chilly, particularly for those whose resting-place is the bare ground and

56

their covering the canopy of heaven. Some walked up to San Diego, four miles distant, but the majority remained where they were, making bonfires of the old hide houses, and of everything which could be torn down. They had not even water to drink, for the place furnishes none, and all that is used here is brought from the town.

Towards evening a steamer was seen coming in, which proved to be the *Columbia* from San Francisco. On the report of the *Uncle Sam*, that she had spoken us, lying-to, disabled in a rough sea, it was naturally supposed that we would get into some place to refit. The *Columbia* was therefore at once despatched by the agents of the company, with a hundred picked men and the proper machinery for a wreck. The Captain had instructions to look into every port on her way down, until he found us, and to render us any assistance we might need. Her arrival certainly was most opportune. The *Southerner* and *Goliah* sailed next morning, with such passengers as chose to go in them, having been chartered by the company for that purpose. As they, however, were small and excessively crowded, our own party were advised to remain and await the departure of the *Columbia*, which would go in a few days, after doing what she could for the *Golden Gate.*

As it was, " the lines had fallen to us in pleasant places." It was my good fortune to recognize in the United States collector at the Plaza, Mr. Bleecker, an old New Yorker, who promptly took every step necessary for our comfort. Our luggage was placed in his storehouse, while he at once mounted his horse, and rode up to San Diego, to charter a large wagon to take us thither. Mr. Bleecker returned towards evening, with an invitation from Don Juan Bandini,

for our party to partake of his hospitality. Our road
wound around the border of the bay, and after crossing the
bed of a river, which at this season is nothing but dry sand,
though a month later it will be a rapidly-rolling stream,
at about eight o'clock we reached our destination.

"My party"—which Don Juan invited—really consisted
of Mrs. Kip and my son; but some of our steamer friends,
hearing there was an opening for obtaining lodgings, at
once joined us and mounted the wagon. I scarcely knew
what to say to them, when I found that "my party," children included, amounted to nearly a dozen. Our host, however, gave us a most hospitable welcome. An admirable
supper in the Spanish style—*tortillas* and *frijoles* of course
included, with native wine from his own ranch—made
amends for the day, while comfortable beds compensated
us for the last two nights of wakefulness on the steamer.
Don Juan is the leading man in this part of California.
Belonging to an old Spanish Mexican family, he has retained much of his landed possessions, and the vast herds
of cattle, which in this country constitute wealth. He has
a number of ranches (or farms), in this State and in the
Mexican province of Lower California, one of which was
mentioned as covering eleven leagues. We were told that
his son-in-law, during the past year, had sold, from one of
his ranches, three thousand head of cattle, at sixteen dollars each, and that he could continue doing this, year after
year, without diminishing his stock. This is a specimen of
the nature of California wealth among the old Spanish inhabitants.

Until the coming of the Americans, these people led
a life of ease and quiet, in the midst of the fullest abun-

dance of everything they could desire. Kind hearted and
hospitable, their houses were always open to strangers
who were worthy of their confidence. Their lives were spent,
indeed, in idleness, for, in this climate and with this soil, but
little was demanded of them. The Indian population furnished them with servants, and their time was passed in
those amusements which their fathers had brought with
them from old Spain. Then came our countrymen, who
robbed their ranches, seized their lands; and drove them
to the wall. At the very time that Don Juan was showing
this unbounded hospitality to a party of American strangers,
who had no claim upon him—several of whom could not
even speak his language—his son arrived from one of his
ranches on the other side of the line, ninety miles distant.
He had ridden in on a single horse in one night, to
announce to his father, that Walker's company of *filibusters*
had killed the cattle, driven off the horses, and completely
stripped the ranch. And this is not by any means the first
time he has been thus plundered.

His residence at San Diego, at which we have now been
domesticated for nearly a week, is just on the edge of the
town. It is built in the Spanish style, around the sides of a
quadrangle into which most of the windows open, and is only
one story high, with massive walls of *adobes* (sun-dried bricks).
Everything here is conducted with such ease that we feel as
much at home as if we had lived here for months. Nothing
is omitted that could conduce to our comfort, and in the
elegance with which the Señora Bandini presides over her
household and entertains her guests, we found our ideas of
the grace and dignity of the Spanish ladies fully realized.

San Diego is a little Spanish town of about a thousand

inhabitants, built in a straggling style, and with a perfectly foreign air. The houses are mostly constructed of *adobes*, except that here and there some white painted, clapboard shop tells us of the occupancy of one of our countrymen. As usual, the town is built around a large Plaza, where the population, Spaniards and Indians, wrapped in their ample mantles, sun themselves and lounge; and here, on Sundays, are their amusements. Through the week, however, it is as quiet as possible. The climate is delicious, said to be the most healthy on the coast, reminding me indeed of that of Naples. The people do not seem disposed to show any activity, except when on horseback. Now and then some cavalier, mounted on a fine horse, dashes across the Plaza, lasso in hand, his huge spurs and stirrups jingling as he goes. The American population, is gradually coming in, and in a few years the place will lose its Spanish characteristics. During the Mexican war, San Diego was taken by Commodore Stockton, and on the hill above, are the remains of the breastwork he threw up to command the town.

Opposite to Don Juan's is a long Spanish house, the residence of the Padre, one end of which is fitted up as a Chapel. I looked into it when passing, but found everything, pictures, images, etc., in the worst possible state of tawdriness. One of our countrymen—a steerage passenger from the ship—followed me in, and lounged round the place with his hat on and a cigar in his mouth! Four miles further up the harbor is New Town, a more recent settlement, where several of our army officers are quartered; while six miles farther back in the country, at the old Mission of San Diego, a force of about one hundred soldiers is stationed. This is at present the residence also of the Rev. Mr. Reynolds, one of our clergy, who is a Chaplain in the United States Army. He officiates there on Sunday morning, and in the afternoon comes down to San Diego and holds service,—the only one, except the Romish, in the place.

San Diego, just now, is unusually lively. Our passengers have most of them moved up to the town, where the cabin passengers provide themselves with lodgings as they best can. The steerage passengers, numbering about three hundred, have been most of them quartered in a deserted hotel, just beyond the town. Here they are divided into messes, and daily rations are given them by the purser of the steamer.

A schooner, chartered by the company, has just arrived. The agent is trying to induce a hundred of the steerage passengers to go in her, to prevent the *Columbia* from being overloaded; but though he offers them five dollars apiece premium, besides a dollar a day during the voyage, they hold back, suspicious of some deception. In the meanwhile, the *Columbia* is exerting all her force to get off the *Golden Gate.*

Sunday has come—our first Sunday in California. Opposite to us, near the little Romish Chapel, are four bells, tied to a frame-work by thongs of ox-hide. When it is time for Mass, two little boys mount the fence by them, and beat them with stones in each hand. They have been ringing at different hours this morning, and the people crowding to the Chapel until it was filled to overflowing. The Indian population are all dressed in their gayest garments, while a party of *filibusters*, armed to the teeth, are lounging in the plaza, preparing to march to-day to join Walker, who is a hundred miles distant, in Lower California. The higher classes are dashing about on horseback, though to-day it is more quiet than usual, as no public exhibition, (bear baiting or bull fight), is to take place. With the Indians, however, it is a day of revelling and intoxication, which often ends in bloodshed. It was so at this time, for, towards evening, seeing a little group collected near Don Juan's, we found, on inquiry, that one Indian in a quarrel had just stabbed another to the heart. Passing one of their mud-houses, a short time after, I heard a sound of sorrow, and, looking in, saw the murdered man lying half-naked on the floor, and his mother wailing over him. Such an occurrence is too common to excite any attention. The murderer was arrested by the American authorities, but suffered to escape during the night.

I was requested, by some of the residents, to hold service, and was, of course, happy to comply. We had the room used as the court-room, which is occupied by Mr. Reynolds in the afternoon. There was no opportunity of giving much notice, and service was not expected, as Mr. Reynolds is never here in the morning; yet there were about fifty persons present, including several of the army officers and their families. We returned thanks for our late escape from the perils of the sea, and, by a singular coincidence, the Psalm for this morning,—the twenty-second day of the month—contained that description so applicable to our late situation:—

"They that go down to the sea in ships, and occupy their business in great waters ;
"These men see the works of the Lord, and His wonders in the deep.

" For at His word the stormy wind ariseth, which lifteth up the waves thereof.

" They are carried up to the heaven, and down again to the deep ; their soul melteth away because of the trouble.

" They reel to and fro, and stagger like a drunken man, and are at their wit's end.

" So when they cry unto the Lord in their trouble, He delivereth them out of their distress.

" For He maketh the storm to cease, so that the waves thereof are still.

" Then are they glad, because they are at rest ; and so He bringeth them unto the haven where they would be."

VIII.

WITH difficulty, we procured to-day something like a large farm wagon, to drive out to the mission of San Diego. It is about six miles back in the country, our road being most of the way through a perfectly level valley between the hills. Just beyond the town of San Diego stands a single palm, which is the only tree to be seen for miles in any direction. The country, like the hills about the Plaza, is covered with low bushes.

Seventy years ago, California was almost entirely divided among these missions, founded originally by the Franciscans. All the arable land for miles around their residences was cultivated for the fathers by the Indians who were under their influence. They pretended to hold these lands merely as guardians of the Indians, though their care was often anything but disinterested. Several years before the occupation by the Americans, these possessions were most of them sequestered by the Mexican Government, and the mission buildings are generally falling to ruin. These old fathers, however, settled themselves with great judgment. They chose fine locations, erected solid buildings, and, by planting immense num-

64

bers of fruit trees about them, did much to advance the agricultural interests of the country.

The Mission of San Diego originally comprehended a large tract of country, embracing in its jurisdiction several minor Missions under its control. The buildings are on a hillside. They have an extensive view down the valley, and are substantially built of *adobe*. In the centre is a fine large church, which at that time they were preparing to transform into barracks for the soldiers. It is well proportioned, with an air of stateliness. The remains of the pulpit, solidly built of *adobe* cemented over—its steps still perfect,—and the chancel—its cross sunk into the wall above the place where the altar once stood—render its present desecration more melancholy. The low grounds around the Mission are covered with old olive trees, remains of the orchards originally planted by the priests.

Here, I had the pleasure of meeting the Rev. Mr. Reynolds, the first clergyman of this Diocese whom I had seen. He had been prevented from fulfilling his usual engagement in San Diego, the preceding Sunday afternoon, so that I had not before become acquainted with him. An hour was passed pleasantly with the family of one of the gentlemen attached to the army.

To-day one of the steerage passengers quartered in town died of the Isthmus fever. Poor fellow, he had just escaped the perils of the sea, to meet his end on land. He was from Pennsylvania, and as he was not a Romanist, they came to me to perform the funeral service. Some distance from the town, there is a little enclosure set apart for the interment of foreigners, and thither, towards evening, about a dozen of his late comrades carried him, when I read the service which committed his body "earth to earth." He had been to California once before, but was now going out again, to make arrangements preparatory to bringing out his family for a permanent residence.

In the course of the morning, I had, too, witnessed the funeral of an Indian child, in the Romish burying-ground. The coffin was covered with a gay-colored paper of the kind with which we cover our walls. The relatives crouched down on the ground around the grave, while the Padre read the service and sprinkled the holy water, and not a sound was heard until he had finished the prayers and turned to go. Then there burst forth a wild wail of grief, and all rushed forward to throw the first earth into the grave with their hands.

Thursday morning, Jan. 26th, arrived the summons for us to repair to the *Columbia,* which was ready to sail for San Francisco; and with regret we took leave of our kind hosts, the Bandinis, by whom we have been entertained for six days with a generous hospitality. Upon reaching the Plaza, we found that the *Golden Gate* was lying in the inner harbor, having got off the day before. Fortunately, during this week had occurred the spring tides, when the water rises to a greater height than at any other time. Taking advantage of this, as the tide rose every night, by carrying out anchors, and having hawsers on board the *Columbia* to pull them, she was at length floated off, though leaking badly. During the past week, we had been accustomed to watch her progress anxiously, every morning climbing a hill back of the town, from which we could see her, though ten miles distant. Here, by taking several ranges with objects near us, we could judge whether her position had changed during the night. She was now anchored with the hulk into which her cargo had been dis-charged by her side, and the *Columbia* (which looked like a mere lighter in comparison with the *Golden Gate*,) next to it. After repairing the principal leaks, she managed to reach San Francisco about a week after our own arrival, and was sent up to Benicia to be repaired. It was a result which few expected at the time we left her, when it was generally supposed she could not be moved, and would have to be dis-mantled. As it was, the whole of this difficulty cost the company a hundred and forty thousand dollars.

We were rowed out to the *Golden Gate*, and after a pleasant dinner with Captain Isham, in the evening we were trans-ferred to the *Columbia*, which sailed for San Francisco. After we got under way, one of our cabin passengers, a Mr. Gib-son, was found to be missing. As he was known to have gone to bed on board of the *Golden Gate*, thinking that we should not sail till morning, his absence created con-siderable amusement, on the supposition that he had overslept himself, and would be annoyed next morning at finding himself left behind. We subsequently learned, that the next day he was found lying senseless in the hold of the hulk. To reach the *Columbia*, it was necessary to descend a plank from the *Golden Gate*, and cross the deck of the hulk to the other side where our steamer was lying. With the most culpable carelessness, the hatches of the hulk were left open, and I remember how, with many warnings, and by the aid of a lantern, Captain Isham piloted Mrs. Kip and myself around them to the steamer. In the darkness, and perhaps confu-sion of being just aroused from sleep, Mr. Gibson must, in crossing, have fallen down a distance of twenty-two feet.

There he lay, undiscovered, from nine in the evening until early next day. One side of his head was almost crushed in and his shoulder was broken. He was removed to the *Golden Gate*, where every attention was shown him, but he lived only three hours. It was he who had come to me, a few days before, to make arrangements for the funeral of the passenger we buried at San Diego, and now he was laid by his side.

The *Columbia* was, of course, excessively crowded, as she was not intended for one-third the number of passengers which were now on board of her. Yet the weather proved to be calm, so that the few days of our voyage passed without inconvenience. The most dangerous part of the passage is through the channel of Santa Barbara, which is only a few miles wide, with the coast on one side and a chain of rocky islands on the other. It is said, there is a variation of the compass here, owing to some local attraction, which renders it useless in passing through the channel. It is generally foggy, so that steamers run great risks in getting through. In this way, the *Winfield Scott* was lost, last month. The Captain, mistaking his position, drove her with a full head of steam on one of these islands, where the passengers remained, under tents, for several days, before they were taken off. As it was bright sunlight when we passed, we saw the wreck at a distance, the bows resting high on the rocks.

Sunday morning, the 29th, the fortieth day since we left New York, terminated our voyage. As day was breaking we found ourselves off the harbor of San Francisco. From its opening the inner harbor is distant several miles, forming one of the most magnificent places in the

world for shipping. As we approached, a gun was fired
from the steamer, which echoed far and wide over the
hills on which the city is built. The first thing which
struck us was the crowd of shipping at the wharves,
reminding us of the wharves of New York. Another gun
was fired, as we drew nigh the pier, when, early as it
was, crowds were seen pouring down from the city.
In addition to the passengers' friends who were anxiously
expecting them, after so protracted a voyage, many
came to learn the fate of the *Golden Gate.* As we
touched the pier, a letter, from the Vestry of Trinity
Church, was passed on board to me, stating that a
committee had been appointed to meet us on our arrival,
and to conduct us to lodgings which had been provided. A few moments after the plank was out, a member
of the committee was on board, introducing himself to
us, and thus, through considerate kindness, our arrival
was deprived of that desolate feeling which can not but
accompany one who comes, for the first time, to a strange
place where there are no familiar faces.

IX.

It is curious to stand on the deck of a crowded steamer, as she is passing through the " Golden Gate " and entering the noble harbor of San Francisco. There are a few returning Californians, who are pointing out every object of interest with which they were formerly familiar; but the majority of the passengers are gazing with earnestness on the untried scene which is to them but the land of promise. Most of them have come as adventurers to that new home, and the result is yet to show whether any of their expectations are ever to be realized. Some are coming to retrieve broken fortunes, and, instead of reaping the golden harvest, how many will find a grave in the already crowded cemetery of San Francisco—dying, " strangers in a strange land "—; or else be glad, in a few months, to take passage home in some returning steamer! Many are ladies and children, whose husbands and fathers, having succeeded in business, have now sent for their families to join them. We belonged to none of these classes; yet none, probably, looked out with more interest on their future home than we did, when on that beautiful Sunday morning, just as the sun was rising over the distant mountains, we found ourselves entering the harbor.

70

The first thing which strikes the stranger with surprise, on passing through the streets of San Francisco, is the excellence of the buildings in this city which is little more than five years old. In Montgomery Street, there are massive edifices of granite and brick which would not look out of place in the thoroughfares of our old cities at the East. The first generation of houses was, of course, of the frailest kind—the mere temporary expedient of settlers, and but one remove from the tents in which they had been living. The great fires which desolated the city swept these away—for they burned like tinder—but cleared the ground for more substantial dwellings. Houses were imported from abroad in large numbers. One, of white granite, seventy feet front and three stories high, was prepared in China, the stone all cut and ready to put up. The first company of Chinamen who came out were imported with it, to erect the building. There is a large wooden house, the second story of which projects ten feet over the first, which to one who has been on the Rhine, suggests at once reminiscences of the "Fatherland." It was brought out by some Germans. There is one from Belgium. That large, chateau-looking building, on the hill, just back of the city, came from France; it is now occupied as the French Consulate. Every little while you meet with a house half composed of minute panes of glass, which unmistakably show its Chinese origin. Walk through Mission Street, and on each side of the way are neat and pretty cottages—there must be a dozen in all—exactly alike, which were sent out from Boston.

Every month witnesses a striking change in the outward appearance of the city—a change so great that a six months' absence seems to have prepared a new city for one who is returning to it. The high hills are levelled and thrown into the valleys—grading is going on in all directions—finer buildings erecting—and, on every side, the night scarcely brings pause to the busy march of improvement. There is, too, a degree of elegance visible in the manner of life, which would surprise those at the East who look upon California as the outpost of civilization. The day, indeed, is not far distant, when San Francisco will be one of the most luxurious cities in the world. It has, in fact, the greatest natural advantages. Even now the fruits of the tropics and of the temperate zones are united in its markets in a way never seen in any other land.

The whole tone of society is rapidly altering, and one who forms his estimate from the accounts of four years ago, must be widely mistaken. Then the city was composed, almost entirely, of men. There were no accommodations for ladies, and the gentler sex would have been sadly out of place among the hardships which marked those days. Then, we are told, a lady in the street was an object of wonderment, and all stopped and turned round to look at her. The great disproportion between the sexes still continues, though it is rapidly decreasing. At the last census, two years ago, there were about thirty thousand males and five thousand females—a curious and probably unprecedented anomaly. In the usual proportion, there were men enough in San Francisco for a city of one hundred and fifty thousand inhabitants. The population is now estimated at about fifty thousand. Every steamer brings out ladies and families, domestic ties are forming or renewing, here as elsewhere the softening and refining influence of female society is felt, and San Francisco is rapidly settling down to be like every other civilized city.

There is something about San Francisco which, strange as it may seem, constantly reminds me of Paris. There is a freedom from the stiffness and conventionalities of Eastern cities, and a liveliness not seen there. The splendid cafés and restaurants on every street are always open and filled with company. Families occupy apartments in the foreign style. The population has come together from every civilized nation on the earth, and from some which can scarcely claim that character. Every state in our country is represented, and every nation in Europe. There are thousands of Chinese who occupy streets entirely appropriated to them, and as you see them at their various employments, you could imagine yourself in Canton. Now and then, you see the Asiatic look of the Malays and Hindoos. The islands of the Southern Sea have contributed their proportion. It is curious how near you seem to be to divers odd places which before you have only read about. Placards are up, giving notice of the sailing of ships for Australia and New Zealand. Last week a steamer was advertised to go on a pleasure excursion to the Sandwich Islands, to be absent but thirty days; and this morning, in the post-office, I was quite startled by hearing one of the porters call out,—" Which is the Sandwich Islands mail ?"

What most astonishes a new-comer is the scale of prices. When I reached San Francisco, it was at its height. Luxuries commanded a prohibitory price. Apples, for instance, I have often seen at five dollars apiece. Rents were startling. Near my lodgings (in Stockton Street) was a two-story brick house, of about thirty feet frontage, occupied as a boarding-house, which rented for five hundred dollars a month (everything here is by the month).

There were many wooden cottages in the city. At the East they would cost about fifteen hundred dollars each. They were without plaster, linen being stretched across the partitions and then papered. They looked very well, but were highly inflammable. It was owing to the character of these buildings that the city was so often entirely desolated by fires. I never dared to hire one, because I was afraid to trust in it my books and papers.

Another disadvantage was, that you could hear noises from one end of the house to the other. If a child cried in the southeast corner, you heard it in the northwest with as much distinctness as if in the same apartment. And yet, these cottages rented, on an average, for one hundred and twenty-five dollars a month. As it was, I took apartments in a brick building,* erected in the style of the continent of Europe, in suites of apartments with a restaurant attached. Here, I felt tolerably secure from fire, which was quite a consideration, as I was so often absent from town. For a parlor and two bedrooms (unfurnished), I paid one hundred dollars a month. Beside this, of course, meals had to be provided, and a servant to take charge of the rooms.

In a few months I was able to procure a house which had just been erected. It was of timber plastered over in the cheapest style, two stories without a garret, twenty-two feet front by thirty feet deep.† For this I paid, for the first year, one

---

* *Virginia Block,* corner of Jackson and Stockton Streets.
† In California Street, just below Stockton.

hundred and seventy-five dollars a month—more in a year than the whole place would have cost at the East.

The ordinary price for meals is one dollar. In the fashionable restaurants of San Francisco, it is, of course, much more for a dinner, but one dollar is the ordinary price in the smallest country towns throughout the State. Gentlemen are in the habit of hiring rooms in one place and taking their meals at another. The ordinary price for good board in this way, (board alone,) is sixteen dollars a week.

Servants' wages were,—cooks', from seventy to one hundred dollars a month, chambermaids', from forty to seventy dollars, and nurses', five dollars a day. Common laborers were paid three dollars a day, and mechanics much more. A doctor's fee was ordinarily about eight dollars a visit.

Life was not less strange to us in its social aspects, and I can best convey my impressions by following closely the very words of my journal, from which this chapter has been taken. It must, therefore, be understood as written in 1854, soon after my arrival.

"People live by fortnights in California." Such is the remark we heard a short time after we arrived, and every fortnight we spend impresses it upon us. At these intervals of time the steamers arrive and depart, and thus twice a month all the old associations with the East are revived and memories of "home," (as they all call it,) are rekindled.

It is a time of some excitement when the steamers go. On the 1st and 15th of each month, two of these magnificent vessels,—one for the Panama and the other for the Nicaragua route—are lying side by side, ready at noon to set off for their destination. Through the morning they are thronged by thousands taking leave of departing friends. On all sides you hear the greeting,—"So, you are going home!" often accompanied by the wish that the speaker could himself set his face thither-ward. So general are these expressions, that I was quite startled one morning by hearing a gentleman reply, when asked,—"Are you going home?"—"Why should I, when I am at home already!" It was something so different from the usual spirit of California.

Few of those who go, however, expect to remain at the East. There are some, indeed, who have achieved a fortune and depart to settle down in its enjoyment "at home." And yet many of these, after trying the experiment, have come back again. They say—"Everything is so tame at the East." They miss, too, this delightful climate, and find the weather too hot in summer and too cold in winter. Although they talk about "home," just as the old English colonists used to, of England, nine-tenths of those now in the country will live and die here. The majority of those who leave on the steamers are merely going on a visit, to return in a few months, or to bring out their families, or on temporary business.

But still greater is the excitement when the steamers arrive. For days beforehand they are looked for and the time of their coming is calculated. If delayed a few days, the community is filled with anxiety, and countless speculations are indulged in, to account for their non-appearance. Friends and relatives are expected, or letters are looked for, and thus everyone has an interest in their coming. To show the amount of correspondence, even at this early day, I will mention, that one mail recently

took out sixty thousand letters from the city of San Francisco alone. At length, a gun is heard at " the Heads,"
followed in a little while by another as the steamer draws
near the city, and at once thousands throng down to the
wharf. The deck and cabin are soon filled with friends,
long-parted, congratulating each other, and at once there is
a sensible change over the whole face of society.

It is at the post-office, however, that this excitement is
greatest. As soon as the mails begin to open, and for
several days after, it is besieged by crowds. To prevent confusion, the direction has been issued, to fall in line in the
order of arrival, and consequently, from each of the half-
dozen openings for delivery, there extend long lines of men,
stretching off into the street and winding around like long
serpents. Sometimes there are more than a hundred in each
line, and thus one slowly moves up, and, after waiting for
hours, finds oneself at the goal, the head instead of the tail
of a long series.

Sometimes an impatient man of business pays a handsome
sum for the place of a person who has nearly reached the
head. A friend told me that he went one morning just before day was breaking, and then found himself No. 11. No. 1
had been there since just after midnight, and when seven
o'clock came had the satisfaction of hearing the clerk say,
in answer to his inquiry,—" Nothing for you."

Such are some traits of California life. A gentleman described it to me lately very truly, when he said: " Everything here is hurry-skurry. It is like living on curry.
But what will the world do for excitement when California
settles down?" The active and energetic have thronged
hither from all parts of the world, and there is a rush and

hurry to grasp sudden fortunes. Blanks in the lottery are of course innumerable, yet they are seldom heard of, while the prizes are published, and are sufficient to keep alive the hopes of all. Men who five years ago were worth nothing, are now millionaires. The changes in the value of property, are almost incredible. I pass every day a square * which five years ago was sold for twelve dollars: it is now worth six hundred thousand dollars. It is impossible, therefore, for dwellers in the East to understand the tone of feeling in this city of fifty thousand inhabitants—all brought together in the last few years, and, as yet, without time to form local attachments or associations.

Public morals, however, are improving. A short time ago Sunday was the great business day. Now, the counting houses and more respectable shops close. It is true the theatres are open, and present their highest attractions for that evening, —horse-racing, bear-fighting, etc., are going on, and gambling saloons are in full operation. Still, there has been a great advance. Through the morning, at least, the streets are comparatively quiet, and the churches are well attended. In this respect, Sunday here has somewhat a Continental character. The gambling saloons now are diminishing in number, and are less and less frequented by the higher class of men. Three years ago, gentlemen were here without their families, and had really no other comfortable places to resort to. They slept at their counting houses and offices, and took their meals at eating houses. When night came, the only bright, cheerful looking places, were the brilliantly lighted gambling saloons, where, too, they had

* In Montgomery Street.

splendid music. Here, therefore, they met, and passed the evenings, even when they ventured nothing at the tables. Now, their families are coming out, they are reconstructing their homes, and home feelings are resuming their sway.

Still, there is much, very much, to be done here, to breast this current of intense worldliness which is sweeping everything before it. In 1852 it was so impossible to procure the conviction of a criminal, that a Vigilance Committee was formed of the first men in San Francisco, who, sustained by public opinion, sat as a private court, forcibly seized prisoners when the public courts would have acquitted them, and hanged them in the streets before assembled thousands. The feeling is still prevalent, that a man must fall back on his right of vindicating himself, and although the duellist is by statute disqualified for public office, this law is a dead letter. The highest public officers have fought, some of them repeatedly, and only last week a member of the Legislature was killed in a duel with a brother member. Public opinion has not yet set its seal of reprobation on such things. As you walk through the streets with one well acquainted with men and matters, he points out to you—"That is the man who killed —— in a duel." "That is Mr. —— who shot —— last winter!" etc. Yet their position, neither socially nor politically, seems much affected by it.

But here, as elsewhere, there is the other side. Here are also the good and the true hearted, the earnest Christian, and those who have retained their fidelity to the principles they learned in their old homes. In no part of the world would the Church, after a time, be better supported. Yet we need the aid of our brethren at the East, till it can be planted in the moral wastes, which now abound throughout this land, and that religious atmosphere can be created, which is to purify and reform these gathering thousands.

I have written this, after reading a letter just received from a friend in England,* dated from "Merton College, Oxford," and it is impossible to imagine the contrast to my mind between the "quiet and still air of delightful studies" which breathes through it, coming out at times involuntarily, and the rush and hurry of life about me. It is strange to look on this exciting scene without sharing in it, being in it yet not of it. My correspondent says—"There is a general rejoicing here at the successful issue of the visit.† The Venerable President of Magdalen College,‡ now in his ninety-ninth year, thanked God that he had lived to see the beginning of a union, which (said he) is the most important step that can be effected for the consolidation and strengthening of Reformed Christendom. He specially rejoiced in your mission, because it recognizes the Bishop as the *essential* to make a Diocese, and does not allow a Diocese to grow up first, and seek a Bishop afterwards."

Another,§ who is widely known in this country for authorship in Church literature, writes me—"I cannot forbear telling you how much I am interested in the success of your undertaking, and how earnestly I hope that God's blessing

---

* Rev. Edmund Hobhouse, Fellow of Merton College, since Bishop of Nelson, New Zealand.

† Referring to the Delegation of the Church of England to ou General Convention in 1853, consisting of Dr. Spencer, ex-Bishop of Madras, Archdeacon Sinclair, and Rev. Earnest Hawkins, Secretary of the Society for the Propagation of the Gospel.

‡ Rev. Dr. Routh. He died next year.

§ Miss Sewell—author of "Amy Herbert," etc., etc.

may be with you, and that He will grant you the bodily health, and the mental and moral strength, needed for so great and important work. You must be so much occupied now that it seems unkind to ask you to write, yet if you could find a few minutes to tell me something about your future plans, I should be very much interested in hearing them."

Doubly pleasant, indeed, to us who are laboring in this "far-off land," are these proofs of the Unity of the Church!

X.

CLIMATE.

WHEN a person feels homesick in San Francisco, he is very apt to say, "Well, after all, one compensation for living here is the climate." The atmosphere is certainly most bracing and exhilarating. Day after day, often for a long period, the air is so pure and balmy that it is a luxury to inhale it. We realize that it adds to the mere physical pleasure of living. Nowhere have I found winter weather so much like that of Naples as in some places on the coast, such as San Diego, Santa Barbara and Monterey, but the summers are very different, as the great heat of the South of Italy is here unknown.

There is, however, no division of summer and winter, but of the rainy and dry seasons. The former takes the place of winter, and the latter of summer. The dry season begins about in May, and after that no rain falls till November or December. All the moisture which vegetation receives is from the dews or the fogs at night. Of course, the country then begins to dry up, the plains in the interior become parched and dusty, and, except where there are evergreens, not a bit of green is seen. In San Francisco, the mornings through this season are generally warm and balmy, but about noon high winds set in from

the ocean, often accompanied with fog. This peculiarity
of climate is confined to some twenty miles on this part of
the coast. It is said to arise from the heating of the
plains in the interior, when by noon the air becomes rari-
fied and a vacuum is produced. To fill this, the air rushes
in through the chasm made by the Golden Gate. Other
places on the coast have the cool breezes from the sea,
but without the chilly winds. In this city, however, no one
goes down to his business at ten o'clock, although the atmosphere be like June, without taking his overcoat with him,
for he knows that, on his return towards evening, he will
need it. In July and August the evenings are often so cold
that a little fire is desirable.

The inhabitants complain of these cold winds, and yet
they are preferable to the heat of our Atlantic States.
They are, too, great preservatives of health, giving us a new
atmosphere every twenty-four hours. Without this, there
would be danger of the plague amid the filth and crowd of
the Chinese quarter. I have seen, too, steamers infected
with cholera come directly to the wharf, after having lost
fifty or sixty passengers on their way up the coast—in one
case patients had died after entering "the Heads '—and
although hundreds rushed on board to meet their friends,
and the sick were carried up into town, this was the last we
heard of it. In any other city cholera would have spread
like wildfire. Here it is not thought necessary even to
make sanitary laws.

In October or November there may be a few occasional
showers, though I have known the rainy season not to set
in until about Christmas. Then the winds have ceased, and
when it is not rainy, the air is so fresh and balmy, that

every breath seems to invigorate and inspire with new life. On the country it acts like the advent of spring in other lands. The dusty plains, and the hills which for months had been waving with the yellow wild oats, are now green, and carpeted with flowers. You see countless acres of them of every hue.

Before I reached here, I expected, during the rainy season, to find it raining almost all the time. There is, in this respect, a great difference in different seasons, yet generally, (and I am now writing after five years' experience,) I do not think more rain falls here during the six months of the rainy season, than usually, during the same length of time, at any period of the year on the Atlantic coast. We arrived here in January, the middle of the rainy season, but for the first ten days we had rain but part of two days, with some showers at night.

I believe no city in the world is more healthy than San Francisco. Consumption never originates in it, and from its high position on the hills, it cannot be liable to chills and fever. Should any miasma be generated, it would be swept away by the high winds of summer. The effect of the climate indeed is very visible on those who have been here for some years. They are larger, more robust, and have a ruddy, English look, which is not so often seen on the Atlantic coast. In walking the streets one is struck with the stout, athletic appearance of the male portion of the population.

Many of these remarks about temperature apply to San Francisco only. In the state there is every variety of climate. Back from the coast a few miles, through the beautiful valleys of Santa Clara, or Sonoma, or Napa, it is warmer, but with a climate which cannot be surpassed in

Italy. Still farther back, where entirely removed from the influence of the sea breeze, it is exceedingly hot through the dry season. At Sacramento and Marysville, for a portion of this season, the mercury rises above 100°, though from the latter place, the Sierra Nevada range is in sight, white and glittering, with its winter drapery of snow. And this range extends through the whole length of the State, affording on its slopes and in the valleys at its base, all varieties of temperature.

I one day came down the Sacramento Valley, when the thermometer in the sun registered 127°, but I did not feel the heat more than I should have done at the East, at 90°. Then, too, it is one peculiarity of the climate of this country, that however hot it may be through the day, it is always cool at night. I scarcely remember to have known in any part of California, a night when it was comfortable to sleep without a blanket. In consequence there is no exhaustion of the system.

Another feature of the climate, and one which prevents the heat from being felt as much as in other countries, is the exceeding dryness of the atmosphere. The old Californians (Mexicans) after killing a bullock are accustomed to cut the flesh in strips, (it is here sold by the yard), and to hang it up for a few days in the open air till it becomes entirely dried. It is called "jerked beef." When passing their houses in the interior, I have seen the piazza, between the pillars, entirely festooned in this way. In any other country beef would be spoiled in a few hours, by this exposure. On the plains I have noticed a peculiar effect of this dryness of the air. In riding over them I have sometimes passed the carcase of a dead animal which had been left where it fell. It did not, however, in its decomposition, taint the air with any disagreeable odor, but seemed to dry up and pass away, until only the skeleton was left to rattle in the hard skin.

And yet, the mortality among those who came to California has been fearful. The two cemeteries at San Francisco—"Yerba Buena" and "Lone Mountain"—stretch far and wide with their almost countless graves, while through the length and breadth of the land, on the hillsides, and in the ravines and gulches through the mines, thousands are sleeping their last sleep, the very spot where they were laid forgotten. The sick have come here but to die. Every steamer brings those in failing health, who resort to this climate as their last hope of restoration. But having postponed the change too long, they come only to swell the bills of mortality of San Francisco. The exposure in the mines, too, is terrible. All day long, men inspired by the " greed of gold " work under the burning sun, standing perhaps up to their knees in water. Their food is insufficient and their accommodations such as give them but little shelter. Is it strange, then, that disease attacks them, particularly when so many are entirely unprepared by previous training to endure such hardships? Many, too, are without friends or any associates who know them or care for their welfare.

One day, at a mining camp, it is noticed that some one who has a " claim " near by has not appeared in the morning to dig as usual. Perhaps a miner, more benevolent than the rest, visits his tent and finds him seriously ill. For a day or two, a little attention is paid him, but the third morning he is found to be dead. No one knows him and he is hastily buried on the next hill. His tools and few effects are divided, and thus ends his history. I have heard of instances where men had been lying dead in their tents for days before their decease was discovered. The tent was closed, the occupant did not appear, no one felt any particular interest in him, and it was supposed he had gone off for a time "prospecting," (hunting for a new digging,) till actually the process of decomposition gave notice of the true state of the case.

This ignorance of each other's names, I found to be particularly frequent with young men of respectable families. They feel, in their present position, as if they had sunk themselves and are willing to live *incog.* until "their pile is made," and they can emerge again into respectability. They, therefore, are known to their companions by some *sobriquet*, often the place from which they come, as "Boston," "Kentuck," "Natchez"—and thus, if suddenly cut off, "they die and make no sign," and no one knows who are the relatives to be informed of their decease.

Many—very many—die on the journey over the prairies; and when their companions arrive at the Pacific, four or five months afterwards, they have entirely forgotten their existence and make no report. Not unfrequently, too, in riding over the wide plains of California, one comes to the bleached skeleton of some human being—all that the wolves have left. He has set out alone from the mines on his return to San Francisco. Weary, and perhaps ill, he attempts to walk across one of those wide-stretching plains between the Sierra Nevada range of mountains and the sea. Standing on its verge, the traveler, deceived by the exceeding transparency of the atmosphere, thinks that he can pass over it in a few hours. But he travels on—and on, while the horizon seems to fly from him and to become no more distinct, until at last, worn out and fainting under the noon-tide heats, he sinks down in his path and dies, alone. Months go by before any one passes that way, and then all that can be known is that these are the remains of a fellow being.

Or, discouraged at the "diggings," he wanders in broken health to San Francisco. Here he becomes worse and is carried to the hospital. Before he has declared his name or residence, the power to do so is gone. In a few days he is numbered with the dead, no papers are discovered about him to show who he is, and his sole record is found in the coroner's report at the end of the week:—"A man apparently about thirty years of age." And thus, in California, hundreds pass away, for whom fond hearts at home are yearning, hoping for letters month after month, always ignorant of the fate of the loved and lost. Constantly the steamers have brought me letters from families, not only in our own country, but in England, making inquiries for members of their little circles who had gone years ago to California and from whom no news had been received. Probably their closing scenes might be described in one of the ways I have mentioned above.

XI

THE FIRST SUNDAY.

I HAVE already mentioned, that it was at dawn on Sunday that we entered the harbor of San Francisco and saw before us the city scattered widely over a series of hills, which seemed like "the seven hills" of Rome. What a contrast to the scene which was presented but a few years before, when there was scarcely a hut on the borders of this quiet bay! The harbor, and afterwards the city took the name of the old Mission of St. Francis, the buildings of which still remain nestling under the hills, about three miles from the city.

The member of the committee who came on board to receive us proved to be Mr. Augustine Hale, whose letters to his sister in Albany had first awakened my interest in behalf of California. A carriage was waiting, and in a short time we found ourselves at the house of William Neely Thompson, Esq., another member of the committee. This, for the next fortnight was our home, where everything was done which kindness and hospitality could suggest.

The Rev. Mr. Wyatt at once called on me and insisted on my immediately commencing duty. I confess, I felt but little like engaging in a service, for I had not recovered from all we had passed through during the previous ten days. But everything in California is *onward;* life does not pause for the accommodation of the tired and the weary, and therefore, I yielded to the request of the Rector, and, three hours after my arrival, found myself standing in the chancel of Trinity Church.

The church was founded by the Rev. Flavel S. Mines. After laboring awhile and having this edifice erected, his health failed and he died of consumption. The church is his fitting monument, and he now sleeps beneath its chancel in the hope of a glorious resurrection. The building was curiously constructed of sheet iron, plastered inside. On the arrival of Mr. Wyatt and his entrance on the Rectorship, about eight months before my own coming, the church was enlarged by widening it some twenty feet. At this time the parish was in the very height of prosperity, with a noble, energetic congregation, comprising as much intellect and cultivation as I ever saw gathered in a similar assemblage. The proportion of gentlemen, (as of course is usual in this city,) was much greater than one is accustomed to see at the East, and before I knew them personally, I was struck with the mere outward appearance they presented. Everything betokened activity and energy of mind. There was nothing among the non-Episcopal congregations which could at all compete with the Church, and as the only other Episcopal congregation in the city, Grace Church, was merely in existence, almost all there was of *the Church* on the Pacific coast was gathered into Trinity.

In the morning I read the Ante-Communion Service and

preached, and in the evening I preached again. My
text in the morning was I Corinthians x. 4, and I here
quote the conclusion of my sermom, to show the feelings
with which I entered on my ministry in this distant
land:

" ' And that Rock was Christ.' It is a text which seems
to embrace within itself the very substance and fulness of
the Gospel. And I cannot but rejoice, brethren, that the
first message I am permitted to deliver in this place is from
words condensing within themselves the whole system of
which our Lord was Himself the earliest herald, and which
He bequeathed to His ministers to publish to the ends of
the world. Commencing now a new era in my public ministry, and with a great gulf separating the past, with its throng-
ing memories, from the shadowy future, it is fitting that
these words should be at once my present theme and the
type of what should be my message in days that are to
come. I would have them go on with me, spreading their
influence over all that I may say when ministering in holy
things, till to me, as to all others, that solemn hour comes
when Christ the Rock shall be the dying mortal's only
refuge.

" In obedience, brethren, to that voice of the Church to
which we can only bow in reverence, I come to you, to labor with you in her cause,—in the words of the Apostle,—
' your servant for Jesus' sake.' I have left the associations
of a life-time, to spend the remaining years which God may
grant me, where the length and breadth of a continent separate me from scenes which the past has hallowed. I have
left the graves of those most dear to me, to find my own

where to me the soil has been consecrated by no kindred dust.   Yet I feel that everywhere, over the wide earth, the Church is one,—the same in her spirit and her holy ordinances,—and wherever, therefore, I can stand, as to-day, by the side of her altar, and surrounded by her members, *there* will be home.   And I know too well the generous and earnest spirit of the Churchmen of this land, not to rejoice that, in the Providence of God, such are to be my fellow laborers.   I know that in the mighty contest which together we are to wage, you will not be wanting.

"There is indeed, my brethren, a spirit abroad in this land which cannot but rebuke the faint hearted and the idler, and awaken him to zeal and energy.   Where worldliness is earnest, and every faculty is braced to the utmost in the strife for the prizes of this perishing life, shall the follower of the Lord be slothful, when he is struggling for the souls of ' a multitude which no man can number,'—when the reward of his labor is to be a crown which fadeth not away?   Everything indeed around you, brethren, summons you to aid those whose cry amid the strife is—' Come up to the help of the Lord !'   Your land, overleaping the natural stages of growth, is springing up at once to a giant manhood with a rapidity never before witnessed, and while this generation is yet on the stage, its spiritual destinies may be determined for all coming time.   You are settling this question, therefore, not for yourselves alone, but for your children and your children's children.

" How noble the cause, therefore, in which we are to labor ! Who could be recreant in such a contest ?   Who can even predict the future which opens before us if we are faithful to these mighty interests which are thus entrusted to our hands? Oh! brethren, let it be so ; and then, when time with you is fading into eternity, the Church of God will rejoice that you have lived : and it will be found written of you in the Book of God's remembrance, that you have done something worth recording."

XII.

GRACE CHURCH.

Now that more than five years have passed since my arrival in this country, as I look back upon them, how many of my most pleasing associations centre in Grace Church! It is to me the most home-like place in California.

At the first settlement of the country, when the Rev. Mr. Mines came across the Isthmus, the Rev. Dr. Ver Mehr, at the same time, arrived by the way of Cape Horn. Each had his friends and supporters, and each party commenced the formation of a congregation. It was a sad mistake, the effects of which the Church in this city feels to the present day. There should have been but one congregation, instead of two, which divided the energies of the Church. I have already mentioned the founding of Trinity Church by Mr. Mines. He was a man of energy and talents, and nothing but his failing health and early death prevented the accomplishment of all his hopes.

Dr. Ver Mehr, too, was a man of talents, highly accomplished, and particularly skilled as a linguist. He was, however, a Belgian, and had never acquired the English language sufficiently to succeed as a preacher. He was a fine writer, and his sermons delivered by any one else

94

would have been very impressive, but owing to his German accent, it was difficult to keep the thread of his discourse.

About 1849, in the first outbreak of the California excitement, I happened to be staying with Bishop Doane at " Riverside," when one evening, Dr. Ver Mehr, then one of the teachers at St. Mary's Hall, came in to inform the Bishop, that he proposed going to California. I listened to the discussion which followed, without having any idea that I should ever be personally interested in the matter. I remember, however, that the Bishop strongly urged him not to attempt it. He stated to him, that he was not personally adapted to a new country, nor was his style of scholarship that which was needed here. In fact, he prophesied to him exactly the result which afterwards happened.

Grace Church was " built in troublous times," in Powell Street, but unfortunately not paid for. For some years there was a constant struggle, and Grace Church was always in the field begging money, either by subscription papers, or though the medium of fairs. Every little while it would be in the hands of the sheriff. The result was, that the fine lot which the church owned, and which, had it been preserved intact, would have been a splendid site for a larger church when prosperous times came, was pared down, and all of it sold but the ground under the wooden church and the rectory next door, at the corner. To gather a permanent congregation seemed out of the question.

In the meanwhile, Dr. Ver Mehr and his family had an equally hard struggle for existence. The church in its depressed condition, could not afford to give them a support, and for several years they endeavored to make up the deficiency by the varying success of a school. At length, the whole matter—church and school—was given up in despair, and they retired to Sonoma, where they opened a Female Seminary, principally for boarders.

This withdrawal took place about four months before my arrival. From that time, of course, the condition of the church was looked upon as hopeless.

There was generally a Morning Service on Sundays, by the Rev. Orange Clark, D.D., (who had come out as Chaplain of the U. S. Marine Hospital), but there was no Pastor, and in fact scarcely any congregation. Most of those who felt any interest in the Church had joined Trinity.

On the second Sunday morning after my arrival I officiated in Grace Church, Dr. Clark reading prayers. There was a full congregation, drawn together, of course, by curiosity, as scarcely any of them belonged there. Outside of the building, the appearance of things was desolate enough. Powell Street had not yet been graded, and the church, instead of standing as it now does, several feet below the street, was then some distance above it. In front a deep gully intersected Powell Street at right angles, through which a small stream of water flowed. The church was therefore only accessible in Powell Street, from the South, and in rainy weather, there being no planking, hardly accessible at all, as there was danger of being mired. On the corner was the rectory—a miserable little shanty. It was shortly after leased for five years to Mr. Vandewater, who, at great expense to himself, transformed it into a tasteful cottage and subsequently purchased it.

That week, the two wardens, Judge Wilde, formerly of Georgia, and Dr. Tripler, chief of the Medical Staff, U. S. Army, on this coast, came to invite me to take the Rector-

ship. I asked them the state of the congregation, when the
Doctor, with a quiet smile, replied, "There are twenty
people inside, and the sheriff at the door." This I subsequently found to be exactly the case. After considerable
discussion with the Vestry, I at length agreed to take the
church, while out of deference to Dr. Ver Mehr he was retained as Assistant Minister, a certain portion of the income
of the church, when it should have any, being allotted to
him.

Thus I commenced my new Rectorship. After a short
time the debt was paid, and the church filled up, so that a
competent support was assured to a Rector. At first, I held
service in the morning and afternoon, but soon found that
the habits of the people would make it impossible to gather
a congregation in the afternoon. I was obliged, therefore,
to have an evening service, and I think that at the present
time there is not in the city any religious service on Sunday
afternoon. For about a year Dr. Ver Mehr remained as Assistant Minister, though living at Sonoma. During that time
he came to San Francisco several times to officiate for me
on Sunday, when I was obliged to be absent from the
city. This, however, was inconvenient, and as, in the
meanwhile, other clergymen had come to the Diocese, so
that I could get an occasional supply elsewhere, his connection with the church was dissolved at the end of the
first year.

From this time, until my return East, in April, 1857, this
was the scene of my labors when I could spare time from other
parts of the Diocese. And of all the twenty years which I
spent as a Pastor, there are none to which I look back with
so much unalloyed pleasure as to the three and a half years'

Rectorship in Grace Church, with a magnanimous Vestry and a kind and generous congregation. The entire period was marked by unbroken harmony.

Our communicants increased in number to about one hundred and fifty, and for some time there were more than twenty families on the sexton's list, waiting for pews. For a long while I had been confident, that by building a large church, so that more room could be afforded, and the pew rents so reduced as to bring them within the means of many who could not take them at the present rates, the congregation could be doubled. In this opinion the Vestry agreed, and a lot was purchased at the corner of Stockton and Sacramento Streets, where it was expected that a new edifice would be erected in the spring and summer of 1857. Unfortunately, however, after one half the purchase money had been paid, it was discovered that the title was defective. The difficulties accompanying this were very depressing and delayed the undertaking two years.

In the spring of 1857, it became necessary that I should go East, and I accordingly sailed on the 20th of April. On the Sunday before, I ordained Ferdinand C. Ewer to the Diaconate, and as he was the only clergyman unemployed, I left him in charge of the church. It was not until the middle of December that I returned, but during all this time I had most encouraging reports of Mr. Ewer's success in keeping up the congregation. On my return, therefore, I resigned the Rectorship, and left the charge entirely to him.

Since then the course of the parish has been prosperous. A lot has been purchased on the corner of Stockton and California Streets, which is now excavating for the founda-

tions of the new church. In a few months this will probably
be rising, the most beautiful church edifice on the Pacific
coast, and I trust that within the coming spring and summer the congregation will begin within its walls a new career
of prosperity. Yet, then, the old church will be swept
away, and with it, so many pleasant associations of my early
years in California.

XIII.

SACRAMENTO.

A few days after my arrival, I had an earnest letter from the Vestry of the church at Sacramento, urging me to take the Rectorship and settle at that place. Although fully aware of the importance of Sacramento, as the second city in the State, very strong reasons impelled me to feel that San Francisco was the proper place for my residence. It is the headquarters of all influence in California, the port at which all from the East must necessarily land, and therefore I could probably do most for the general interests of the Church in this Diocese, by a residence at San Francisco. I determined, however, that Sacramento should be the first place in the interior I would visit, and arrangements were therefore made for my holding service there on the third Sunday after my arrival.

On Friday, February 4th, at four P. M., I left San Francisco for Sacramento. The steamers on these rivers are beautifully arranged, with staterooms, a handsome saloon, and every comfort that is found on the fine steamboats at the East. Travelling is, however, expensive in this country, either by land or water. To Sacramento the distance is one hundred and twenty miles, much less than that

100

from New York to Albany. Leaving San Francisco in the afternoon you reach Sacramento at one or two o'clock the next morning. The fare is ten dollars, a stateroom three dollars more, and supper a dollar and a half.

After crossing the wide-spread bay of San Francisco, we reached the entrance of two straits. The most westerly leads out between the high opening known as the Golden Gate, and in the distance we can see the white waves of the Pacific rolling along with their heavy swell, and dashing up against the rocks. We took the other strait, which is about six miles long and leads into an inner bay called San Pablo. The strait is studded with little islands, which vary in color, some of them being of red rock, while some are perfectly white with guano. Toward night they are covered with the sea birds. The Bay of San Pablo is about twelve miles in diameter, and would furnish anchorage to the largest navy in the world. Several little streams empty into it, and on one side is an island which has received the name of Mare Island. In the early settlement of the country, before the wild game had been driven off into the interior, they who coasted along by these shores were accustomed to see roaming over this island a herd of elk, always accompanied by a wild mare, who seemed to act as leader and gallop at their head. She had left her natural associations with the wild horses pasturing on the neighboring hills, and made her home with these new friends.

We then entered the Straits of Carquinez, with the little village of Benicia (a military station) on the one side, and Martinez on the other. Seven miles distant on Napa River, is another little town—Vallejo. General Vallejo, who was military governor of the country before its occupation by

Americans, so named these towns after his wife—Benicia Vallejo. Señora Vallejo thus has her name perpetuated on the coast.

For the whole distance, after leaving San Francisco, the ranges of mountains by which we were surrounded had the same appearance. Their shape impresses you with the idea that they have been formed by volcanic action. And so, undoubtedly, they were. The strata are rent asunder and piled up in confusion, showing traces of great convulsions. Since we have been in San Francisco there have been several shocks of earthquakes; some of which seemed to us quite severe, though no damage was done. There is something unmistakable in the motion. The tremulousness of the earth is unlike any other shock. In the southern part of the State they are more frequent. Sometimes, we are told, the earth rocks like a cradle and great damage ensues. The old Californians shake their heads significantly when they see the three and four story houses of San Francisco, and prophesy that one day there will come an earthquake which will shake them to the ground. Their own plan of building was certainly more suitable for the country,— houses one story high, with *adobe* walls two or three feet thick. These walls might crack, but could not easily be shaken so far from their centre of gravity as to come down. They are also warm in winter and cool in summer.

But to return to the mountains about San Francisco. No rocks are seen,—nothing but the round knolls and glades on the hill-sides, generally without a single tree. The meadows, however, at the base are fringed and dotted with clumps of trees, which sometimes extend up the little glens. But on the higher parts of the hills, which are exposed to the sweep of the summer winds, all is bare. As the rainy season was now closing, they were beginning to look green and fresh, and later they will be perfectly carpeted with flowers. Through the dry season they are covered with wild oats, yellow and almost golden, as if significant of the mineral treasures within. This furnishes abundant food to the numerous herds of cattle which are scattered over them, needing no shelter through the whole year, for even in winter—if the word is a proper one here —the mildness of the climate allows them to graze at large.

Above every other object towers Mount Diabolo, three thousand feet high, rugged and scathed, bearing all the marks of an extinct volcano. It is probably for this reason that the early Spaniards bestowed upon it the name it bears, while everywhere else along the coast, they scattered the names of Apostles and Saints. On one side, blue and irregular, stretches the Coast Range, and then far on the eastern horizon, as the declining rays of the sun fall on their snowy peaks, we see, like a silvery chain, the mountains of the Sierra Nevada.

After the first fifty miles, our course was through broad plains, on which at times little groups of antelopes were seen grazing, or through waste marshes covered with rank vegetation. Through this, "the slough," as they call it, winds in every direction. We sail for ten miles, and have really advanced but two. We look over it and see the white sail of some vessel peeping out, as if it were anchored on the land. The slough is so narrow that at times it seems as if two vessels would hardly have room to pass, and so close do we often run to shore that it would be possible to jump from the deck of the steamer to the meadow at our side.

Sometimes, we turn angles so sharp that the stern of the boat grounds, and it requires some manœuvering to get round the corner. Here and there a squatter has established himself on the shore, and prepared a little patch of land to raise a crop of vegetables; or where the plains are interspersed with trees, a woodman has planted his shanty on the bank, and there the smaller steamers stop to "wood up." Then there is seen a scattered village of the Digger Indians, their little huts built of the *tules*, or thick reeds which cover the marshes.

Occasionally, on the way, we had pointed out to us the site of projected cities which existed on paper only. In the first rush of adventurers to this country, amid every other kind of speculation, that in land was very prominent. It was seen, of course, that there must be some large cities, and the only question was, "where." Speculators seized on sites which seemed to offer good anchorage for commercial purposes, and cities were laid off, and diagrams published, and the lots offered for sale. Unfortunately for their golden dreams in this part of the country, San Francisco and Sacramento have monopolized the commercial business, and the other promising young cities have faded away into nothingness. We passed one of the most famous of these schemes, in Suisun Bay, about fifty miles from San Francisco. On a level plain, with the range of barren mountains behind it, stand three or four houses, which were intended to be the germ of a future metropolis rejoicing in the awkward name of "New York of the Pacific." As there is no particular reason why anyone should live there,—no trade, no productions but mosquitoes,—these houses will probably be abandoned before long, and the silence of the marshes will once more reign on the site of this aspiring city.

I awoke in the morning to find myself at Sacramento. It lies on a beautiful stream, Sacramento River, about three hundred yards in width. The country all about it is perfectly flat. There are no wharves, but hulks are moved close to the shore and fastened to the roots and trunks of trees which grow along the edge. Over these, steamers make their landings. A few hundred yards above, is the confluence of the American and Sacramento Rivers. Here the shore is lined with trees, so that looking away from the young city to the north, as the rays of the rising sun fell upon the masses of foliage, there was nothing to remind us that the busy haunts of men were growing up so near. With wonderful rapidity Sacramento has grown to be the second city in the state. It is laid out with the streets at right angles, those running north and south being named after the numbers, those east and west, after the letters of the alphabet. Standing, as it does, on a level plain, removed from the sea breezes, it is exceedingly hot during the summer months, the mercury rising to over a hundred degrees. Still, it is very healthy, for in these inland places there is a purity and a dryness in the atmosphere which seem to prevent the heat from being felt as much as it would at the East, when of the same degree. At the first settlement of the city, many of the forest trees were preserved, and oaks and sycamores, frequently six feet in diameter, lined some of the streets, throwing widely their boughs and furnishing in summer a most grateful shade. Shortly after, however, the city was swept by a desolating fire which left little of it standing, and the fine old trees shared the fate of the new wooden buildings which had been run up at their side.

Sacramento is one of the most bustling cities in the State. It is one of the principal points from which the mines are supplied, and as you walk through its streets you see the huge wagons, with their six or eight mules, loading with goods ; or you meet them on the plains in the broad Sacramento Valley, slowly toiling on to the mountains. Twenty-two lines of stages leave the city every day. The inhabitants have shown a degree of enterprise and energy in building up this place for which it would be difficult to find a parallel in any part of the world. They have been desolated, not only by fire, but by water. During the rainy season the river rises above the level of the plain on which the city stands, and there have been times when the streets were passable only in boats. A levee has, however, been thrown up on the river bank, so high, as, probably, effectually to remedy this evil. In addition to these drawbacks, the city commenced with a competitor. Three miles down the river, the town of Sutter was founded, which it was supposed would be a formidable rival. It stands on rising ground, and seems to be in a more pleasant situation than Sacramento. But it did not prosper. There was need for one town only, and therefore, as Sacramento grew, Sutter dwindled away. It is now almost depopulated Four or five brick buildings, one of them as large as a first class hotel, stand in lonely dignity overlooking the plain below—mere memorials of disappointed hopes.

It seems strange that in a city of this size and importance the Church has not been securely established. I find many Church people scattered about among its population; some, for the present, are attending the services of the different denominations, with the danger of becoming entirely alienated, and, at all events, having their children grow up in utter ignorance of the Church in which their fathers were reared; while others go nowhere and are relapsing into utter indifference on the subject. The Church in Sacramento has indeed been singularly unfortunate. In September, 1849, the Rev. Mr. Burnham, of New Jersey, came here in feeble health, and after officiating for a few weeks, became too weak to continue the services and died in the early part of the following year. It is a strange proof of the facility with which we are forgotten, that I found it difficult to obtain the name of this young missionary, four years after his death. Even the gentleman in whose house he died could not recollect it! Then, the Rev. Mr. M. visited the parish and held occasional services for a few months, when he abandoned the ministry and left the country. In October, 1850, the Rev. Orlando Harriman assumed the charge, but his health failing, he returned to New York in March, 1852. Then occasional services were held by the Rev. Mr. Pennell, a clergyman of the Church of England, the Rev. Orange Clark, D. D., chaplain to the U. S. Marine Hospital at San Francisco, the Rev. John Reynolds, chaplain of the U. S. A., the Rev. Augustus Fitch, and the Rev. John Morgan. The three last mentioned returned to the East. None of these seemed to find sufficient encouragement, and abandoned the field. At one time the subject of the permanent establishment of the Church was taken up by the people with considerable energy, and a sufficient sum of money subscribed to purchase a lot. While deliberating on its location, in November, 1852, occurred the fire which swept off a great portion of the town, and for a time paralyzed everything. Everybody had lost heavily,—some everything,—and it became with many a struggle for their very existence. All the minutes of the meetings of the Vestry with other parochial papers, (including the subscription paper,) had been burned, the hopes of Churchmen were destroyed, and for a time nothing further was done towards founding the Church. In this state I found them at this visit in February, 1854.

Standing at the foot of J Street, the principal business street, it presents a strange appearance. There is scarcely a house in it more than one story high.

These slight wooden 'structures with canvas partitions were put up hastily after the fire, and their occupants have not yet been able to replace them with better buildings.

Not knowing any one in Sacramento, I went to the Orleans Hotel, where shortly after breakfast, Jos. W. Winans, Esq., called on me and invited me, with my son, to stay with him at a house, where in company with several other young men, he was keeping bachelor's hall; an invitation which we accepted. This indeed is the usual style of living, even the married men having in few instances, as yet, brought out their families, as they are only trying an experiment here. There are therefore but few ladies, and the number of families is small.

I spent Saturday with Mr. Winans in visiting the principal people who were known to have been attached to the Church at home, or who had shown any predilection for it, to kindle up anew their zeal and prepare them for exertion it its favor. Sunday morning came, rainy and cold. The flat, unpaved streets were lying in pools of water, and

it seemed almost impossible to get from one side of the
city to the other. Yet we had a good congregation. The
Methodist place of worship, (only the basement story of
which had been erected), was kindly offered for our use,
a courtesy which was extended to us on all my future visits
during the year—subsequently, on the arrival of their
clergyman, the congregation worshipped in a public hall.
In the afternoon I baptized two infants, and again had service in the evening.

The next day I met several of the gentlemen of the church,
with reference to its re-organization. As a result they
shortly after procured a new incorporation, (Mr. Winans
and Dr. J. F. Montgomery, Wardens,) and a clergyman
was called from the East.

While at Sacramento, I drove out with a gentleman over
the plains which compose the Valley of the Sacramento.
It extends—I think about sixty miles—to the foothills, and
is covered with scattered oak trees, like a rolling oak prairie
in some of our western states. About a mile above the
city, on the river, we passed an old *adobe* house at what was
the *embarcadero* (or place of landing,) when General Sutter
first came into the valley. Two miles farther, on the plain,
is Sutter's fort. It is a parallelogram, about four hundred
feet each side, thus giving room within for the buildings and
also for enclosures for the cattle. Here, in the early days of
California, the old General ruled like a feudal lord. With
grants from the Mexican government of many leagues of
land, he had a territory much larger than most of the German principalities, and with a small band of determined
white men about him—trappers and hunters from their
youth,—from his fort he controlled the Indians on the

plains. When gold was discovered and the rush of Americans came, he received the hundreds of immigrants who arrived, with open-handed hospitality. His cattle were killed for their use, and often his land was freely given to them. He became thus the prey of sharpers, who gradually stripped him of his possessions. The patriarch of California and the pioneer—all she has given him is the empty title of Major General of the militia, a cocked hat and a pair of epaulets! His fort, which is historical in the annals of California, is now deserted,—the wall broken down,—and the annual rains are gradually destroying the *adobe* walls.

The old General now lives at the Hock Farm, on Feather River, some ten miles below Marysville. As he happened to be in Sacramento at this time, he called on me, but as I was absent, he saw my son. He talked over his past history with him and "fought his battles o'er again." A Swiss by birth, he had served in the European armies, and at one time occupied the same tent with Louis Napoleon. But the old General's day is over. He could not contend against the tide of Anglo-Saxon energy which is sweeping over this land, and it is probable that not an acre of his once vast possessions will be bequeathed to his children.

May 11th.—Wednesday, I was again in Sacramento, for the purpose of holding a service the next evening. The claims of business are so great, that it is hard for many to break away from their week-day cares and devote themselves for an hour to the calls of the other world. The Legislature, too, was just breaking up and held an evening session. Notwithstanding, the attendance was good, and everything I see convinces me that they need only a clergyman of proper spirit and talents, to build up a strong congregation.

It is strange how unexpectedly persons' paths in life cross each other. Two years before this, in the depth of winter, I had been lecturing at Rochester, N. Y., before the Young Men's Association, when, the next morning, on entering the cars for Albany, I met one of the Mr. Rochesters. He requested me to take charge of his cousin, Mrs. B., who had come with her children from Kentucky, and was on her way to New York, to sail for California, where she was to join her husband. I did so, and when we reached Albany, at evening, took her to the ferry-boat by which she was to cross to take the night train for New York. Here I took leave of her, feeling that she was going to the ends of the earth, and certainly never expecting to see her again. From that time she scarcely crossed my mind until unexpectedly I met her at Sacramento, which is now her home.

In the course of the day, I visited the Legislature, a body which in this State seems to have the power of locomotion to a great degree. The primary meetings, when the Constitution was formed, were held at Monterey. Then it met at Vallejo, and then at San Jose. Then it removed to Benicia, and in the middle of this session it transported itself to Sacramento. As the Governor, of course, follows the Legislature around the State, by remaining in office for a few years, he has a good opportunity to become acquainted generally with his constituents in various parts.

I saw the Legislature to disadvantage, as just at the close of the session every member is striving to have some favorite bill taken up. The election of a United States Senator, too, was absorbing all attention, and every other question was bending to it. These circumstances, therefore, doubled the confusion which often prevails in a legislative body.

The speaker of the assembly was introduced to me as Mr. Fairfax. As in my youth I had spent a winter in Virginia, and knew all his family, I inquired to which branch he belonged, and found that he was the present holder of the title, as "Burke's Peerage" entitles him, "Lord Fairfax of Cameron, the tenth baron." When I last saw him at his father's, he was three or four years old. Another curious meeting in this far-off land!

September 23rd. Summer had come and its heat was prevailing throughout the interior, when I found it necessary to go again to Sacramento, in answer to the appeal of a member of the Church, who, just recovering from a lingering illness, wrote to me of her "very great desire to join once more in the beautiful service." There were others, too, who needed spiritual services, and I felt I could not neglect the call.

The hills about had put on their deepest golden hue, as the wild oats had dried, it being five months since they had had any rain; and the evergreen trees which grow in the valleys and defiles were thrown out into strong relief. I awoke in the morning to find myself at the wharf, and in as different a climate as if I had dropped suddenly from the temperate into the tropic zone. When I left San Francisco the afternoon before, the cool sea breezes were blowing, and I wore an overcoat. At Sacramento I found it oppressively hot, and during the three days I was there, the mercury must have risen above 100°.

A month previous, another sweeping fire had desolated the city, when twelve squares were burned over. Some public buildings were destroyed, including the court house where the Legislature met, and the Congregational meeting house. Yet with Californian energy, the citizens at once began to repair their loss, which will prove a public benefit, as more substantial buildings replaced those that were burned. The walls of the Capitol were already several feet above ground.

The Vestry have lately had an answer from the clergyman to whom the call was forwarded. He declines the invitation, and they are again seeking an incumbent.

Saturday was spent, as usual, in visiting members of the congregation, and particularly one young man who was ly-. ing at the hotel, in the last stage of consumption. He had been confirmed at home, where he knew some members of my family, and had a few days before asked his attendants to procure for him, if possible, the attendance of a clergyman of the Church. Being sensible of his situation, it was a source of great consolation to him, to have her solemn rites brought to him in that hour. There is something indeed dreadful in thus dying, away from home, without a friend or relative to stand by the bed-side—to feel the longing for "old familiar faces" in that last hour of nature's feebleness, as, in this case, where, resigned to all that should befall him in the coming world, the sick boy declared his only regret to be that he could not see his family. And yet, how many die in this way in California—without even a friend to close their eyes,—abandoned to servants— or more frequently, in the interior, without any attendance at all. How many thousands, for whom friends at home are anxiously looking, have died without leaving even the record of a name behind them, and now are lying in nameless graves on the hill-sides or river banks!

On Sunday, I had two services as usual, and administered the Holy Communion to twenty-one communicants. I also baptized two children. In the afternoon I administered the Communion to the young man I have mentioned, it being the first time he had received that Sacrament. Three days afterwards, he died, and, as I had left the city, a layman read the burial service at his grave.

This was my last visit to the parish while it was without a clergyman. On the 19th of November, two months afterwards, the first Rector, the Rev. Horace L. E. Pratt, arrived and entered on his duties. From that time, the history of the parish is written in the annual parochial reports.

On Monday at noon, I left for home. The steamer was crowded with miners—stout, hairy, athletic fellows, most of them having revolvers strapped at their sides. Upon conversation with one of them, I learned that a flume had broken in the mountains a fortnight before, and as the supply of water was thus cut off from extensive "diggings," more than a thousand miners had been thrown out of employ. Some were going down to San Francisco for recreation; others were going home. Very few had succeeded in "making their pile."

XIV.

STOCKTON.

My first visit to Stockton was by appointment for Sunday, February 17th, 1854, in the month after my arrival. The steamer leaves San Francisco at four o'clock in the afternoon, and reaches there before daylight the next morning, unless detained by fogs or lowness of water in the river. After proceeding for some hours by the same route as to Sacramento, passing Benicia, we turn aside and enter the San Joaquin River. Until dark, I found the scenery the same as that of the Sacramento River,—broad meadows covered with *tules*, and the river winding tortuously.

I arose at daylight, and learned that we were still a few miles from Stockton, while the mist which had detained us was gradually rolling off the wet marshes as the sun's rays penetrated through it. The whole scenery below Stockton —meadows covered with rank, luxurious vegetation—reminded me vividly of the Pontine Marshes. Formerly, they were tenanted by herds of elk, which were often lassoed by the native vaqueros, but the increasing population has driven them farther into the recesses of the country. Antelopes, at some seasons of the year, are still seen in bands, feeding on the herbage,—the coyotes (a small species of wolf) make there their home—while innumerable

115

large gray squirrels and flocks of water fowl find their hiding places in the weeds and tall reeds.

As we approached Stockton, we entered a "slough" of the river, which leads up through the centre of the town, where it is crossed by several bridges. The town itself, like Sacramento, stands on a level, and although it would seem from its situation that it must be exposed to a deadly malaria, yet it is tolerably healthy. Some intermittent fever prevails in the autumn, but it seems to be of a mild type and readily to give way to medical treatment. During the summer, a breeze from the sea sets up the valley in the latter part of the day, which moderates the excessive heat and at the same time sweeps away malaria.

The earliest white men who visited this place were the trappers from the North,—they were hardly permanent enough to be called settlers. These sloughs of the river once abounded with beaver, which are still occasionally seen in their waters. Thither came little parties sent out by the North West Company. They penetrated through the country wherever traces of beaver were found—encamping by the side of these streams,—leading a wild life, like that of the Indians themselves, to whom they assimilated in their habits, and whose squaws often became their wives. When the season closed, loaded with pelfries, they repaired to the nearest trading post of the Company. There, the winter was often spent in revelry, until spring found them penniless and ready to set out once more on a new expedition. Many of those who came to Stockton were Canadian French, some of whose descendants still remain at a little settlement on the plains, about six miles from Stockton, called French Camp.

The first permanent settler, however, was Mr. Webber, a German gentleman, who in 1844 obtained a Government grant of a tract of land, covering the country for about eleven leagues, and embracing within its bounds the whole site of the present city, which he took active measures to have colonized. His residence is just below the town, on the borders of the slough. At immense expense, he has thrown up banks to protect himself from the rising of the water, and formed flower gardens which give a cheerful air to his place. Few persons, however, would have chosen the location he has selected, when, by going back a mile on his grant, he might have found beautiful sites covered with old oak trees.

Stockton is admirably situated for inland trade, being surrounded by mining districts to which it furnishes supplies. The *placers* and gulches on the Stanislaus and the Tuolumne Rivers are less than seventy miles distant; while those on the Mokelumne, on Carson Creek, and at "Murphy's Diggings," are less than sixty. To some of these places the supplies can be carried by mules only, while to others, huge wagons, drawn by a long train of mules, can find a road. We saw them loading at the store-houses in town, and preparing to set out on their toilsome journey across the plains and up through the ravines of the mountains. The drivers are generally Mexicans, whose Spanish opposition to change is seen in the very equipments of their mules. Their harness was probably unchanged since their fathers came to this country. It is found of the same pattern now on the plains of Andalusia—the same array of tinkling bells and plated ornaments, as perhaps in the days of Cervantes.

We reached the wharf on the slough at seven o'clock, when I was met by the warden of the church, Mr. Eastman, and

conducted to the Magnolia Hotel, where I was to stay.
Saturday was spent in investigating the situation and prospects of the Church, and in making preparation for service
the next day.   The parish here was organized in August,
1850.   The Rev. O. Harriman, Jr., (the same who was at
Sacramento for a time) officiated for about a month, when,
not receiving an adequate support, he abandoned the field.
In 1851, the warden, Mr. Bissell, commenced lay reading,
which he continued for about two years, when, to the great
regret of the parish, he returned to Philadelphia.   From that
time, except during visits from Rev. Dr. O. Clark, Rev.
John Morgan and Rev. John Reynolds, Chaplain U. S. A.,
there were no services, and while the organization was
preserved, the Church existed only in name.   On Saturday,
in company with the warden, I visited those who were known
to be favorable to the Church, to awaken their interest in its
behalf.   This, indeed, is the only way in which anything can
be done in this country.   Men are too much immersed in
business, to give heed when addressed in masses.   They
must be sought out and appealed to, personally, to enlist
them in any cause, particularly one which is removed from
the interests of this lower world, and which holds out no
prospect of a golden harvest.

Notice of our service had been given in the public
papers, and a large room in the court house was provided, where the judge's seat made a good pulpit and
the jury room answered for a vestry room.   There were
about three hundred persons present.   The number of
Prayer Books produced, and the nature of the responses,
gave evidence of a degree of churchmanship which ar-
gued well for the founding of a strong congregation

in this place. We had service both morning and after-noon.

Monday also was spent in visiting the members of the Church, and particularly one who was exceedingly ill. It was a great satisfaction to me to be able, in the last closing hours of life, to repeat in her hearing those familiar prayers to which for so many years she had been a stranger. She died that night, after my departure, and the burial service was read by the warden of the church.

I left in the steamer, at four o'clock. Through the whole evening, and as long as I remained on deck, the scenery around us was lighted up by fires. The dry *tules* which cover the marshes are thus burned over every season. Any accident which starts the fire—the carelessness of a party camping out, or even the sparks from a passing steamer, begins a conflagration which spreads over a wide extent of country. Sometimes the flame swept down near the river bank by which the steamer was passing, then it rolled away toward the horizon in lurid masses, lighting up the whole sky, and furnishing a spectacle which reminded us of Fenimore Cooper's descriptions of the burning of the prairies.

June, 1854. I went to Stockton a few weeks ago, to per-form the marriage service, and again, last week, to spend Sunday. Until a Rector arrives, the only way of keeping the Church alive is by services of this kind.

The vestry have been endeavoring to get a lot, but owing to the unsettled land titles in this part of the country, they have been discouraged from attempting to acquire property. Nothing can be done until there is a legal decision on the validity of Mr. Webber's grant. They wrote me lately, how-

ever, that they had subscriptions for the support of a clergyman, to the amount of two hundred dollars a month.
They have secured, too, for their services, the use of a
larger and finer room in the court house.   It is the hand-
somest and most convenient room for the purpose that I
have seen outside of San Francisco,—windows curtained,
handsome lamps hanging from the ceiling,—and without the
desolate appearance which public rooms generally have.
At our service, on Sunday, the whole floor of the room
was filled with chairs, and the congregation, as in the
winter, numbered at least three hundred.   As in my
former visit, I spent Saturday and Monday in visiting
where anything could be said or done to advance the interests of the cause for which I went to Stockton.

On this occasion, I stayed with the Resident Physician of
the State Insane Asylum.   This institution is situated on
the side of the river opposite that on which the greater
part of the town is built, but, as I mentioned before, connected with it by bridges.   This side is now building up
with dwelling houses, which will make it the finest part of
the city.   The asylum is about a half a mile out, where the
rolling prairie commences, and is surrounded by trees.
From this place, for miles the country is covered with
clumps and groves of oaks, just as it is in the Sacramento
Valley.   I rode over it, one day, for several miles, and found
the same characteristics of scenery.   Unless a person had
some distant landmark in sight, he might easily lose his
way on these extensive plains.

The asylum is a long brick building, having now only
two stories, though an appropriation has been made, at the
late meeting of the Legislature, to enlarge it.   At present

its one hundred and fifty patients are inconveniently crowded. I went through the wards with the Doctor, and was rather startled by overhearing the following conversation with a patient who had been scrutinizing me for some time.

" Doctor! is that one of the directors ? "

" No."

" Who is he ? "

" He's a Bishop."

" What sort of a Bishop?   A Methodist ? "

" No; an Episcopal Bishop."

" I'm glad of it. If he had been a Methodist Bishop, I should have had to kill him. I'm commanded to kill all the Methodists."

In proportion to the population, insanity is perhaps five times more frequent in California than in any other country.   Adventurers come here from every quarter of the globe, with extravagant hopes of speedy fortune.   When these fail, the restless, undisciplined brain is easily upset.

The following is one of many instances I have known. One morning I was summoned to the door by a man in the dress of a miner, who said he wished to have some conversation with me.   I, of course, invited him in, and, after we were seated, he took out a small Bible, and said that he had just come from the mines and desired to ask me some questions on religious subjects.   I found in five minutes, that he was entirely deranged, his topics of conversation being a mixture of religion and mining.   He had met with something in Job, about "the vein of gold and silver," * and also about "the island of the innocent," † and he wished to find

* Job xxviii. 1.   † Job xxii. 30.

them again. He wanted an explanation of the Book of Revelations, and also of the mystical connection between Job's " seven sons " and the " seven seals" of the Apocalypse. I said what I could to calm him—advising him to let the prophecies alone, and to confine his reading to the Gospels —and he left me, stating that he would soon return. Two days after, I recognized him in a description in the newspaper of a person who had committed suicide—as the coroner's jury correctly stated—" while in a state of insanity, arising from sickness and disappointment in the mines."

There is one peculiarity of the California Insane Asylum (which I trust will have been altered before these pages see the light), that should awaken the indignation of all the other states sending their citizens to the Pacific. In every other Christian country where I have been, the physician who presides over an insane asylum is carefully selected with regard to his fitness for the post, and then holds his office for life or during the continuance of good behavior. Here, the position is made a prize to reward political partisans. At every change of politics in the State, out goes the physician of this institution. Then commences a course of lobbying at the Legislature, and exertions of friends, and the place is finally given to one whose supporters can command most party influence. Thus, the life and intellect of hundreds of these poor invalids are made the sport of politicians.

Of course, if the power changes every two years, so often must the doctor. Even if he should be a good physician, (and this does not enter into the calculations of the politicians), he may have no particular skill in the treatment of insanity. This is a special gift. And even if he should have

it, he has no time to study the cases, to watch their changes
and conform his treatment to their peculiarities. The
whole matter is a disgrace to humanity, and when it
has been in agitation, and I have heard the claims of
the incapables urged because their relatives had done
service to *the party*, I have felt my blood boil at this in-
famous violation of all the laws of decency.

In November, the Rev. James S. Large arrived in Stockton and entered on his duties as Rector. With this visit,
therefore, ended my charge as furnishing an occasional
supply to the parish. For the future, my visitations were
the usual ones made by a Bishop to the Church.

XV.

MY FIRST CONVENTION.

The earliest Convention (so called) was held in Trinity Church, San Francisco, in July, 1850, as it is expressed in the report,—"for the purpose of organizing the Diocese of California." The opening sermon was preached by Dr. Ver Mehr, and the Rev. Flavel S. Mines was appointed chairman. The Convention met for eight evenings in succession, and adopted a constitution that could have been expanded to meet all the wants of a Diocese the size of New York. Besides the ordinary Standing Committee, they appointed a Board of Trustees of the Episcopal Fund; a Board of Trustees of the Diocesan Fund; Trustees of the College and Theological Seminary; and a Board of managers of the Presbyterium, (a place for disabled clergymen,) and of the Sanitarium, (a home for infirm widows). Most of these institutions, after a lapse of years, have not yet commenced their existence.

It is a fact but little known to the Churchmen of this day, that the early founders of the Church on this coast had no idea of uniting with the general Church at the East. There is no recognition of it in any of their proceedings. They ignored the name of the " Protestant Episcopal

124

Church," and called their organization "the Church in California."

Knowing that while in this position no Bishop would be consecrated for them, the question of attempting to procure the episcopate from the Greek Church was discussed, previous to the meeting of the Convention. The Missionary Committee had cut off the stipends for California. Dr. Ver Mehr and Mr. Mines were of the opinion that the ecclesiastical authority at the East had no jurisdiction over the doctor, who never had been a missionary, or over Mr. Mines, whom by their action they had discarded; and that, therefore, they had a right to organize independently.

But, apparently abandoning the idea of recourse to the Greek Church, the Convention elected as their Bishop the Rt. Rev. Horatio Southgate, who, having been consecrated for a Mission to Turkey, from which he had lately returned, was already a Bishop. He, however, declined the invitation. Then three years passed away, during which time nothing further was done to organize the Church. And when the Convention met in May, 1853, in their report they say: "The Diocese of California, organized in 1850, has remained about stationary—we are obliged to confess it; nay, it may in the eyes of some have seemed to be defunct. It exists, but in verity we cannot say more." The Rev. Flavel S. Mines had been removed by death. Marysville, where the Rev. Augustus Fitch had commenced a parish, was vacant, by his removal to the East in the previous year, and the Standing Committee reported: "At this time the parish at Marysville is defunct." The same was the case with Sacramento and Stockton. The two parishes in San Francisco—Trinity and Grace—alone were reported by the committee as being "in a progressive condition."

Still no advance had been made in procuring Episcopal supervision. The idea was entertained here, that as they had regularly organized themselves into a Diocese, the General Convention could not appoint a Missionary Bishop over them. They therefore appointed a committee to correspond with different Bishops, and procure from some one of them a visit for temporary services. The report of the Standing Committee contains the following equivocal language: "As a Diocese we ought to manage our own affairs. *Whether we ask for admission into union or not,* we can no more rely on missionary help." A resolution, however, was finally passed, "to apply for admission into union with the General Convention," but without any declaration that they subscribed to the government of the Church general in the United States.

At the General Convention of 1853, therefore, California was regarded in the House of Bishops with an evident feeling of distrust. The impression seemed to be, that the Diocese wished in some way to be independent, and that its organization was made to prevent the appointment of a Missionary Bishop. The General Convention, therefore, entirely ignored the action of the Diocese, on the ground that it had not subscribed to the Constitution of the Church,—refused to receive its delegates, (two lay delegates being present,)—and the House of Bishops proceeded to the election of a Missionary Bishop.

Before I left New York, considerable doubt was expressed as to the state in which I should find things on my arrival on the Pacific coast. The last conver-

sation I had with one of the members of the Missionary Committee, (Rev. Chas. Halsey), on board the *George
Law,* just before she left the wharf, was on this point. He
said to me:—" If there is any opposition, we will at once
send into the Diocese half a dozen missionaries, who will
give the majority to right principles, and be *the* Diocese."
I subsequently learned, that on the news of the election
reaching California, some, whose schemes had been thereby
defeated, held a caucus to discuss the question, whether or
not they should nullify it. Fortunately for them, they determined to bow to the decision of the Church. For my
own part, I came prepared for whichever course they might
take. If I should be met in a proper, Churchlike spirit, I
was ready to respond to them with like feelings. If they
took the opposite course, I should have refused all recognition of the recusants, as Churchmen, and, regarding them
as schismatics, should have considered the Church in this
Diocese as including those only who paid a proper respect to
its authority.

I, however, had no cause of complaint. The day after my
arrival, the Standing Committee waited on me to present a
series of resolutions of welcome, and at our Convention,
four months later, the following preamble and resolutions
were adopted.

" Whereas, this Convention, at its session in May, 1853,
adopted measures to obtain an Episcopal visitation of the
Diocese of California, by some one of the Bishops of Dioceses in union with the General Convention, under the supposition that California, being an organized Diocese, was
precluded from the privilege of having a Missionary Bishop
placed in charge over her; And whereas, the General Con-

vention, at its session in October, 1853, judged it canonical and expedient to send a Missionary Bishop to this Diocese, therefore,

"*Resolved,* That this Convention desires to express its devout thankfulness to the overruling Providence of Almighty God, and its very cordial satisfaction, that this Diocese has thus so soon been permitted to enjoy the benefit and consolation of a Bishop's care.

"*Resolved,* That this Convention eagerly embraces this first opportunity to express its hearty approval of the action of the Standing Committee as the representative of the Diocese, in promptly receiving the Rt. Rev. Wm. Ingraham Kip, D.D., Missionary Bishop to the Diocese of California, with a reverent and affectionate welcome, to be the shepherd of the sheep in this portion of Christ's fold and our beloved Father in God."

On arriving in California, the question for me to decide was, whether I should regard the Church as still without an organization—mere missionary ground—(which the very action of the House of Bishops in electing me would have justified my doing), and thus begin *de novo;* or, accepting the legislation of the Diocese as it stood, go on with it. As a matter both of prudence and convenience, I determined on the latter course.

My first Convention in the Diocese met May 3rd, 1854, in Trinity Church, San Francisco. But two Clergymen were present, the Rev. Orange Clark, D.D., late Chaplain of the U. S. Marine Hospital, and the Rev. C. B. Wyatt, (the only parochial clergyman in the Diocese,) of Trinity Church, San Francisco. There were lay delegates from three Churches, Trinity and Grace, San Francisco, (I had taken the rectorship of the latter,) and St. John's Church, Stockton. The first and most important business was to place the Church in this Diocese in a proper attitude towards the Church general in our country. I therefore brought this forward in my address:—

"In concluding this address, my brethren of the clergy and laity, I would ask to call your attention to one point connected with the organization of the Church in this Diocese. You are aware that the application for admission to the General Convention, at the late meeting of that body, was not favorably received, nor were the delegates from this Diocese admitted to seats, on the ground that there was no provision in your Constitution, or in the resolutions requesting admission for your delegates, which subscribed to the Constitution and Government of the Protestant Episcopal Church in the United States. The omission of this clause was, of course, inadvertent, and, it seems to me, that the very application to be admitted into union, was *ipso facto* a declaration of your assent to the Constitution of the Church general. So, however, it was not regarded by the House of Clerical and Lay Deputies, and your admission, therefore, into union with the Church at the East was necessarily postponed until the meeting of the next General Convention.

"There is nothing, that I can discover, in the Constitution of the Church here, which impeaches the validity of its past action or its present organization as a Diocese. To prevent, however, any further mis-construction and to remove any obstacles which may thus exist in the way of our entire union with our brethren at the East, would it not be well for you to remedy this omission in your Constitution? 1

would, therefore, submit this question as a subject for your consideration. In that mighty conflict which the Church finds each year gathering more closely about it, the sources of its strength are the ties which link together those who are fighting under the same banner and whose cry amid the strife is, 'Who is on the Lord's side?' While, therefore, we are seeking to brighten once more the chain of brotherhood which unites us to our Mother Church beyond the seas, doubly pleasant is it to strengthen every tie which binds us to the altars in our own land, where once we worshipped, and where our earliest vows were uttered."

A committee was thereupon appointed,—consisting of the Bishop, Rev. Dr. Clark, Rev. Mr. Wyatt, and D. S. Turner, Esq.,—who reported an addition to the proper article in the Constitution, by which this omission was supplied. And then the Church in this Diocese was prepared to take its proper place in the Church in our country.

XVI.

LENT and Easter were over when I determined to see something of the mining regions of the state. On the after-noon, therefore, of Easter Monday, April 17, 1854, I left San Francisco, in company with Mrs. Kip and my son, in the *Bragdon*, which was to go through to Marysville. It was with some little compunction that we selected her, for her engine is high pressure, and on one of these boats, only ten days before, the boiler had burst and killed thirty passengers. However, as the result proved, she carried us both safely and pleasantly to our destination. As we left our wharf, the *Columbia*, for Oregon, with Bishop and Mrs. Scott on board, (who had been spending a short time in San Fran-cisco, on their way to his Diocese,) fired her gun and set out on her voyage.

On the following morning, at Sacramento, we left the river of that name and entered the Feather River. The old Californians called it the *Plumas*, on account of the myriads of wild fowl seen on its waters, but Americans have anglicized it to *Feather* River. The scenery here begins to change in one respect. In a former chapter

131

in describing my visit to Sacramento, I mentioned that the lower part of these rivers, above San Francisco, was almost destitute of trees. Here they are again seen, reminding us of home and the East. Broad, prairie-like plains stretch out on each side, which are occupied with a constant succession of *ranches*, but the narrow river is fringed with fine trees, and often the boat approaches so close to them that they brush her guards.

We had not more than eight or ten cabin passengers. One of them, with whom I became acquainted, was going up to the mines as one of the partners in a grand company which was spending fifty thousand dollars in laying bare about fifteen hundred feet of the bed of the Feather River. Out of twenty feet square of the bed, they, last year, took one hundred and seventy-five thousand dollars, and, in this proportion, he expected to make some millions out of their grand operation. As I never heard anything further of the company, I suppose it exchanged— as most mining companies did—golden hopes for leaden realities.

About ten miles below Marysville is the ranch of the old pioneer, General Sutter. It is one of the most beautiful places as to situation that I have seen in any country. The house, except in the centre, is but one story high. It extends perhaps a hundred feet,—the portico in front covered with vines,—and has a very picturesque appearance. It stands on a perfectly level plateau, which rises eight or ten feet above the river and stretches back for miles to the mountains. Here and there, over the whole extent, are clumps of large oak trees, and the country, dotted with groups of cattle, presents the appearance of a wide-spread

English park. The General owns several leagues of land about his residence.

We should have reached Marysville at ten o'clock, but owing to some accident in the machinery, we did not arrive till three hours later. We felt, however, that this was an advantage, for the day was beautiful and we had a good opportunity of seeing the varied scenery of the river. Had we made the proper time, much of the river above Sacramento would have been passed before daylight. About half a mile from Marysville we left the Feather River and turned into a narrow, rapid stream, called the Yuba, so fringed with trees at its mouth as entirely to conceal the town, nor did we see it until we were close upon it.

Marysville is a thriving, growing town of about eight thousand inhabitants. The hotels are well filled and a constant stream of trade passes through it. The Presbyterians and Methodists have congregations established here, and the Baptists are making an effort to obtain a footing. An appointment had been made for me for Tuesday evening, and I found the Methodist house of worship had been courteously offered for our service. The attendance was exceedingly good, as on a week-day evening most persons in California are too busy to attend to anything but matters which are "of the earth earthy." There is evidently a large number of Churchmen at Marysville.

In the afternoon I walked down to the Feather River, and, crossing by a primitive ferry-boat attached to a line stretched across, went on a visit to the Indian village on the other side. The inhabitants are a remnant of the Digger tribe, and are the most degraded Indians I have ever seen. They dig a cellar room about three feet deep, then place a mound of earth over it, so that there is just room to stand upright, and this forms their house. There is an opening about two feet square, through which they crawl into it. On one side they erect a staging on poles, a few feet from the ground, and on this place their provisions, making it a store-house. They were lounging about in the warm sun, some of them almost entirely naked, the men with sticks thrust through the lower part of their ears, which adds to their savage appearance. They are dying off fast, and will soon be entirely extinct.

They have one curious custom. When a member of the family dies, they burn the body, and mix the ashes with pitch procured from the pine tree. This is smeared over their bodies and particularly over the head. I have sometimes met them in the mountains, entirely naked, and with the whole head, except the eyes, ears and mouth, coated an inch thick, causing them to look like demons. This is left to wear off and its permanency regulates the length of their mourning.

At six o'clock next morning (Wednesday), we took the stage for the mining country. It was a long wagon with a wooden top, holding twelve persons inside. About half of the passengers were Germans, and as they chattered away in their native gutturals, I could imagine myself in an *eil wagen* in Austria. For the first seven miles the country was perfectly flat table-land, but it is rapidly being fenced in and appropriated. We passed immense fields of wheat and barley, some of them nearly a mile in length. Here and there were clumps of grand old trees, while the distant hills formed a fine background to the picture. We began, in a few miles, to ascend the hills, after having forded two small streams; and, descending again, came to the Yuba, of mining celebrity, which we crossed by a scow and rope. On its banks commences the mining district. All along are hillocks where the ground has been dug over, and troughs are seen which have been used by miners to convey water to the diggings, while occasionally we passed the wrecks of some of that expensive machinery which at different times was introduced, but generally proved useless.

Along the banks of the river, for several miles, extend flats of sand and gravel, well known as the "Long Bar." The whole space has been dug over, sometimes two or three times, until it is covered with piles and mounds of earth, like gigantic sand hills. Most of the miners, we were told, had lately left for some new and richer mines recently discovered at Iowa Hill, but some were still scattered about through the whole length, working singly or in small companies. Most of them use the common old-fashioned rocker. They fill it with earth and water, and rock it back and forth like a cradle, until the earth is washed out; while the gold, being heavier, sinks to the bottom. Some had long sluices—wooden troughs with a stream of water running through them. Into these they shovel the earth, and in the bottom are slats which catch the gold as it sinks, while the earth runs off with the water. When the gold is as fine as powder, they are obliged to resort to quicksilver to separate it from the sand. The miners, we found, were making only from two and a half to three dollars a day. The expense of living, however, is now much less than formerly. Meals are given at the shanty eating-houses for eight dollars a week. The charge two years ago was twenty dollars.

Mingled with these miners are Chinese, who live on the merest trifle, and therefore can afford to work for a smaller remuneration than Americans.

All along the river are tents or log cabins, or, at best, hastily built board houses, in which the miners are living. The population, is, of course, exceedingly fluctuating, and on the rumor of a richer mine, two-thirds of the people will emigrate. The only way for the Church to reach these districts, is to have itinerating missionaries who can go around among them and preach from cabin to cabin. Still, each of the inland villages is the centre of a mining population, and a Church established in any one of them would reach hundreds who are laboring in the vicinity. Many of them, too, were members of the Church at home, and need only to be sought out and recalled to their old associations.

We were all day passing through hills covered with noble timber. Sometimes there would be a wide expanse of country, beautifully rolling and set with clumps of trees— giant old oaks, the largest I had ever seen. For a gentleman's residence here are the most beautiful sites, entirely free from all underwood and presenting an unequalled park ready made by nature. The oaks were at times interspersed with pines, sometimes an hundred and fifty feet high, straight as an arrow, each fit to be "the mast Of some great ammiral." The fields, too, and open spaces were covered with the wild flowers which abound in such profusion in California. The prevailing colors were yellow and purple, though others were mingled with them. Sometimes there would be several acres of the same hue, completely covering the field. At times, as we rose on the side of a hill, we could see, stretching before us like a panorama, a

wide expanse of valley and hill-side. In the plain beneath
us rose *the Buttes*, as they are called, three or four strange
elevations, thrown up apparently by some volcanic action
in the very middle of an immense prairie which reaches almost as far as the eye can discern. They rise rough and
ragged against the sky, entirely isolated, about half way
on the plain between the Sierra Nevada Mountains at the
east, and the Coast Range at the west.

We constantly passed the sluices or flumes built by miners
to carry water from some distant stream to the " dry diggings." These are ditches about two feet square, excavated
from the ground, where it is possible, but often passing over
the valleys in wooden aqueducts. They are tapped, and a
stream is let out to each company of miners that hires from
the company. The Flume Company get about six dollars a
day from each company taking their supply. One of these
which we repeatedly passed,—the Deer Creek Ditch,—is
twenty-five miles in length.

There is a peculiar code among the miners, and they are
strong enough to enforce their own laws. One principle is,
that no mineral lands can be held by proprietors. A village lot can be, but not a field for agricultural purposes.
An individual may therefore have a fine field in grain,
when it is discovered to be a "gold digging," and at once
a hundred men encamp upon it, cut it up in shares, and
turn up the whole surface for their own benefit. As soon
as miners arrive in a new digging, they elect an alcalde.
Any individual has then a right to appropriate a claim,
varying from fifteen to sixty feet square, according to the
richness of the mine. He drives a post at each corner,
another in the centre having on it his name, pays the al-

calde a dollar for registering it, and the claim is his. When he leaves, he can sell it. The real owner of the soil is not consulted.

Sometimes, when a hill is equally rich throughout, it is entirely leveled to the plain. If there is a plentiful supply of water, they begin at the top and cut down until they fairly wash it all away. In some places, we saw excavations twenty and thirty feet deep, which had been made by the miners. In others, they sink shafts to even a hundred feet in depth, until they strike the right vein; then they will follow a vein from one hill-side to another, and trace it on through a wide extent of country. Often, rocks have to be blasted, and perhaps weeks and even months spent in making tunnels and preparing to wash, when "the lead" is lost and the whole scheme proves a failure. The finding of the gold, indeed, sets at naught all ordinary geological laws. It seems as if the whole country had been turned up by the action of fire, its strata thrown into confusion, and gold makes its appearance just where all scientific men said it could not be found.

There is no record of the countless deaths which are taking place from exposure in the mines. Laboring under the hot sun and in the water, sleeping on the bare ground with only canvas overhead, and with unwholesome provisions, the miner, reared, perhaps in ease, sinks into sickness "which is unto death." A young friend of mine lived, one winter, for weeks in the mines, on bread he made from pounded acorns. Unlike the majority of his companions, however, he lived to tell of it.

At noon we reached Rough and Ready—a straggling village of five hundred inhabitants. It has been built up

entirely as a mining centre. We stopped here to dine, and
at the same time I made inquiry to see if it were possible
for me to arrange a service for that evening. I found, however, that I could not, nor could I hear of a single individual
attached to our Church. I therefore determined to go on to
Grass Valley and make that my first stopping place. This is
but four miles distant. We therefore resumed our seats after
dinner and went on. It was an exceedingly rough road over
the mountain. In walking up a steep hill to relieve the horses,
I stopped to talk to some miners who were shovelling earth
into a sluice. I found, however, they were only " prospecting," and it would take several days for them to decide
whether or not it was worth while for them to work that
spot.

We reached Grass Valley at four o'clock. It is said to
be one of the most beautiful places among the mountains,
and is surrounded by some of the richest mining spots.
On one side are the famous " Gold Hill " mines, and near
are the quartz crushing mills. The population of Grass
Valley is estimated at about two thousand, though this must
include the floating mining population. We stopped at the
hotel (a third-rate country tavern), but on inquiring for
rooms, I found that Madame Anna Thillon was "starring"
it here at the little theatre, and, with her troupe, had taken
all the best apartments. The host at last showed us two
miserable rooms, which were all he had for us. I then inquired for the ladies' parlor, and was informed that
Madame Thillon had engaged it for her dining-room.
" Where then "—asked I—" is the lady to sit ? " He opened
the door of the desolate looking, uncarpeted dining-room,
with a close stove at the end, and intimated that this was the

only place he had.   For the first time since I have been in California, I saw Mrs. Kip's countenance fall, but I did not wonder at it, for the prospect was dismal enough.

I knew no one in Grass Valley, but a friend in Marysville had given me the name of Mr. Winchester, and had written to him the day before, to announce my coming, though without knowing whether he was a Churchman.   So, my next step was to seek Mr. Winchester.   I found his home pleasantly situated on the verge of the town, and on sending in my name had a most cordial welcome.   I was further delighted to hear that he was an attendant on the Church. Learning that my family were with me, he walked down to the hotel to insist on our taking up our abode with him.

We found Mrs. Kip not in the most cheerful frame of mind, and after some faint expressions of reluctance, she consented to accept his hospitality.   We accordingly moved our quarters to Mr. Winchester's pleasant residence.   His family are at the East, and we were inducted into their place.

Upon consultation with Mr. Winchester, it was thought best that I should go to Nevada (as I wished to visit there), on Friday, hold service in the evening, and then return and spend Sunday at this place, where a large public hall could be procured for that purpose.

Thursday, 20th.   In the night we heard the sound of rain, somewhat to our surprise, as we supposed the dry season had commenced and we should see no more rain till next November.   However, Grass Valley is in the mountains, three thousand feet above the level of the sea, and therefore an exception.   It has poured all day, and at times there has been heavy thunder.   How strange it is to realize where I am !   I sat in the window and looked out over the diggings, beginning in the very next field, which was filled with sluices and mounds thrown up by the miners, and just back, all along the edge of the woods and under the gigantic pines, are their log cabins. Last evening, when they were ending work for the day, my son went down to see what they had gained. One party of five had gold which they estimated at about twenty dollars. This is probably the average wages.

In the afternoon, during a temporary lulling of the rain, we walked over to the quartz crushing mills. These are established by a stock company in London, and are the most perfect in California. Their machinery, sent out from England, bore on it the name so famous to machinists—" James Watt & Co., Soho," and is exceedingly beautiful. The company has spent about half a million of dollars, and the result of the experiment is yet to be reached. They can crush about seventy tons of ore a day. After being crushed several times, till reduced to a powder, it is passed through sluices where the gold and black sand are caught in the lining of blankets. These are then washed out, and the gold is separated by quicksilver. A few hundred yards distant is the celebrated " Gold Hill," from which several fortunes have already been made. The top and surface have been worked over by miners, while at the base it has been honey-combed with tunnels following the veins of gold quartz. We entered one about five feet high, extending into the heart of the mountain for six hundred and fifty feet, with lateral passages. At the end of it the miners were then getting out quartz.

Mr. Walsh, the superintendent, mentioned to me a fact which shows what a lottery mining is. He pointed out a log cabin, built on one of the gulches or ravines of the hill, over one of the richest spots upon it. It was built by a man who made it his headquarters, and from thence went "prospecting" over the whole adjacent country. Meeting with no success, he finally sold his cabin and claim for a trifle, and went elsewhere. The purchaser excavated under his cabin, and actually dug twenty thousand dollars from beneath the very floor on which his predecessor had been sleeping.

Friday, 22d. Rain still pouring down. At eight, the stage called for me to go to Nevada. The distance is but four miles, over a mountain of the Sierra Navada range, Nevada being situated on the other side of it. We toiled up the mountain and through the old woods, by a road which this sudden torrent of rain had cut up, so that our vehicle rocked from side to side, and constant orders were given for all to lean to the right or left, to prevent it from going over. All this was sadly to the terror of the only lady passenger, who most earnestly wished herself in San Francisco. On the summit of the mountain, the storm, for a time, changed to snow, and then back again to rain as we descended to Nevada.

Nevada is unlike any other American town I ever saw. Built up by the miners, without any plan, its streets are narrow and irregular, and it seems crowded into a defile of the mountain. The hills tower around it on all sides, covered with gigantic pines, one of which was lately cut down measuring two hundred and fifty feet in length. Change its wooden houses to heavy stone and surround it with a wall, and it would be exactly like some towns perched up in the recesses of the Apennines. Everything looked gloomy enough as we entered it—the rain pouring in torrents, and the swollen Deer Creek roaring as it passed through the centre of the town.

I entered Nevada without knowing what success I should have in arranging a service for the evening, or that any steps had been taken for that object. The manner in which I was obliged, on this journey, to *feel* my way from place to place, is a fair specimen of the way we, here, must " seek for Christ's sheep that are dispersed abroad." When I left Marysville I did not know an individual at Grass Valley or Nevada, or whether anyone there was attached to the Church. I have already stated how I found Mr. Winchester and had made arrangements for Sunday. But what was to be done at Nevada? It was then Wednesday, and my service would have to be on Friday evening— short time, at the best, for arrangements and notice—and Mr. Winchester did not know the name of a single individual there, likely to be connected with the Church. At a venture, however, he wrote to a Mr. B——, editor of the *Nevada Journal*, and requested him to give notice for Friday evening, in his paper, which was to be published that day, and see that the friends of the Church secured a place for service. When I arrived, therefore, I called on Mr. B. and found that he had accidentally stumbled on one Churchman, who engaged the Congregational meeting-house for that evening, and that the proper notice had been printed.

This publication brought out other Churchmen, who seemed rejoiced to hear that the Church was to take some notice of them. Still, the advertisement would be seen by but few, as it was issued within only a few hours of the time—it was raining violently—and Nevada, being without sidewalks, was covered with mud. Not a promising prospect, certainly!

Just before evening, the weather cleared. Still, the mud rendered the streets almost impassable. As they were not lighted, there was no such thing as picking our way. The Congregational meeting-house (since burned down) was a neat little building, holding about two hundred. Our attendance was about fifty, being forty-five more than I expected under such circumstances. But as they came dropping in, and I saw from their dress that a number of them were miners, I felt an earnestness and interest in preaching, greater even than I have felt in some of the splendid churches at the East. After service several of the congregation, who proved to be among the leading men of Nevada, were introduced to me, and they expressed a strong desire to organize a Church and have regular services. And thus ended the first service ever performed in Nevada. Years hence, should the Church be established and flourishing in this place, its members will look back with interest to our initiative on that rainy evening.

Saturday, 22d. The situation of this place, crowded between the mountains, prevents its being built in the straggling style usual when we commence a town with "magnificent distances." It is perfectly compact, and contains some seven thousand inhabitants, a part being the floating population of miners who surround the town. There are small Congregational and Baptist societies, and a little handful of Methodists, divided, as usual in this country, between two chapels,—Methodist North and Methodist South. Such are the beauties of schism! The number of those, however, who attend any service is lamentably small.

I asked a gentleman, whether he supposed all the congregations collected on Sunday morning would amount to five hundred persons? He answered, he did not think they would. Sunday is the great day for business, as the miners generally, owing to old home associations, do not work their claims on that day, but spend it in town purchasing their goods. All the shops, therefore, are open, and this is the day for brisk trade. In all mining towns I have found that the merchants generally wished to close. They would lose nothing by it, were all to do so, for the miners must purchase a certain quantity of goods, and if the shops were not open on Sunday, they would be obliged to buy on some other day. There are always, however, some Jews, who will keep open, and the rest think themselves obliged to do so, to prevent the Israelites from having the monopoly of trade. The passage and enforcement of a Sunday law would make an entire revolution in the moral and religious life of these places.

Around Nevada are the most extensive mining operations in the State. The whole land is rich with gold, and even a part of the town has been undermined, and the houses are propped up by beams. It is said, there is not a foot of ground but contains gold; but as labor is too high to have it all worked, only the rich veins are followed out.

We walked out this morning a few hundred yards beyond the limits of the town, and suddenly found ourselves on the edge of a precipice on the side of the mountain, down which we looked an hundred feet. It is an immense excavation made by the miners, who have thus literally washed away half the mountain. The earth is gradually carried away in their sluices, down to Deer Creek, which runs through the ravine below, and thus the whole mountain will eventually be removed and reduced to the level of the plain. In this excavation, called Lands' Mine, one hundred and fifty men were working. They are hired by the company and have no interest in the mine.

There is a rich deposit of gravel, from fifty to one hundred feet broad, which runs through these hills. It was once the bed of a river. It winds from hill to hill like a serpent, and to trace it tunnels are driven, so that these hills are all perforated and honey-combed. When it is struck at a distance below the surface, a shaft is sunk, up which the earth is drawn that it may be washed out. These shafts again are all connected by tunnels, to give a circulation of air and to prevent the collection of noxious gases. We saw one, a hundred and thirty feet deep, at the bottom of which five men were working, while the earth was drawn up by horse power. The gold here is all of the best kind, but never found in lumps or grains, only in powder as fine as flour. It can be collected, therefore, by quicksilver only, which is placed in the sluices through which the water and earth are poured. The quicksilver, by its natural affinity, attracts the gold and amalgamates it while the earth runs off in the water. By application of heat to a retort, the quicksilver is then evaporated, leaving the pure yellow metal.

It is never safe in California to judge of a person by his dress. You are thrown into contact with rough-looking people in a stage coach, and before you have travelled five miles, find they are college-bred,—perhaps professional men at the East. You speak to a miner in a red flannel shirt, about the geological formation of the mine in which he is

working, and the first sentence of his answer—the very
wording of it—shows him to be scientifically educated, and,
by his training, an accomplished man. The proprietor of
a book store in one of the mining towns told me, that the
roughest looking men came in to ask for classical works
on these and on every other scientific subject. Astronomy
seemed to be a particular favorite with them.

We were looking at a deep excavation, when a person
ascended from it dressed like a miner, and, coming forward,
called me by name. His face seemed familiar, but I could
not recognize him, and he was obliged to introduce himself.
Six or seven years ago he was a vestryman of my church in
Albany, being then a merchant in extensive business. About
five years ago he came out to the mines, where he had
suffered all kinds of reverses, and endured the usual hardships, until now he was beginning to reap a reward in the
prospect of fortune. He had extensive claims on these hills,
and employed fifteen or twenty workmen in his "diggings," which he was preparing to work by machinery.
His family had joined him a few months before, and were
living in a board cabin he pointed out to me, which he had
erected on the hills near his claims. His wife and daughter
had been communicants in my church in Albany, and I
walked over to see them. The home in which I had last met
them, was a three story brick house. Such unexpected en-
counters are common in California, and this was the second
I had had in Nevada in twenty-four hours.

Among the vegetable productions of California peculiar
to this country, is the soap plant, which the gentleman with
me pointed out growing on these hills. It looks like a lily,
and has a large bulbous root. He pulled up one, crushed

it with a stone, and then proceeded to wash his hands in a neighboring pool of water. His hands and the water were at once covered with a lather like soapsuds. It is an excellent substitute for soap, and is used for that purpose by the old Californians.

After spending the greater part of the day in visiting those who were favorable to the object for which I had come, and making the necessary arrangements to establish the Church, at four o'clock we set out in the stage on our return to Grass Valley. The day had been beautiful ; the roads were already drying up ; the air was pure and bracing ; and there could be no greater contrast than between our ride this afternoon and that through the storm of the day before. We wound in and out among the old patriarchs of the forest, and everything had an air of freshness, as if we were in a newly discovered land. I cannot remember that I ever enjoyed a ride more. In about an hour we reached Grass Valley, and found ourselves again at the hospitable residence of Mr. Winchester.

Sunday, 23rd. As beautiful a day as ever shone! The diggings which I see from my window are nearly deserted, only a solitary miner here and there using his pick. A few Indians and Chinese are scattered about. In the village a few shops only are open, together with some gambling saloons kept by Frenchmen, whose object is to decoy the miners into spending the hard-earned wages of the week.

We had a morning service in a public hall, and a congregation of about fifty, among them some of the most influential families in the village. Quite a number, too, were young men of the class adapted to form the strength of a congregation. In the afternoon we removed to the Presbyterian house of worship, which had been offered to us the evening before, their congregation having no service at that hour. Our attendance was over one hundred. Out of the two thousand persons in Grass Valley, not three hundred are found at one time in the different places of worship on Sunday. The congregation at the Presbyterian house of worship varies from fifteen to fifty. I found numbers of persons who acknowledged to me that they never went anywhere, for there was nothing to interest them ; but they assured me if the Church was established here, they would support it and attend regularly.

There is some society to be found in this distant village as refined as any in our eastern states. On Thursday afternoon I had spent a very pleasant hour at the house of Mr. Melville Atwood. He is from England, and has come out to direct the scientific arrangements of the English Quartz Company. His wife is a sister of Prof. Forbes of London, who, in science, has a world-wide celebrity. We had promised to dine with them on Sunday evening. In addition to his family, we found a guest staying with him—Sir Henry Huntley. Sir Henry is a captain in the British navy and was formerly Governor of Prince Edward's Island. He was sent out from England, in command of a company of Cornish miners, to superintend the quartz works belonging to an association there. Of course the company went to pieces, as the courtly Sir Henry was not intended by nature for such work.

Monday, 24th. We did not send to the stage office till last evening, and then found that every place was taken and we must remain another day. Willie has been out in the diggings trying mining. He washed out several pans of earth, but, not being very skilful, did not get more than twenty-five cents worth of gold.

Mrs. Kip had been with me, making visits and perfecting our acquaintance with the people of Grass Valley. We passed, in the village, an exceedingly pretty cottage, inhabited by Lola Montes. It has a conservatory behind it, and flowers and bird cages about it, giving it an air of taste and refinement. She is said to have a pension from the King of Bavaria, who, when she was his *chere amie,* gave her the title of Countess of Landsfeldt. Among her pets, —and we were told she has a number,—is a young grizzly bear which was chained to the stump of a tree just outside her front court-yard. We stopped for a moment to look at it, and while so engaged, Lola came out on the porch to arrange her flowers. She has a rather fine countenance, as well as we could judge at the distance. We cannot imagine what induced her to select this retired village for her residence, after the kind of life she has led in Europe.

Tuesday, 25th. The rain came on again last evening, and it has literally poured through the night. This morning was not much better; but as these mountain storms sometimes last for a week, nothing remained for us but to set out for home. The stage—a long wagon—came at seven o'clock, and, ourselves included, there were twelve inside. Just as we set off, the rain ceased and we had no more that day. Through the morning, however, it was like a fitful April day,—alternate clouds and sunshine. We took a different road through the country, from that by which we came, traversing the side of the mountains and directing our course towards Sacramento. The mountain streams had been swollen by the rains, and in several through which we passed, the water came up to the body of the carriage. Then, too, we were constantly kept on the *qui vive* by the directions of the driver,—" To the right, or the stage will be over ! "— " To the left ! " etc.—obliging us continually to " trim ship," to the manifest terror of the two ladies within. We passed, every few miles, traces of mining and excavations, or saw long flumes stretching across the landscape. The country is what at the West they call " oak openings," covered with large trees without any under-brush. Occasionally there were large fields under cultivation, where the settler had devoted himself to the certainty of agriculture instead of the lottery of mining.

At noon we reached Auburn, so named by one of the first settlers, who came from Auburn in the State of New York. Situated, however, as it is, among the mountains, it cannot be called

" Sweet Auburn, loveliest village of the plain."

It is now a stirring mining town, surrounded by extensive diggings ; but let the mines give out or better ones be discovered five miles distant, this would soon be " the deserted village." As we left the town, we passed through a street inhabited entirely by Chinese, who are to be met with in all parts of the mines.

Descending into the plain below, we had magnificent views of the Valley of the Sacramento which stretched far as the eye could reach, seeming to be an unbroken expanse of forest land. The sun was shining brightly, and every pleasant little nook we passed appeared to be occupied by miners. Sometimes there was a neat cabin, as if the occupant had made up his mind to a long residence, but gen-

erally there were only canvas tents. They looked so pleasant, however, this bright afternoon, the men working in the
gulches, that a passer-by would imagine mining to be a
most agreeable employment.

A few miles farther on we reached the level of the plain
—the distance from the mountains to Sacramento is about
thirty miles,—a rolling country covered with clumps of old
oaks scattered about. Here would be a single tree, there a
clump of half a dozen, then a wide grove. We passed hundreds of sites where I could not help imagining how beautiful some of the old halls in England would look, if they could
be transported to these spots. It extended, too, as far as
the eye could reach, often for miles without a habitation or
a fence. The late rains had laid the dust, everything was
fresh and green, the atmosphere was just cool enough, and
altogether it was a delightful drive. Now and then we came
to a ranch house kept as a hotel, where we changed horses,
or to the cabin and little enclosure of a settler.

Of the land which belongs to the United States Government, any actual settler may appropriate to himself a hundred and sixty acres, free of purchase; and as we looked at
this wide expanse of magnificent unsettled country, with its
fine agricultural advantages, and remembered the millions of
toiling farmers in the old world, who are laboring year after
year for a mere subsistence and are crushed down by taxes,
I asked myself, why will they not come over and "possess
the land" which seems to be waiting for their occupancy.
And one day the Valley of the Sacramento will be thus
filled.

The great drawback in the greater part of this Valley is
the want of water. Late in the summer the herbage is en-

tirely dried up, and the country loses its livery of green till the rainy season comes again. Perhaps the experiment might be made which has been so successfully tried in the Valley of San José, and water provided by digging artesian wells. Were this to be done successfully, it would supply the only deficiency which is felt here.

As the twilight deepened, we could see the teamsters, in different parts of the plain, kindling fires by the side of their huge wagons and preparing to camp out for the night; while the little prairie wolves (coyotes), startled by the noise of our vehicle, sprang up and dashed away into the darkness. It was just at evening that we crossed the river by a bridge, and entered the streets of Sacramento, having driven about seventy miles since breakfast.

XVII.

SAN JOSE.

IT was in May after my arrival that I made my first visit to San José and the first service of our Church was held there. This was followed by other visits at intervals, and although five years have now elapsed, and, owing to the want of clergy, we have never had a resident minister there, yet, in pursuance of my plan, I record the visit as the first effort in behalf of our Church in that place, and, therefore, when the Church is established and San José has lost all its old California features, to be a matter of interest.

We left San Francisco, on Monday morning at eight o'clock. The stage had nine inside, all but ourselves being French. For the first few miles the road was over hills like those which immediately surround San Francisco, with scarcely a tree to be seen. Then we came to the wide-spread plains, stretching, far as the eye can reach, towards the edge of the ocean. For miles there will be no fences or enclosures—no houses, only one vast prairie. Here and there we see herds of the wild cattle, easily distinguished from the domestic by their large branching horns, or groups of wild horses grazing about. Then, a herdsman, wrapped in his *scrape*, would pass, with his huge spurs jingling like bells.

Having been up very early and finding the monotony of the road rather tiresome, I had fallen asleep, when, shortly after eleven, I was awakened by the stopping of the vehicle. I roused up, and opening my eyes, seemed to have dropped into another country. The stage was standing before a tasteful house and around us were groves of noble trees. On the other side of the road were cultivated pleasure grounds, while through the foliage was seen a country seat, with its conservatory on one side. I rubbed my eyes and asked where I was. I found we had reached San Mateo, one of the favorite summer resorts of the San Franciscans. With a mild atmosphere, freed from the high winds which prevail nearer the ocean, these secluded valleys furnish a pleasant change from the city.

Beyond San Mateo, the country is diversified with fine rolling surface and groups of old trees extending to the horizon. Occasionally we passed noble ranches comprising thousands of acres. Sometimes a single field of grain will contain three hundred acres. It was a delightful drive through the mild and balmy air, and at three o'clock in the afternoon we reached Santa Clara. This is a little village, the houses of which are about equally divided between the old Spanish *adobe* buildings, as usual one story high, and the new, pert looking residences of the late American settlers. At the edge of the town is a three-storied, red brick building, without an attempt at ornament, or a tree or a shrub near it; looking very uncomfortable and very much out of place, as if it had wandered away from some city. This, I was told, was a school belonging to the Methodists, which rejoiced in the magnificent title of—" The University of the Pacific."

This place is the seat of the old Romish Mission of Santa Clara. The old church, with its low walls, covers a great extent of ground. The front has a coat of white plaster gaudily painted with figures in the Spanish style. The old mission buildings attached to the church have been converted into a college, which contains a large number of pupils.

The *Alameda* from Santa Clara to San José—three miles in length—is exceedingly beautiful, being arched the whole distance with trees. They were planted by the old priests, in the days of their rule, and stand in three rows, one on one side, and two on the other where the footpath ran. You look down the road, through a vista of foliage, far as the eye can reach, and so it continues to the very entrance of San José.

This place is considerably larger than Santa Clara, and has the same mixture of American and old Californian population. The valley in which it is situated is about twenty miles broad by a hundred long, hemmed in by mountains. With a climate of perpetual summer, it is considered one of the garden spots of California, and when the projected railroad connecting it with San Francisco is finished, this valley will be filled with the villas of citizens who will take refuge here at times from the crowded city. The legislature once met here, but it proved to be too dull a place for their taste and they preferred the bustle of Sacramento. It is indeed as quiet as can well be conceived, presenting a strange contrast to the usual excitement of California. We look out from the balcony of the house where we are stay-

ing, and opposite are Spanish *adobe* houses, the inmates of
which seem to be lounging about, enjoying the "dolce far
niente," never excited except when on horseback. Afternoon comes, warm and quiet; the whole population seems to
be taking its siesta; and you hear no sound except the insects
wheeling round and droning in the air.

Tuesday. We drove out for about a mile, to a ranch on which
is an artesian well. The proprietor was boring for water,
when, at about seventy-five feet below the surface the instrument fell out in a stream of water three and a half feet
deep, and a rapid current at once gushed forth. The head
of water is seven inches in diameter, and placing in it a
pipe five feet high, it rose at once with great force to the
top. There is sufficient volume of water to irrigate a
farm of one thousand acres. On the next ranch, a short
distance off, the experiment was tried again with the same
success. These were the first efforts of the kind, but since
then water has been obtained, not only for the town, but
for any part of the valley, thus supplying the only need
which was felt,—water in the dry season. There is evidently a subterranean stream running under the valley.

On the *Alameda* we passed a splendid tract of land of
three thousand acres, surrounded by a wire fence, which was
purchased by Commodore Stockton at the first annexation of
the country. It was then an old Spanish grant owned by
Ignacio Vallejo. The greater part of it is now under cultivation.

In the afternoon a gentleman called to take me driving.
We crossed the plain to the mountains about seven miles
distant. For the greater part of the way there was no
road, but we were guided by taking for our direction the

point in the mountains to which we wished to go. Part of the way was through grass which almost concealed our horse and wagon, and then we would drive over a large unfenced tract, the crop from which had just been reaped and was lying on the ground. It was what they call "the volunteer crop." After the grain has been gathered in, there springs up at once, without any planting, another crop which can be reaped in a few months, not of course equalling the first, but yet often surpassing the ordinary yield in the Atlantic States.

We were going to visit a gentleman from New York, who was owner of a wide tract of land at the base of the hills, which he was placing under cultivation. We found his primitive wooden house on the first knoll at the base of the high mountains rising stage after stage behind it. From the front we had a magnificent panoramic view of the plains, bounded at the distant horizon by mountains, except at one spot where we saw dimly the blue line of the ocean. Below us stretched out his wide fields—thousands of acres under cultivation, without a single fence. It was agriculture on a scale which dwarfed into insignificance most of our Northern and Eastern farms. His cattle had free range over the mountains, and we saw them several miles distant coming over the hills, driven home by his herdsmen on horseback, to be shut up for the night. His *corral* (enclosure for cattle) was in a ravine through which a stream of water flowed. The great advantage of farming here is, that no forage need be hoarded up for winter. Stock feed out the whole year and take care of themselves. In the dry season, they find food in the ravines through which the streams flow, or feed on the wild oats on the hills. The winter, too, is so mild that they require no shelter. At the East, the prominent object on a farm is the barn. Here, you never see one. "All out doors" is the barn, and for the cattle the *corral* is all that is necessary.

We reached the village again at evening, often puzzled to determine the direction we should take, as we were so buried in the tall grass as to be able to see nothing about us. I can readily understand, how on these, to the eye, boundless plains, travelers are often lost, and wander for days before they regain the proper direction.

On our way, we passed a little wooden building, which my companion pointed out to me as a school-house, in which a curious assembly meets two evenings in the week. It is composed of grown up and even middle aged people,—generally Westerners who had originally no advantages of education—gathered there to learn spelling. Though the object was highly praiseworthy, their efforts—he said—were sometimes most ludicrous.

Wednesday 24th. At San José the Romanists have founded the largest female seminary they have in the State. It is an extensive brick building, with one side left unfinished that a wing may be added. Its cost, so far, has been about seventy-five thousand dollars. On visiting it, we were received by one of the sisters, who conducted us through the different departments. There is one room for the California (Spanish) girls, who bore on their countenances the unmistakable marks of their race, another for the English girls, and a third for the smallest children. The dormitories and other rooms are all exceedingly neat, and the charges, as shown by their printed circular, apparently very cheap. I understand, however, from those who have had daughters there, that "extras" make the school as expensive as any other.

There are fourteen sisters in charge of the establishment, and about one hundred and fifty pupils. Of the latter, one half are Americans and very many are Protestants. All are obliged to attend Mass, and I satisfied myself, that, notwithstanding great professions to the contrary, the sisters do exert a constant, although silent, influence to draw pupils to their faith. Of this we had a convincing proof before our visit was ended. When we entered the little chapel, I was surprised to see the young lady (a pupil) who was conducting us around, kneel and cross herself most devoutly. Upon inquiry, I found she was a "convert," made so before she had been there three months, and baptized without the knowledge of her parents. These women, therefore, to whose care her training had been committed, instructed her to begin her religious life by violating one of her first duties. But while Protestant parents will continue sending their children to such places, they must expect like results.

From there we walked to the parish church of San José. It was locked, but a *sub-pretre*, whom we found in the porch of a cottage near by, sent a boy to open it for us. Like all other churches of the kind, it is of *adobe*, and is built in the shape of a cross. Its very thick walls and small square windows remind one of the crypts in old Italian churches. The paintings and engravings on the walls are crude. There are perhaps not more than six pews on each side of the nave, while, scattered over the floor of the transepts, are the little square carpets on which the Spanish women kneel to pray.

At evening we had our first service. The Presbyterian

house of worship had been courteously given us for the occasion. The building, which was small, was well filled, and I found later that there were many Church people in the neighborhood. Among those present was a classmate of mine at Yale College—Mr. Douglas— whom I had not seen since we graduated in 1831. He became a Congregational minister and had since been a teacher in the Young Chief's School at the Sandwich Islands. He came here in 1847, to join his brother, who is the owner of a ranch in the neighborhood.

Thursday. A party was formed to-day to drive out to the celebrated Almaden Quicksilver Mines. After going a few miles, we crossed the plain and entered the mountains, where the scenery was beautiful, as we drove around the hills covered with park-like oaks. The road wound by a running stream, and now and then we passed the ranch of a Californian.

The quicksilver works are very extensive, the mine being the richest in the world. This year, the company makes one million of dollars worth of quicksilver. The cinnabar is so rich that it yields seventy per cent. The works are of brick, and we were shown the large reservoirs filled with quicksilver. The atmosphere is most stifling, and must be destructive to health, as we were told that breathing it sometimes salivated the workmen.

The ascent to the mines is by a winding path leading up the mountain for more than a mile, and then there is a descent of some three hundred steps. I did not attempt this entrance into the bowels of the earth, but contented myself with the report of those who did go. Most persons make such expeditions merely to boast of them. Chateaubriand,

when a week at Cairo, could not spare an extra day to visit
the pyramids, but begged a friend to write his name on
that of Gizeh, that it might hereafter be believed that he
was there.

From the side of the hill a spring wells out. The water
has a strong medicinal quality, resembling soda water, and
effervesces in the same way, when mixed with syrup.

We lunched under the trees, picnic fashion. By the side
of us ran a stream, and just within sight were some canvas
and reed houses which the Californians erect for the hot
weather. Their inmates, however, make but little use of
them, except for sleeping, their days being spent in the
open air.

The drive back was delightful, the air as balmy as that of
Italy. In San José everything was so quiet that it seemed
as though the whole town must be asleep. Likely most
people were taking a siesta, as enough of the old Spanish
population remains, to counteract in a degree the restless-
ness of the Americans among them.

Friday. We left in the stage at seven in the morning,
to return to San Francisco by a different route on the other
side of the bay. For almost the whole distance, the road
led over wide-spread plains, sometimes for miles without
a fence or a house. The country has a "sealike sweep,"
while the hills are set round it like a mighty frame. Often
the road could hardly be marked, while the wild mustard,
with its yellow flowers, was higher than the horses' backs.
Occasionally, nestling in a sunny nook, we would pass
some *milpas,*—Indian huts of weeds or brush,—or an old
California house with the occupants lounging out of doors—
or the more comfortable looking wooden house of some

American settler, who had "located" on the plain and enclosed his garden about him. Several times we drove over the dry pebbly beds of the *arroyos*, showing the places of streams which in the rainy season it would perhaps be difficult to ford.

After a ride of about twelve miles, we turned aside to what was once the Mission of San José. The Mission house, a spacious *adobe* building, with long corridors, is now occupied by Mr. Beard. The church, like all the old Spanish churches, covers a great deal of ground, and bears on its front traces of once having had fresco paintings. It is still held by the priests. The little settlement around it consists of a tavern and a few *adobe* houses, occupied principally by Spaniards and Californians. Everything around them is primitive—even the low carts standing at their doors, with two wheels about two feet high, each cut in the most clumsy style out of a solid block of wood. The long ranges of native huts, once occupied by the Indian converts, are still visible, but broken down and roofless, while each rainy season wears away the *adobe* walls, so that they will soon be reduced to the level of the plain. A little beyond the settlement is the old burying ground, but its fence is gone and the tall black cross in the centre is tottering to its downfall.

Mr. Beard, the present owner of the Mission building, is one of the greatest agriculturists in California. He claims the whole plain for some leagues around, and from the Mission you see his fields stretch over the lower ground for miles. They are well fenced in and show the energy of American cultivation.

Here we took in two new passengers—Spanish women,

with their *rebozos* over their heads in place of bonnets, and dressed in rich silks and ornaments, as if for a ball. They conversed in Spanish and smoked their cigarettes. At one place we passed a vineyard surrounded by a hedge of roses which served as a fence. The whole country seemed covered with potatoes or wheat. The latter was in fields of sometimes a thousand acres each, often the volunteer crop, but promising abundantly. A railroad is greatly needed to open a market for these crops, as, with wages and freight at present rates, it does not pay to transport them to San Francisco. At one place, we saw a mound of potatoes, about five hundred feet long, by ten wide and five high, left to rot upon the ground.

We stopped once at a little hamlet called Union City, to change horses, and again at a tavern built upon Castro's Ranch, to dine. At three o'clock we reached the Bay— passed through the growing towns of Alameda, Clinton and Oakland, within a mile of each other, situated among groves of oak trees, and soon to be covered by the villas of the San Franciscans—and taking the ferry, in three quarters of an hour, arrived at home.

XVIII.

A severe illness in the summer, probably the result of my passage over the isthmus and change of climate some months before, had quite prostrated me; but having made an appointment at Monterey for the 30th of July, I determined to endeavor to fulfill it. I hoped that the change of air and a short sea voyage would, before Sunday came, fit me for my duties.

On the previous Thursday afternoon at four o'clock I left San Francisco, with Mrs. Kip, in the steamer *Sea Bird*. We had about thirty passengers on board. We passed through the Golden Gate, which just six months before I had entered for the first time with such a feeling of loneliness—a feeling which the kindness of many friends had since so entirely dissipated—and when night closed about us, we were already far out at sea.

When I left my stateroom at seven the next morning, I found from the revolution of the wheels that the steamer was going very slowly. The Captain supposed us to be opposite the Bay of Monterey; yet being unable to see

165

any headlands, we were feeling our way into the harbor.
Above us was the bright blue sky, lighted up with the clear
sunshine; but all around was a thick fog which completely
obscured the land and prevented us from seeing our position.
And so we slowly went forward, till about nine o'clock; when
the heat of the sun seemed to melt away the mist, and we
found ourselves, where we should have been, at the entrance
of the harbor.   Point Lobos was on our right; the placid
bay, without a single sail, was before us; and there, in that
beautiful basin, was the old town of Monterey.   In a few
moments the steamer's gun was heard echoing from the
neighboring hills, waking unusual sounds in that quiet scene;
and we came to anchor within a few hundred yards of the
sandy beach, on which the tide was gently rippling.

Monterey is a straggling Spanish town, built without any
regard to order, at the head of the bay.   Back of it, on
three sides, the ground rises into hills, the slopes of which
are richly wooded with old oak trees.   Under the Mexican
rule it was the capital of California and the residence of the
principal families, who were attracted hither, partly by its
delicious climate and partly by its being the headquarters
of the gayeties of the province.   Under the American government it retained, for a short time, its importance.   Here
in 1850 was held the first convention, which adopted the
State Constitution and took measures for obtaining admission
into the Union.   Delegates thronged to it from all parts of
California.   It was held under the authority of Gen. Riley,
the Military Governor, and for a time Gen. Sutter, the pioneer
of California, presided over its deliberations.   The staring
wooden taverns which were run up at this period are still
standing, some of them now closed and unoccupied.   The

capital was then removed to San José, and this destroyed the political importance of Monterey. For a time it was the headquarters of the army; but these too were removed—to Benicia and San Francisco—withdrawing, in the officers and their families, much of the agreeable American society for which the town had been distinguished. Most of the nfluential California families moved away, out of disgust for the intruders who had taken the power from their hand. Some went to their ranches, stretching over leagues of country, where they could still practice sovereignty; and some returned to Mexico.

Monterey is now as quiet a place as Zimmerman himself could have desired in which to realize his dreams of solitude. Business has departed, except the little trade necessary for the daily wants of its population. You see no one in the streets, but a few Spaniards and Indians, who seem to have, as is really the case, nothing to do. There are scarcely any vehicles; and all is quiet until some Californian dashes along at the usual head-long speed. The houses, scattered without much regard to order, are mostly of *adobe*, with tiled roofs, one story high. The centre is generally occupied by a large hall, to which other apartments are in subordination, as it is used for dancing, the great amusement of these people. The dining and sleeping rooms open out of it, but are mere appurtenances. In a population of over a thousand, there are not two hundred Americans. The Spanish language is of course generally spoken.

No sooner had we dropped anchor than a shore boat came off for passengers and landed us on the rocks at the edge of the basin. I had come to Monterey, principally at the request of Mrs. Boston's family, one of the American families longest in the place, the members of which took a great interest in the Church. One of them met us as we landed, and in their hospitable home we spent the next week. Their house was just below the town, overlooking the bay; and from the windows of my room a scene spread out on which I was never tired of gazing. There I spent the greater part of the next two days, feeling still too weak to make much exertion, and endeavoring to recruit strength for the services of the approaching Sunday. Before me was the peaceful bay, stretching round in a beautiful semi-circle— no wharves—nothing to interrupt the silvery line of the sand on which the spray broke and glittered. Some distance from shore, imbedded in the sand and almost covered by the water, lay the wrecks of two vessels which long years ago must have grounded there and been dismantled. They alone broke the glassy surface of the basin when no breeze was sweeping over it. Besides these, two or three fishing boats floated lazily near the beach.

Bayard Taylor, in his "Letters from California," dwells much upon the peculiar sound of the surf, as it rolls and breaks upon this shore. I know not whether it was mere imagination, but it has often seemed to me, as I listened to these sounds, that they had a quality all their own. Even when the surface was unbroken, there was a constant swell which lined the borders of the bay, far as the eye could reach, with a brief display of silver foam; and every moment it broke upon the shore with solemn regularity, as if the ceaseless pulsations of the mighty Pacific. This seemed to me more impressive, thus rolling up the bay with a long, dirge-like moan, than the wilder dashings of the waves upon Point Lobos; and doubly so at night, when I have lain awake hour after hour, the silence broken only by these monotonous beatings.

It seemed, too, as if the town was as quiet as the bay. No sound came up from it. The bustle of Yankee energy seemed not yet to have broken in upon its primitive repose. Except some children playing about, the cattle lazily feeding, or an occasional foot-passenger,—generally a Spanish woman with the *rebozo* over her head,—we saw no signs of vitality. In its utter want of all life and energy, and in its foreign aspect, it reminded us, more than any other place we have seen on this continent, of some of those quiet towns in the South of Europe, which had not yet been reached by the progress of modern innovation.

The most exciting scene that passed before the window during my stay was the capture of one of the wild California cattle by a Spaniard on horseback who had attempted to drive it forward without success. The animal seemed obstinately bent on going in a direction contrary to his wishes, when, with the utmost rapidity, he threw his long lariat with the slip knot at the end. By some sleight of hand which I could not understand, it struck the fore-leg, and encircled it at once, the horse planted himself firmly on the ground to enable him to sustain the shock; and in an instant the animal was lying helpless on its back. This was repeated several times, and always with the same unerring precision. It is their usual way of capturing cattle on the wide plains or hill-sides. The animals are suffered to run wild until wanted; when the *vaquero* rides up to the herd, selects the one he wishes, and while the terrified animal is thundering along at full speed, by a whirl of the hand which is hardly perceptible, the lariat strikes his foot, and he is thrown down with a shock that for a few moments disables him. Before he recovers, he is tied, so as to be completely hampered. The horses are sometimes so well trained, (as I have seen in Southern California,) as to stand perfectly still after a bullock has been lassoed and the rider has dismounted to bind him. He seems to watch the motions of the animal, and when he moves, draws back and tightens the lasso tied to his saddle-bow, as if guided by reason. Two of the native Californians will sometimes capture the fierce grizzly bear even, in this way, with lariats round his fore and hind legs drawing him different ways until he can be secured. Beginning with this exercise in childhood, as soon as they can sit a horse, they attain a perfection which would be inconceivable to one who had not witnessed it.

The only walk on which I ventured during these two days, (and this sent me exhausted to bed, before dark,) was to the Fort which is not far from Mrs. Boston's house. It is on high ground overlooking the bay. The breast-work which has been thrown up, surmounted by several large cannon, surrounds the space devoted to barracks, arsenal and parade ground. There was once a large garrison stationed here; but although the United States' flag still floats gaily over it, its glory has departed, and a single officer, (in charge of the military stores remaining in the depot,) and a sergeant, are the only occupants of the barracks.

The climate is perfectly delicious. I was delighted with its balminess the day I landed, and every day of my stay increased my appreciation of it. The temperature seems to be equable, differing but a few degrees throughout the whole year. During this, which is the dry season, no rain ever falls; but early in the morning and in the evening, a fog prevails for a few hours; while through the middle of the day the soft breeze which comes in from the sea tempers the heat so that it is never oppressive. Nowhere else have I breathed an atmosphere so favorable to invalids. In my own case I found its influence beneficial beyond my expectations. The two days which passed before Sunday seemed to have the effect of so far restoring my strength, that when the time came, I felt able to go through the varied duties of the day with as little exhaustion as if they had been preceded by no illness.

The service of our Church had never been held in Monterey. Some years ago, on the first occupancy of the town by the Americans, the Rev. Calvin Colton, Chaplain in the U. S. Navy, a Congregational minister, was stationed here. He was appointed Alcalde, and while here erected a stone building for a Town Hall, which is now called "Colton Hall," and is one of the most substantial public buildings in California. He also published "Three Years in California," a diary of life in Monterey which gives a good picture of the society and life in this country. Subsequently, another Presbyterian minister, Mr. Willy, resided here for a short time as Chaplain to the garrison, but for some years there have been no Protestant services of any kind. The old Romish Church is the only place of public worship. On Saturday we heard the bells ringing violently, and were told it was to notify the inhabitants that the next day was Sunday. Perhaps this is necessary in the perfect tranquillity of Monterey, where they "take no note of time," where nothing disturbs the quiet of the day, but the moaning of the wind through the pine trees and the breaking of the waves upon the beach.

On Sunday morning the sound of these bells came floating over to us in the perfect stillness. The Church is on
the opposite side of the town, standing where the ground
begins to rise into the hills, and from my window I can see
group after group winding their way up to its doors. For
our service we had the Court Room in Colton Hall, the
room in which the convention which adopted the first Constitution of this State, held its meetings. The Congregation numbered about sixty, and at the Holy Communion
four came forward, some of whom had not for a long time
enjoyed this privilege. " Your sermon," said a gentleman
to me, after service, " is the first I have heard for four
years." In the afternoon the attendance was much larger,
as many of the Spanish ladies came in to witness the services, though unacquainted with the language. After the
second lesson, I baptized five children; and having given, in
place of the sermon, an extemporaneous address explana-
tory of Confirmation, I conferred that rite on one lady who
that morning received the Communion for the first time.
In the early part of the week I visited many of the Americans, particularly those who had brought their children for
baptism. They all expressed themselves anxious to have
the services of the Church; but they are too few in number
to take any steps towards this, nor is there any reason to
suppose that Monterey will increase or strengthen its American population. In fact, since my visit it has diminished;
and the removal of Mrs. Boston's family has taken away the
only one of any influence. Twelve miles distant, on Salinas
Plains, I am told an agricultural population is settling, but
of course it is scattered at the ranches.

As the steamer was not to return from San Diego till

Thursday, we had several days to spare, on one of which we drove out to Point Lobos. It is doubtful whether in quiet Monterey we would have been able to procure a vehicle; but an officer of the coast survey whose station is here, kindly placed his horses, wagon, and steward at my service during my stay. The vehicle was capable of carrying an indefinite number, and on a pleasant morning, when there was just fog enough to keep the heat of the sun from being felt, a party was formed to visit Point Lobos. The wagon was filled, while some of the gentlemen went on horseback.

As soon as we left the town, we found ourselves in the old oak woods. Then, there would be a space destitute of trees—then we would drive through the forest by a road on which the grass was growing, while the branches on each side swept against us as we passed. There was every variety of scenery, as we went over hills bare of trees, and through valleys into whose tangled foliage the sun could not penetrate. These woods are filled with game; often grizzlies are met there, but we saw nothing except innumerable squirrels, and a solitary prairie wolf (coyote) which crossed our path. We forded the Carmel River, at this season a shallow stream, but in the rainy season filled to the banks with an impassable flood. During the drive of seven miles, we passed but one house, the owner of which had cleared extensively around him for a farm. At last we approached the seaside, and after driving through woods where there seemed to be no road, we emerged a few hundred yards from the beach, in an open space dotted with scattered trees.

The scenery around is of the wildest character. It seems as if some mighty convulsion had rent the rocks asunder,

and thrown them about in the greatest confusion. Huge
masses, weighing tons, were placed with the strata at right
angles to other masses, as if a giant had tossed them in his
sport. Deep fissures and ravines passed through them, up
which the waters of the ocean dashed and roared, as the
waves swept against their openings. One of these fissures
extended two hundred yards, in some places narrow, and
then at the extremity opening out a wide chamber into
which the water rushed at every swell of the tide, until it
broke against the end with a sound like thunder, filling the
cavity with spray like the steam of a boiling cauldron.

The rocks here are covered with shells, some very beautiful, and also with the greatest variety of sea-weeds that I
have ever seen. Among them is the mucilaginous plant
which is so much used by the Chinese for soup. It is here
collected in great quantities, and has become an important
object of export.

There is, however, another natural production at this
place which excites much more attention. Long before we
reached the margin of the sea we heard an indistinct roar
and bellowing which seemed something different from the
booming sound of the waves. It proceeded from the sea
lions with which this is a favorite resort. A few hundred
yards from the shore is a ledge of rocks, forming an island,
on which they crawl up to bask in the sun. There, hundreds
of them, of every size, can be seen at once, and their roaring
is heard above the sound of the waves. They are huge,
unwieldy masses, sometimes eighteen feet in length, appearing like great lizards as they crawl up on the rocks or slide
back again into the water. Sometimes, a monster who
seemed the patriarch, would raise himself up and bellow,

when the whole herd would unite, till it seemed as if the " bulls of Basan " had been let loose. They are sometimes shot from the rocks on the shore, though, as they are so fully covered with a coating of fat, it is rarely that the ball penetrates to a vital part. The inhabitants, when they can capture them, obtain considerable oil from the carcass.

We returned for about four miles by the same road over the Carmel River, and then turned aside to visit the old Mission of Carmel. To find it, however, seemed no easy work; as the road had been so long disused that it was overgrown with grass, and difficult to distinguish from other paths in the woods. We tried several, where the branches almost met from the sides and swept over us as we passed, but they ended in the dense forest and we were obliged with difficulty to turn and regain the main road. We at last found the right one, and after driving for two miles emerged into the cleared fields which surround the old Mission Church. The situation is beautiful (as are always the sites of the old missions), surrounded by the hills, and with a distant view of the ocean. The church still stands unaltered in its front, having on one side of it the range of offices unchanged. On the other side, the huts which once formed the habitations of the Indian converts have entirely disappeared, as have the other outbuildings, and corrals in which the old fathers once herded their thousands of cattle.

We drove into the quadrangle, about four hundred feet square, formed by the deserted offices of the Mission. They are built of *adobes* and are now rapidly falling to decay. A gentleman who visited the church a few weeks before, found it entirely open, the doors swinging loosely on their hinges, and all the old relics of former worship left as they were years ago.   After the Mission was secularized in 1835, there seemed to be no one to take charge of the building and no definite owner for the property.   The priests had departed, trusting that a feeling of reverence would prevent any from molesting its contents.   This was effectual enough with the old Californians, but probably had no weight with the Americans who wandered that way; so that articles once devoted to sacred uses were carried off, and lately it was found necessary to lock up the building.

At this time it was open, as the Padre from Monterey was here, removing some of the ornaments and furniture to his church.   The church itself is lofty, with a Gothic arch, and some parts of the ornamental stone work are carved with considerable skill.   It is nearly two hundred feet in length, so that there is something stately in its appearance as you stand at the lower end and look up.   The wall of the chancel has been elaborately gilded and painted, but the colors are now fast fading away, from exposure to the air and weather. The whole building is of stone, except the chancel end, which is unfortunately of *adobes*.   The roof over the end where the altar once stood has fallen in, and a few more rainy seasons will finish the dilapidation of the building. At the left hand is a small chapel for the Baptistery, where the large font, carved from a species of yellow stone, with a heavy wooden cover, stood as it did the day the last child received from it the waters of baptism.   Next to it is a pretty little chapel which was used for the daily Mass and Vespers.   The altar is still there, with a picture of angels over it, some of the heads of which are very well executed. On the altar was the printed Gospel with prayers, framed and glazed.   It seemed as though the officiating priest had left it there but yesterday. On the walls were painted the *Te Deum, Gloria in Excelsis,* and other anthems, with the musical notes, so that the whole congregation might sing them correctly.

In the sacristy—a large room on the other side of the church—we saw the old paintings and images. I turned over the former, but found most of them to be daubs, portraits of saints and martyrs. Among them was one of a Padre landing on the coast, with a violin in his hand. In the background are seen the Indians, whom tradition asserts he attracted by the music of his instrument before beginning his sermon. The images are about four feet high, of wood, well carved, some with gilded mitres on their heads, and one, (whose name I could not learn), representing an African, perfectly black, with woolly head.

A wax figure as large as life, representing the dead Christ, had been left lying in the nave of the church. It was uninjured, except that some of the panes of the glass case which covered it were broken. The Padre had now brought out some Indians to carry it to Monterey to ornament his own church. They were placing poles under it, to carry it as on a bier. On our way home we passed it, and as we approached Monterey we met groups of señoras, who had gone out to receive it. A few hours afterwards, the bells of the Church rang out a loud peal, and we heard there had been quite a service for its reception.

This was the Padre's first visit to the place, and he therefore knew little about it. He was a Mexican, speaking only Spanish. In front of the altar many of the priests had been buried, and he removed the slab from a tomb in the pave ment to show us the coffin below in a narrow cell of masonry. Several of the tombs were lately opened by direction of the Archbishop of San Francisco, to find the remains of Padre Junipero Serra, the founder of this church and one of the earliest Missionaries in California. In this, however, they were unsuccessful.

In the tower still hang the three old Spanish bells, one of which is yet perfect, but the other two have been broken and are now useless. Thirty years ago, their sound, as it swept over these hills, called hundreds of Indians to daily prayers.

After leaving the church, we walked over to an extensive pear orchard, planted by the Padres, the fruit of which some Californians were employed in gathering. A small house had been built in the orchard, where lived an American, who, having married a Mexican wife, had settled down here, usurping the grounds of the Mission. As we were looking over the gate, his wife came out and welcomed us in with the grace which seems peculiar to these Spanish women. She was exceedingly handsome, and from her appearance I supposed her to be a young girl. She had, however, been for some years a wife, and was the mother of three children. She conducted us into her house, a single room, with a little partition to conceal the bed, and an earthen floor; but where she presided with a dignity not often seen in aristocratic saloons. It is a trait, however, we have often remarked in the native women.

Our road home led for some way through the deserted clearings of the old fathers, by their ruined corrals, and then through the thick chaparral where the birds alone broke the silence of these solitudes, until we emerged in the groves of old oak trees which overlooked the town. Interspersed among them occasionally, are lofty pines, from which hangs the long gray moss waving mournfully as the sea breeze sweeps by it. Thus all the hills about Monterey are thickly wooded, while among them wind little ravines or cañadas, into which the sun's rays seem scarcely able to penetrate. Thick vines stretch up among the trees, while the laurel groves grow rankly and luxuriantly below; so that it seems a twilight around, nor is any light seen, except when you look up, directly over your head, to the calm blue heavens above.

Beneath, Monterey was spread out, covering a gentle slope of land for three quarters of a mile. Two miles below was seen Point Pinos at the southern extremity of the harbor, from which the bay curved round to Año Nuevo, its northern side, twenty miles distant. Behind, the country rose in ridges to the Toro Mountains, while through the clear air without a cloud, could be seen far off on the northern horizon, the mountains of Santa Cruz and the Sierra de Gavilan, beyond the Salinas plains where the virgin soil is already broken by the enterprise of American immigrants.

The next morning we took another drive, to Point Pinos below the town. The road is through the pine forest, often scarcely to be traced in the open glades, and then through dense chaparral which still furnishes a lurking place for the grizzly bear. The point projects out into the ocean, with irregular masses of sand-stone, which, like those at Point Lobos, seem to be thrown into every fantastic form. Among these the waves dash up, while the foam and swell roll over them, and break upon the shore with a shock which seems to make the earth tremble. In the coves we found the rocks covered with shells; the avelone with its many hues and fine coating of mother-of-pearl, and the star-fish of orange and scarlet; myriads of muscles and snails; and sea-weeds of every brilliant color.

A short distance from the shore is a substantial stone lighthouse, which only waits for the lantern to be forwarded from San Francisco, to commence its duties. It is much needed at this place, for although the bay is more than twenty miles wide at the entrance, owing to the fogs at night, vessels frequently go ashore.

Every morning at nine, the sound of the bells is borne to us, across the little plain, from the church which is situated on the rise of the hills beyond, and one morning we walked over to it. It is of stone and a good-sized building, very much resembling the church at the Carmel Mission, but not kept in good repair. For some reason,—perhaps to save trouble—the windows on one side have been entirely closed with *adobes*. In front of it, on the ground, was lying one of its bells, hopelessly cracked. A group of Indian children were playing about, and as we came up, one of them crawled out of the bell where he had been hiding from his companions. The other two bells were still hanging in the tower. On one side against the walls is a tomb enclosing the remains of one of the priests, but without any inscription.

The interior of the church is like that of most chapels I have seen in this country. There was nothing remarkable except a curious picture of Heaven and Hell, one of those poor paintings so often seen in the Romish churches which attempt to bring down the future state to the most sensual minds. Heaven is represented by a pyramid on which are some melancholy looking beings, who seem to be not at a enjoying themselves, while in Hell are depicted devils tormenting their unhappy victims with pitchforks.

We crossed a little lagoon that flows up from the harbor and walked up for a mile to a beautiful headland which projects out on the opposite side of the bay. I had often looked at it from my window, and been attracted by its picturesque appearance, covered, as it was, with old oaks. We found it as peaceful and quiet as it seemed in the distance; and that most appropriately it had been selected as the Romish burying ground. The low wall which surrounded it had been concealed from us by the trees which threw their shade over every part of it. There were no monuments, generally only wooden head-boards and graves to mark the place where the former inhabitants of the little town were quietly sleeping. Outside the wall, under the shadow of a noble tree whose branches entirely cover it, is an enclosure surrounding the marble altar-shaped tomb of the wife of Lieut. Sully, U. S. A. She was a member of one of the old California families residing at Monterey and died at the early age of seventeen. A more peaceful spot could not be found. Nothing breaks the stillness but the notes of the birds, or the sound of the "old unchanging ocean."

A delightful degree of good feeling is evinced towards Americans by the highest class of California families residing in Monterey. Some of them are the old landed families who occupied an influential position under the Spanish and Mexican governments. Others are refugees from Lower California. One of them was Governor of Lower California, but espoused the American cause during the war with Mexico, under the supposition that on the return of peace the United States would insist on the cession of that country also. As this was not done, he was obliged to exile himself and take refuge under our flag. Californians have been so abused and cheated by the Americans, that we wonder they can be polite to any. Yet they are most remarkably courteous towards those entitled to their respect. There is a degree of cordiality and warm-heartedness in their manner which I have never found exceeded. The ladies still retain the old Spanish costume, with the *rebozo* thrown over their heads when they leave the house. They have generally had few advantages of education, yet some, from associating with Americans, have become sensible of their deficiencies and are endeavoring to remedy them. Some of them have married Americans or English who came here many years ago, even before the cession of the country. I was at the home of one Scotch gentleman who had married a California wife and resided in the country for thirty years. The ladies, we were told, generally prefer Americans for husbands. They see the difference in energy and enterprise between them and the old Californians, and in the lower part of the State, when one marries a peculiarly good Californian, the congratulation given her with regard to her intended is,—" He is as good as a Yankee."

We do not wonder at this, for most of the male portion of the Californians do not seem to have the good qualities possessed by the women. They retain much of the old Spanish character, with the evils of the Mexican disposition engrafted on it. They are generally idle and without energy, caring for nothing but horses and doing nothing which cannot be done on horseback. Bull fights, bear fights, and particularly gambling form their amusements. For the last their passion is intense and they will pass entire days and nights at *monté*, as long as they have anything to lose. Neither do they share in the admiration of the other sex for the Americans. They feel that they have been driven by them from their seats of influence, will scarcely ever learn the English language, and generally there is but little association between the young men of the two races.

The size of the California families would astonish our countrymen at the East. I became acquainted with some members of one family in which there were twenty-two children by the same father and mother. In another there were eighteen, while the ordinary number would be more than twelve.

On the last morning of our stay in Monterey, we drove into the country, about five miles, to the ranch of Don José. He and his wife accompanied us on horseback. The Donña rode well, as most of the California women do, many of them being even skillful in throwing the lariat. Their style of riding appears awkward to an American, as they sit on the right side of the horse, though this is really the more natural way. The left hand is thus used for holding the reins, while the right arm is free. Our road lay directly through one of the ravines which run up among the hills back of the town, through the unbroken forest, except in one place where the old trees were lying prostrate on the hillside, cut down by some enterprising American who intends to set out a vineyard on that spot. The farther we advanced into the country removed from the influence of the sea breeze, the warmer it became; but there is a freshness about this soft vaporous atmosphere which keeps it from being oppressive.

Don José's ranch stretches over several miles.   The house is in a hollow among the hills, with some living springs behind it, which are sufficient, in the dry season, to irrigate the gardens.   The servants were Indians, among whom we saw a woman ninety-six of age, born before the first coming of the whites or even of the earliest Franciscan Missionaries. Her hair was long and gray, and her face deeply wrinkled, but she seemed to have as much elasticity and strength as most persons at sixty.   She can carry—Don José told me—a burden of a hundred pounds.   These Indians are slaves.   Frequently, when in the country, finding young Indians about the house, I have asked the proprietor where he got them, and received for answer,—" I gave five dollars apiece for them "—or, " My friend Mr. P. purchased them of some of the tribe and presented them to me."

On our return we stopped at Don José's house in town to lunch, where we were most hospitably entertained.   His daughter played some pieces on the piano for us, with great taste and skill.   As American habits creep in, this instrument is, in many California houses, taking the place of the guitar, whose music they inherited from their Spanish ancestors.

While we were at dinner on Thursday, we heard a gun— the notice that the *Sea Bird* had again arrived.   During the afternoon she took on board her freight, and at about six o'clock, after saying good-bye to our kind friends, we were rowed over to her.   Another hour and we were out of the harbor and in the swell of the ocean, which soon sent most of the passengers to their staterooms.   After rather a rough night, we found ourselves, at breakfast time, once more entering the Golden Gate, and by nine o'clock were again alongside the wharf at San Francisco. I had set out to keep this appointment at Monterey with strong misgivings as to the prudence of the attempt, weak as I then was, but, thanks to a kind Providence, I had not only performed the duties I wished to, but returned perfectly restored in health.

XIX.

THERE is a grave defect in our present canon on Missionary Bishops. When six presbyters have been one year in a Missionary Jurisdiction as parish priests, they may organize a Diocese and elect their own Bishop. They may choose the Missionary Bishop who has been over them or not, as they please. If, through prejudice or intrigue, his own clergy decline to retain him as their permanent Bishop, they place him before the Church as unfit for the office in which he has been tried. Professionally, therefore, he is ruined.

Almost invariably, too, a frontier Diocese is one to which unruly and unworthy clergymen have resorted, as most removed from the reach of Episcopal authority. Over these he must exercise discipline; yet as soon as he attempts it, he arrays them against him and they at once look forward to the approaching election as the opportunity for retaliation. As six clergy are sufficient to elect, it places the matter in the hands of a very small clique. Four men combining against their Missionary Bishop can drive him from the Diocese.

Our venerable pioneer, Bishop Kemper, the first Mission-

186

ary Bishop appointed, had this experience. After the whole North-west had gradually been formed into dioceses, and Indiana, Missouri, and Iowa, cut off from his jurisdiction by electing Bishops of their own, he was narrowed down to Minnesota and Wisconsin. In the latter State his residence had always been fixed. Here, therefore, a party intrigued to elect a diocesan Bishop of another shade of Churchmanship. Clergymen were sent in to it from the East, and every step taken to ensure a majority. The friends of Bishop Kemper discovered the plots, and at the next Convention elected him Bishop, insisting upon his acceptance. It was after my coming to California that I received a letter from him mentioning these facts, and stating that to preserve the peace of the Diocese, in fact to prevent himself from being driven out of it, he was obliged to accept the office of Diocesan of Wisconsin.

From his letter, dated "Lake Superior, Aug. 10th, 1855," I make some extracts : " They collected many hundreds to induce men to come to my Mission to accomplish their object. I can however rejoice, even in advancing old age, that the Lord reigneth and that no weapon formed against this Church or the purity thereof shall prosper. . . My all but determination never to retire from the Missionary field was really altered by these intrigues. The efforts were begun in Wisconsin, and the candidate even named for its Episcopate. Then, at the solicitation of the clergy, I consented to accept."

Four or five years have now passed, and when I look back upon these schemes, (of which I heard at this time from other sources), so disgraceful and unchristian, I realize how time has rectified all these evils. Even the "candidate for the Episcopate " who suffered himself to be involved in this matter has now been for two years in his grave. What would he have gained had he succeeded ?

To remedy this, the canon should be amended to provide that when a Missionary Jurisdiction attains sufficient strength to organize as a Diocese, the Missionary Bishop may continue in charge as Diocesan if he so elect, as now the Assistant Bishop succeeds the Bishop of a Diocese. This would place a Missionary Bishop in an independent position, and by freeing him from the influence of intriguing clergy and future elections, would enable him to enforce the proper authority of his office. Such an amendment was passed by the House of Bishops in the General Convention of 1853, but was thrown out by the Lower House in their jealousy of the authority of the Bishops.

My own experience was very much the same as Bishop Kemper's. Before I had been two years in the Diocese, I found myself surrounded by a network of plots. Any little disaffection arising in consequence of my official acts, which if left to itself would soon have died away, was seized on and fostered to give it strength. In two instances where clergy had difficulties with their vestries, and where justice compelled me to decide unfavorably to them, their influence was at once enlisted against me.

When Convention met in 1856, these schemes, although they exerted no influence, had gone so far that as soon as the session was over, I felt it necessary to crush them out. One of the clergy engaged in them was presented for trial for falsehood and slander, and was suspended from the ministry. The testimony at the trial, placed in my hands full proof of the conspiracy and forever ended it. Some months afterwards, I removed his sentence, and he returned to the East. The other two who were involved with him, left the Diocese, and from that time all was peace.

The clergy took precisely the same course which had been adopted by their brethren in Wisconsin. They determined to elect me Diocesan Bishop at once, and thus remove all occasion of scheming. As I expected to return to the East in April, and could not therefore be at the annual Diocesan Convention which met in May following, it was resolved that I should be asked to call a Special Convention to meet before my departure. I accordingly received the following request:—

To the RIGHT REV. WM. INGRAHAM KIP, D.D.,
                    Missionary Bishop of California:

RIGHT REVEREND AND DEAR SIR:—The undersigned, Presbyters and Lay Members of the Church in California, respectfully request of you to call a Special Convention of the Diocese of California, at as early a date as may be convenient for you to preside in the same.

San Frncisco, Nov. 5th, 1856.

CLERGY.

Rev. James W. Capen,	Rev. Frederick W Hatch, D.D.
Rev. Edmund D. Cooper,	Rev. William H. Hill,
Rev. Orange Clark, D.D.,	Rev. David F. Macdonald,
Rev. Elijah W. Hager,	Rev. J. Avery Shepherd,

Rev. John L. Ver Mehr, LL. D.

PARISHES.

Christ Church, Auburn.—R. D. Hopkins, John Russell.

Emmanuel Church, Coloma.—George Searle, P. B. Fox, H. W. Miller.

Emmanuel Church, Grass Valley.—Melville Atwood, G. A. Montgomery, St. George Scarlett, C. J. Lansing, James Walsh.

Grace Church, Sacramento.—J. F. Montgomery, M.D., C. Theo. Hopkins, Jos. W. Winans, P. B. Cornwall, C. I. Hutchinson, F. W. Hatch, Jr., L. F. Reed, Jas. L. English, J. B. Harmon, Samuel Youngs, Jno. S. Bein.

Grace Church, San Francisco.—David S. Turner, J. D. Farwell, Stephen Smith, R. J. Vandewater, Wm. Blanding, Kenneth McLea.

Church of the Sacraments, Sacramento.—Henry Harc Hartley, Charles D. Judah, Thos. M. Logan, M. D.

St. John's Church, Oakland.—John F. Schander, Andrew Williams, Rob't Worthington, E. A. Suwerkrop.

St. John's Church, Stockton.—R. K. Eastman, B. Walker Bours, John Ferris, R. Manning, Allen Lee Bours, Lewis M. L. Hickman.

St. John's Church, Marysville.—W. Wilson Smith, W. P. Thompson, John W. Reins.

St. Paul's Church, Benicia.—Paul K. Hubbs, Joseph Tuttle, John Currey, Eugene Van Ness, U. S. A., T. Jefferson Cram, U. S. A.

Trinity Church, Nevada.—Chas. W. Mulford, Thos. H. Caswell, J. H. Gager.

Trinity Church, Folsom.—A. C. Donaldson, James S. Meredith.

From a feeling of delicacy, I hesitated some time before I complied with this petition, well knowing that their object

was my own election. I received, however, so many private
requests from the laity of the Diocese, who took the ground,
that the wish was so nearly unanimous that I had no right
to refuse it, that finally, December 5th, I called the Convention to meet February 5th, 1857.

It accordingly met in Grace Church, Sacramento. The
sermon at the opening of the Convention was preached by
the Rev. Dr. Hatch, the oldest clergyman in the Diocese.
After the preliminary exercises, I made the following
address:—

" MY BRETHREN OF THE CLERGY AND LAITY:

"For the first time since the organization of the Church
in this Diocese, you have been called to assemble as a
Special Convention. So widely are our parishes separated
that I realize what great personal sacrifice both clergy and
laity make to gather at any one place in this diocese, espe-
cially at this season when facilities for travel are diminished.
I would not, therefore, without some urgent reason, issue
any summons which should call you together.

" In the present case, however, I am relieved of all responsibility. In the end of November, I received a request
'to call a Special Convention of the Diocese of California
at as early a date as might be convenient for me to preside
in the same.' A copy of this paper will be handed to the
Secretary to be published in the Convention report. This
request was signed by every clergyman now in the Diocese
having a seat in Convention,* and by members of the vestry of every Parish (with one exception), in union with

* Of the only clergymen in any way connected with the Diocese
whose names were not signed, one was absent in the Atlantic States,
and the other suspended.

the Convention. Members of the vestries of two other Parishes, which had been organized since the last Annual Convention, and which have just asked for admission into the Diocese, had also added their names.* In complying, therefore, with this request, I felt that I was responding to the almost unanimous voice of the Diocese.

"There was, in addition, my brethren, another consideration of a personal nature to myself, which caused this request to harmonize with my own views and feelings. It will not be in my power to be with you at the Annual Convention of the Diocese in May next. An absence of now more than three years from my former residence at the East, renders it necessary that I should be there in the end of May, to attend to some matters of private business. I shall be obliged, therefore, to return to the Atlantic States (Providence permitting), by the steamer of April 20th. I am happy, therefore, to avail myself of this opportunity to meet you once more united as a council of the Church.

"Notices were issued on the 5th of December for the Special Convention, and this day was chosen, thus affording two months for the preparation and careful consideration of any business which it may be judged expedient to bring before you.

"And now, brethren, I commend you, in all your deliberations, to Him 'who by His Holy Spirit did preside in the councils of the blessed Apostles, and has promised, through His Son Jesus Christ, to be with His Church to the end of the world.'"

* Christ Church, Auburn, and Trinity Church, Folsom.

Calling the Rev. Dr. Clark to the chair, I then left the Convention. After appointing a committee to bring in a report on the power of the Diocese to elect and the expediency of doing so, the Convention adjourned till evening.

In the evening, the committee reported in the affirmative on both points submitted to them, and it was determined at once to proceed to the election. The choice was unanimous, both with the clergy and laity, nine clergymen being present and nine parishes represented.

I was at that time the guest of John B. Harmon, Esq., and at about nine o'clock in the evening, he drove up to his house to say, that the election was over and the members of the Convention desired that I should return to their meeting. As I entered the church they all rose, and when I reached the chancel the election was announced to me by the Rev. Dr. Clark. I then made them an address of which this was the substance:—

"Called, my brethren, by your request, to meet you once more in this Convention, I am happy to avail myself of the opportunity to thank you for the mark of confidence you have given by the unanimous election which your President has just announced to me. It is not the mere absence of any dissenting voice which causes me to regard it with so much satisfaction. It is the hearty feeling which has characterized all your proceedings, and which, since the first calling of this Convention, has been displayed in the expressions volunteered to me, not by the clergy only, but by the laity also, in every part of the Diocese. You have now officially placed on record a declaration of these feelings, and I regard the manner in which it has been done as a compensation for the labors and trials incident to this office, during the last three years.

"This endorsement of the course I have pursued is the more valuable from the peculiar circumstances in which we have been placed. I have no hesitation in saying, that the difficulties which surround us in laying the foundation of the Church in this portion of the Pacific coast, are without a parallel in any other region of our country. We have a population, earnest and intellectual, gathered from every quarter of the world in the last few years, as yet strangers to each other, and engaged in the hot and eager struggle after gain.

"This is a land of intellect, yet of intellect devoted to this world's purposes. It is a land of gold, yet but little of the gold thereof is consecrated to the service of Him whose are the treasures for which men dig and delve. Few, too, will interest themselves in the great interests of the country, for the majority have little intention of founding here their permanent home. Yet to this population, so excitable and fluctuating, we are to bring the gospel, and ours is the task to endeavor to mould them into a united and Christian people.

"But if these things render the work difficult to you who minister in holy things, the difficulties are doubly increased which gather around him who is to act as your Bishop. He is to be the arbiter in every dispute, and the reference for every complaint; and if he cannot remove every evil, remedy every disappointment, and obviate difficulties which are often the result of the folly or the inefficiency of the sufferers, he is denounced as not worthily discharging his high duties. Unlike an old community, there is here no established Churchmanship, or even settled religious tone, on which he can fall back.

" The spirit of insubordination, too, which reigns around us is liable even to infect the Church. There is a constant need of discipline, and yet the very authority to enforce that discipline must be vindicated against the unruly and the evil. In such a state of things how difficult becomes the duty (inculcated upon him in the consecration service,) to ' be so merciful, that he be not too remiss,' to 'so minister discipline, that he forget not mercy! '

"Under these circumstances, my brethren, more than three years have passed. They have been the most important years of this Diocese, when the foundation of the Church has been laid, and those principles have been settled, (sometimes not without contest,) which are to guide us in our future course. And now, that your unanimous vote has stamped the approval of the Diocese upon my administration in the past, I feel that it is a pledge for your support, should we be fellow laborers in coming days. And what I have been, you will always find me. The warfare in which we are engaged is one of principle, and from that I cannot swerve. Should opposition arise, I can only say to the gainsayer—' With me it is a very small thing that I should be judged of you, or of man's judgment; he that judgeth me is the Lord.

" With regard to my acceptance, it is impossible for me at present to give an answer. The decision of this question depends upon considerations which cannot be settled here. On my return to the East I shall be able to determine; and should it be the will of Providence that we are again to be fellow laborers in this land, I trust when the summer months have passed, we shall be found 'with one mind striving together for the faith of the Gospel.'"

During the summer, the election was confirmed by the Bishops and Standing Committees of the different Dioceses, and then the Church matters of California settled down into a peace which to the present time has remained unbroken.

XX.

BENICIA.

BENICIA is about thirty miles from San Francisco. The Stockton and Sacramento steamers, leaving this city every afternoon at four o'clock, stop there at six o'clock; so that it is of easy access from here. At the first settlement of the country great efforts were made to constitute it the emporium of the Pacific, but San Francisco took the lead, owing to its superior situation, and Benicia settled down into an inconsiderable place. For a little while the Legislature met there, but the members found it too quiet and the assembled wisdom of the State was transferred to Sacramento.

Benicia is now a scattered town, with "magnificent distances" between the houses. About a mile distant, connected with the town proper by straggling dwellings, is another settlement which has gathered around the works of the Pacific Steamship Company. A mile beyond this, and behind the hills, is the United States' Reservation, occupied as a military post. If the townspeople, the steamer employées, and the army people could be gathered into one place, they would together make quite a town.

197

As it is, they present materials for missionary work, and a a strong reason for establishing a parish at that point.

On account of its easy accessibility, Benicia has been chosen as a site for several schools; as not only do steamers stop there, but stages run from that point to the valleys above. There is a large seminary for girls and another for boys, while the Romanists have established the convent of St. Catherine, the inmates of which devote themselves to the education of their boarders.

Shortly after my arrival in California, this was made the Army Headquarters, and General Wool and staff were removed thither from San Francisco, very much to their dissatisfaction. By this order, both Churches in this city lost some of their most efficient supporters, among whom were Dr. Tripler, warden of Grace Church; and Major Edward D. Townsend, Assistant Adjutant General, who belonged to Trinity. These gentlemen, upon settling at Benicia, soon made a move to have the services of the Church; and I accordingly licensed Major Townsend to act as lay reader.

My first visit to this place—and, I believe, the first occasion on which service was performed by a clergyman of our Church—was in the first year of my residence in the Diocese, October 21st, 1854. I reached there at dusk; and being met on the wharf by Dr. Tripler and Major Townsend, I was driven out to their quarters, as I was to be their guest. During the time they were stationed there—for the next two years—this was always my home, and there are few scenes in this land to which I look back with more pleasure, than to my visits to their quarters. In long talks, protracted far into the night, some of my most agreeable hours were spent.

The next day, Sunday, we had service in the Court House.
A good congregation was present and after service and
sermon, I administered the Holy Communion to eight
persons.

Then a few months passed, during which I was unable to
repeat my visit. Major Townsend, however, was laboring
with all the earnestness of a most devoted parish priest,
seeking out children for Baptism and so preparing candidates
for Confirmation that I found my seeing them previous
to the rite was only a form. A large room, formerly used
as a Masonic Lodge, was hired, and converted into a pretty
chapel, with vestry room adjoining. The chancel was prop-
erly fitted with altar and other necessaries and the walls
were covered with oaked paper. In my Convention Address, the following May, I make this mention of Major
Townsend's efforts: "Since my former visitation to this
place, a suitable room has been provided, and furnished in
a church-like manner. It will be remembered that no services of the Church have been held here, except those of
the two Sundays I was able to spend in the place. Everything else,—the Sunday services, the seeking children for
Baptism and preparation of candidates for Confirmation—
has been done by the lay reader. I cannot refrain, my
brethren of the laity, from calling your attention to this
little parish, thus organized and kept in existence by the
exertions of one of your own number, as an evidence of
how much can be effected by the laity when the lack of
clergy prevents their having the services of an ordained
minister."

On the 22nd of February, 1855, I made another visitation.
In the previous week the parish had been organized by the

name of St. Paul's Church. I went up on Friday evening
and after spending Saturday with the major, in visiting the
different families, on Sunday I held service in their new
chapel. In the morning I preached, and administered the
Holy Communion to twelve persons. In the afternoon, I
again read service and preached, baptizing after the second
lesson one adult and eight infants, and after sermon con-
firming six persons.

In July I again visited them, and held service one Tuesday evening, remaining for several days to visit the
families. On the following Friday, I went over to Vallejo
with the Major, and in the evening held the first service of
our Church in that place. It is about seven miles from
Benicia and separated by a narrow river from the Navy
Yard at Mare Island. The population of the place was then
about one thousand, many of whom are workmen employed
in the Navy Yard. A Methodist chapel had been erected
there, which was offered for our use, and notwithstanding
the notice of but a few hours before, there was a good attendance, consisting of the officers and their families from
Mare Island and the people at Vallejo. I returned the
same evening to Benicia and the next day to San Francisco.

During the following January, 1856, we lost the aid of
Major Townsend, as he was ordered to Washington. A
more devoted and valuable layman I have never known;
not only regularly discharging the Sunday duties of lay
reader, but also the weekly and daily duties of "seeking for
Christ's sheep that are dispersed abroad" and inducing
them once more to place themselves within the hallowing
influence of the services of the Church.

Providentially, at the time of Major Townsend's departure, I was able to supply the church by sending as Missionary, the Rev. David F. Macdonald, who had come to me as a candidate for Orders, from the Bishop (Eden) of Moray and Ross in Scotland, and had lately been ordained Deacon. He usually officiated on Sunday morning at Benicia, and in the afternoon at Martinez, on the opposite side of the Carquinez Straits, and also held occasional services at Vallejo.

During the next three years but little progress was made. The officers and their families, on whom we chiefly depended, were constantly changing, and after about six months Mr. Macdonald removed to Coloma. Then there was a succession of lay readers, Dr. Tripler, Capt. Gardiner of the First Dragoons, Dr. Murray, U. S. A., and Lieut. Julian McAllister of the Ordnance Corps.

During the winter of 1858-9, I frequently spent Sunday there, having service in Benicia in the morning, and at Martinez in the afternoon. At the latter place the Methodist chapel was always offered for our use. I generally had also a third service at night. The Female Seminary, Miss Atkins principal, contained at that time about seventy pupils, the majority of whom attended the services at the chapel and indeed took charge of the music. They collect here from all parts of the State and in a year or two scatter to their homes, to be the future mothers of our people. Feeling how great an influence they might exert, I arranged for a Sunday evening service whenever I should be in Benicia. My service at the school was a familiar, extemporaneous lecture, prefaced by singing and the reading of some collects. During the last season (August, 1859), I held a special Confirmation at the school the evening before the term ended, to confirm two young ladies who were the next day to leave for their homes.

In May, 1859, the Rev. E. W. Hager became Missionary here, officiating on alternate Sundays at this place and Napa. As, however, he returned to the East in September, but little was effected.

During the following autumn, a lot was procured and subscriptions made for building the church edifice. The project was carried through, and a neat wooden church of Gothic architecture erected at a cost of about fifteen hundred dollars. It was consecrated in January, 1860. The day was beautiful and balmy, and the services were admirably conducted. The Rev. Messrs. Thrall and MacAllister of this city took part in the service. The Rev. Messrs. Ewer and Chittenden intended to be present, but, having trusted to the Suisun boat of that morning, arrived too late. Thus the parish is established on a firm basis and will be supplied by services from this city until it can procure a permanent Rector.

XXI.

I. Los Angeles.

I HAD several times had urgent requests from the few Americans at Los Angeles, to pay them a visit; and also letters from Captain Gardiner, our Lay Reader at Fort Tejon in the south-eastern part of the State, expressing the same desire. He reads service on Sunday, but they wished to have the Holy Communion administered and some children baptized. He offered, as travelling is unsafe in that part of the country, to send an escort of Dragoons down to Los Angeles to accompany us on our return. I had therefore made arrangements to take the journey. At Los Angeles we were to be joined by the Hon. Edward Stanly (late of North Carolina), who went down by the previous steamer.

I had been prevented during the whole of the past year from visiting the southern part of the State, as it is infested by the worst class of whites and Mexicans, who often rob in large parties, and render it unsafe to travel, except with a party thoroughly armed. Major E. D. Townsend, U. S. A. (whom I have already mentioned as our lay reader at Benicia), having been or-

203

dered to inspect Forts Tejon and Miller, had to pass through the country, and I availed myself of the opportunity to go with him. Some other friends had offered to join us, for the purpose of seeing the country, so that we expected to be strong enough in numbers to dispense with Captain Gardiner's Dragoons. Besides Mr. Stanly and Major Townsend, the party consisted of my youngest son, Willie, and myself, James E. Calhoun, (son of the late Vice-President, John C. Calhoun, of South Carolina) and Jas. T. Smith* of San Francisco.

My objects were, to spend a Sunday at Los Angeles, where the services of the Church had never been held, for I was the first clergyman of our Church in Southern California, except Mr. Reynolds at San Diego—another Sunday at Fort Tejon,—another at Fort Miller, where there had never been a service,—and generally, to see what is the character of the southern half of the State, with reference to the future prospects of the Church.

October 1st, 1855. At four P. M. we were on board of the steamer *Republic* for San Diego. The last time Captain Baby and I voyaged together, he was mate of the *Golden Gate* when we were wrecked at San Diego, and I found therefore that he looked rather suspiciously at me. The clergy, in such cases, are regarded by sailors as Jonahs. We had about fifty passengers. The fog was rolling in when we sailed, and no sooner had we passed the Heads and struck the swell of the ocean, than we plunged into a dense bank, in which it was impossible to see for twenty feet. The Captain says, he never went out in so thick a fog.

---

* Afterwards Rev. J. Tuttle Smith of New York.

At intervals, all night, the bell was kept ringing, and at about three in the morning, we were, as the Captain supposed, off Monterey. We therefore came to, and as the sea was heavy, we were left rolling in its trough for the rest of the night. At daybreak the fog still continued, but we kept slowly drawing in to land until about ten o'clock, when it lifted and we saw the coast, so that we could find the mouth of the harbor.

We anchored at the usual place in the bay, when the boats came off and took us to shore. Monterey is unchanged since I had service here in August of last year. Everything is as quiet and beautiful as formerly—a perfect Spanish town. Major Townsend and I went to see Mrs. Boston's family, (with whom I stayed on my last visit), and then took a walk through town, and visited Colton Hall and the old Church.

Mr. Calhoun and Willie in their walk saw a characteristic California scene. Two men who had been quarrelling, proposed settling the dispute on the spot by the duello. So they drew pistols and prepared to take their ground. It was just in front of a house, the owner of which came out and objected to their selecting that spot for the fight. This brought on a kind of triangular contest, when the last comer seeing a magistrate leaning against the fence a short distance off, appealed to him to stop them. Instead, however, of doing so, he threatened to arrest the pacificator for interfering. The quarrel had now diffused itself and got into other hands; and perhaps the hot blood had time to cool, so the difficulty was made up.

The last half hour on shore was passed with the Hon. Mr. Wall, collector of the port.

Three weeks afterward, his dead body pierced by seven balls, was found on the road a few miles from Monterey, and at a short distance from it the body of a gentleman, his companion. They had been attacked by a party of five mounted Senorians. Later, in attempting to capture these men, Mr. Layton, another of our Churchmen here, was killed with two others. I mention this to show the necessity for my armed escort in travelling in this southern country.

At three P. M. we sailed, but the sea proved to be rough, and most of us were soon in our state-rooms. The rest of the day, and through the night, we were pitching about in a dreamy, uncomfortable state of being, afraid to move for fear of consequences.

Wednesday, Oct. 3rd. The sea smoother, but the fog still dense. In the morning the Captain found he had run too close in shore, and was near the spot where, last year, the unfortunate *Yankee Blade* was lost with many passengers. During the morning the fog cleared off, and we got on our true course. At one P. M. we anchored opposite to Santa Barbara, and went ashore in the steamer's boat, generally a difficult feat on account of the heavy surf. As there is no wharf, the boat has to be run up on shore, while the passengers watch their chances, and jump before the wave returns.

Santa Barbara has its old California population, and there seem to be few Americans settled there. Everything, therefore, is primitive and quiet. The houses are all open, as if they people lived out of doors; and the agricultural implements, scattered about, are of the same clumsy patterns their fathers used in Mexico a hundred years ago. The town is about half a mile from the bay, and is said to contain twelve hundred inhabitants.

A mile and a half back, on the rising ground at the base of the hills, stands the old Mission of Santa Barbara. We walked out to it; and found the same evidences of decay and dilapidation which characterize all the California Missions. There is, as usual, an extensive range of buildings, once occupied by the priests, and terminated at one end by a large church. Around were the remains of their vineyards and gardens, with a few slight houses, about which some Indians were lounging in the sun, the relics of their once numerous bands of converts.

As we found there was a solitary priest still residing here and keeping up the services of the Church, we knocked at his door and brought him out,—an old man in the coarse gray Franciscan dress. Calling an Indian boy, he sent him to unlock the church for us. It was like all the other Mission churches, with little to recommend it but its size, and having, at the entrance, the usual horrible pictures of Purgatory and Paradise. In front of the building was a circular reservoir with a carved stone fountain. It is now dry and dusty. We found there was a series of these reservoirs on the mountain side, on successively rising planes, and connected by canals. In this way water was brought fourteen miles from its source in the mountains. Now, however, most of them are dry, their stone ornaments are broken in pieces, and the surrounding country, which the old Padres thus irrigated and made like a garden, is fast relapsing into its former wildness. It is a lovely spot, however, commanding a wide view of the country and bay, and was selected with the usual good taste of the friars.

We walked back again to the shore. The *Ewing*, U. S. surveying vessel, had just come in. Her Lieutenant took us off to our steamer, in his boat, and at seven P. M. we were again under way.

Thursday, Oct. 4th. At about seven A. M. we anchored opposite to San Pedro, four hundred and twenty miles from San Francisco, and the end of our voyage. Here we leave the steamer, which goes on to San Diego. At the edge of the water is a high bank, and from this the plain extends far as we can see. There are three *adobe* houses on the bank, and everything looks just as it did when Dana described it in his "Two Years before the Mast," more than twenty years ago. We landed in the steamer's boats, and after an unsavory breakfast at one of the houses, a wagon was produced, to which four half-broken California horses were harnessed. The men hung on to their heads, swayed about, and at times raised themselves off their feet as the animals struggled, till the signal for starting was given, when they sprang off, simultaneously, and the released animals dashed away at full speed. The driver occasionally looked in to ask us, on which side we wished to fall when we upset. This seemed to be his standing joke, and one which I thought it not improbable might become a serious question with us.

The plains were covered with thousands of cattle and horses, quite reminding us of the descriptions of old California times. In the twenty-five miles of our journey, there were but two or three shanties, erected by squatters who were raising cattle, and not a fence or enclosure, except the *corrals* about them. We reached Los Angeles in about two hours and a half, having changed horses once on the way.

As we approached the town there was a marked change from the treeless sterility of the plains. We found ourselves winding through the midst of vineyards and gardens, and on all sides saw workmen engaged in the manufacture of wine.

Friday, Oct. 5th. Los Angeles has all the characteristics of an old Spanish town. It contains about five thousand inhabitants, two thousand of whom may be Americans or English. The houses are almost invariably one story high,—a style of building which an occasional earthquake has rendered advisable. All around it is a perfect garden, luxuriant with every kind of fruit. We visited one vineyard, which, besides a profusion of other fruits, contained fifty thousand vines of a large blue grape. Part of these grapes are each week sent to San Francisco by the return steamer from San Diego, and part are manufactured into wine.

Saturday, Oct. 6. Availing ourselves of this day to see something of the surrounding country, we drove out about eleven miles to the San Gabriel Mission. It stands in a most lovely country, but like all the others I have visited, is now in a state of decay. The single priest remaining here,—a Frenchman speaking no English,—took us into the sacristy and showed us the rich fabrics, heavy with gold embroidery,—remains of their former glory,—and probably brought originally from Spain. We entered the large church, once filled with their Indian converts, but now of a size entirely useless. Several children were on their knees before the chancel, who went on with their devotions without seeming to notice our party. The eldest was reading aloud from some devotional book, while the others responded at intervals. The heavy stone walls of the church were hung with the usual pictures.

Around the Mission is a country unsurpassed for fertility. It is well irrigated by little streams from the mountains, that have been led through the fields by the labor of the old Padres. The only settlers, however, are the lowest class of Spanish Californians or Indians, whose little huts are scattered about, among which the children were running around in a state of entire nudity. In the hands of our Eastern farmers, this country, with its perpetual summer, would become a perfect Eden.

About a mile from the Mission is a rich tract of wooded country, called the *Monte,* and celebrated for the luxuriance of its crops. Corn grows here to a height which seems fabulous to strangers. It is peopled by a wild class of settlers from our Western States, whose only religious instruction is derived from an occasional Methodist camp-meeting.

On our way home we stopped at the vineyard of a gentleman, (Hon. Mr. Wilson, who is one of those most interested, in Los Angeles, in the establishment of the Church,) and I describe it to show what Providence has done for this country. It is about seven miles from town. The house stands on rising ground, and from the front of it there is a view of many miles of rich landscape, much of it dotted with oak trees. His men were all busy in the manufacture of wine; and while some of them were bringing in the grapes in baskets, others, standing in the vats with their naked feet, were literally "treading the wine press." The proprietor receives eight thousand dollars a year from the sale of his wine alone.

In the vineyard, besides the grapes, we found a collection of fruit which I had never seen equalled in any part of the world. There were melons of all kinds, figs just bursting, delicious peaches, pomegranates, tunas, (the cactus fruit,) pears and Madeira nuts. Strawberries are raised throughout the year.

✓ *Sunday, Oct.* 7th. Until within the last six months, there had been no religious service of any kind in Los Angeles, except that of the Roman Church. As the preaching there was in Spanish, the Americans never went to it, and were without anything to mark the coming of Sunday. At that time the Presbyterians sent a minister here who officiated in one of the public court rooms, while the Methodists erected a small building and commenced their services. The latter place had been offered to us for our services on this day.

We had service morning and evening,—the first time our solemn liturgy was ever heard in this section of the country. At the morning service there were about eighty present, and a much larger number in the evening. The next day, just before leaving the place, I baptized the four children of a gentleman, whose family, at the East, had been attached to the Church.

I found several such families in this place, whom I sought out and visited. They are literally "Christ's sheep dispersed abroad in this naughty world." Before leaving, I had an opportunity of conferring with a number of the inhabitants. They told me, the persons present had been much impressed with the dignity and solemnity of our service,—that neither Presbyterianism nor Methodism could exert any influence on this population,—but they had no doubt the Church could be established under very favorable circumstances. They wanted something which did not preach Nebraska or Kansas, slavery or anti-slavery, and that was not identified with any of the *isms* of the day.

I have no doubt they are right, and that they would be able to support a clergyman, as they professed to be ready to do so as soon as the right man could be sent. This work, however, calls for a man of zeal and energy, with considerable ability as a preacher and knowledge of the world as well.

Our Church people at the East, residing all their lives in a settled state of society, have no idea of the difficulty of forming a congregation from a population who have not heard the gospel preached for years, who are living under no religious restraints, and among whom the religious element is yet to be created. It is a work of faith, and time, and patience.

Yet to how many of our energetic young men this should present a noble field! Here they would be the first heralds of the Church; and instead of wearing out their lives in a severe and changing climate, they might make a home in one of the healthiest places in the world. A perpetual summer reigns; and for this reason, perhaps, the early Spaniards named it the City of Los Angeles, (the City of the Angels). I certainly have never seen a country which more fully realizes Bishop Heber's description—

> "——every prospect pleases,
> And only man is vile."

II. *Fort Tejon.*

Monday, Oct. 8. Captain Gardiner had sent down from Fort Tejon (about a hundred miles distant,) a large, heavy ambulance wagon, for no other is adapted to the mountain passes through which our road leads. It was drawn by four mules, and had Bell, a dragoon, as driver, who was well acquainted with the country.

Bell was well armed, and all the gentlemen with me had their rifles and revolvers. I was the only one of the party without any weapon. As the party was so strong, Captain Gardiner had not thought it necessary to send any escort, as he had intended, believing that we were able to take care of ourselves.

It may seem strange to an Eastern reader to hear of a Bishop's visitation made with such accompaniments, but here there is no help for it. The country through which we are to pass is infested with California and Mexican outlaws, whose trade is robbery, and who will often shoot down a traveller for the sake of the horse on which he is mounted. Our friends in Los Angeles warned us, when we left the vehicle to walk, as we were often obliged to do for miles at a time, not to straggle off, but to keep together. Sometimes these banditti attack in troops, as in the murder of Mr. Wall at Monterey, which I have mentioned. At other times a single Mexican on horseback dashes by the unsuspecting traveller. As he passes within twenty feet, suddenly the lariat, which he carries coiled up at his saddle bow, is whirled round his head, and ere the traveller can put himself on his defence, its circle descends with unerring precision, and he is hurled senseless from his horse. Then, too, in camping out at night, our rest may be invaded by a grizzly bear, as they abound in these mountains. They often exceed sixteen hundred pounds in weight, and are so tenacious of life that an encounter with them is more dangerous than with an African lion.

We left at eleven o'clock and had hardly got out on the plains, about two miles from Los Angeles, when, in descending a gulch, part of the harness broke, the mules whirled around, and we were saved from an overturn only by the snapping off of the pole. Nothing could be done where we were, so Bell had to take a couple of mules, return to town and have a new pole made. We were therefore left for some hours with the wagon and the other mules. I read, or looked out over the apparently interminable plains, while my companions practiced rifle shooting. About three in the afternoon our driver returned, and we made a new start. We shortly passed through a chain of hills, and then again over the plains for seventeen miles. Not a living object was seen for hours, till, toward evening, the coyotes came out, and we saw them loping along, as they followed us, with their long gallop. They were often in troops, in one of which we counted seven.

In consequence of our delay by the accident, night closed long before we reached our destination. We drove on some time in darkness, till the appearance of a single light, a long distance ahead, showed that we were approaching some habitation. After a time we reached enclosures,—the first we had seen since leaving Los Angeles,—and found ourselves at the old Mission of San Fernando. The buildings are the most massive I have seen in this country. Along the whole front runs a corridor, which must be three hundred feet in length, supported by heavy square stone pillars. Some of the apartments are forty feet long, with thick stone walls and stone floors, reminding me of old castellated mansions in the south of Europe.

Several other travellers arrived late at night from different directions. One of them—an example of the varied characters to be met with here—was a Scotchman, a graduate of the University of Edinburgh, who had been for some years in South America, and was now seeking his fortune in this new land. He arrived almost exhausted, having had no food or water for twenty-four hours. His horse had given out in the mountains, and while pursuing his way on foot, he suddenly saw a huge grizzly in the path before him. Afraid to fire at him, he unslung his tin prospecting pan, and drawing his ramrod, commenced a clatter on the pan, which soon drove the grizzly off.

We had letters to Don Andreas Pico, the present owner of the Mission, and as he was absent, presented them to his major-domo, who treated us with all the hospitality in his power. We had a regular Spanish supper, *olla podrida*, *frijolas* and *tortillas* with native wine. At night our party were all put in a room forty feet long, with one bed in the corner for the six. This, they insisted that I should occupy with my son, while the rest lay on the stone floor wrapped in their blankets.

Tuesday, Oct. 9. We were up at dawn, expecting to be off early, but were detained an hour for breakfast. Our morning ablutions were performed at a little stream in front of the door, which the old Padres had led there to irrigate their gardens. We availed ourselves of this delay to inspect the buildings. The church is like all other Mission churches, except in one particular. It forms one side of a quadrangle, the other three sides of which are buildings about ten feet high. This space was formerly used for bull-fights, and the spectators were accommodated on the roofs of these buildings. There are two very extensive vineyards, abounding also with other kinds of fruit. The grapes here are said to be of a finer flavor than those at Los Angeles. The workmen at the mills were making wine at the time.

We had a Spanish breakfast exactly similar to our supper the night before. Upon offering to pay the major-domo, he refused to receive anything. We then urged him to take a present for himself, but he said, "No ; when strangers come along, if they make me a present, I receive it; but not from the friends [of Don Andreas." And all this was announced with the highest Castilian manner.

It was seven o'clock before we left the Mission, and after proceeding a few miles, we reached the San Fernando Pass, where the road has been cut through a deep defile in the mountains. Here we had to get out and walk for some miles, and the scenery was the wildest I have seen since I crossed the Alps. How our heavy wagon was to get over, was a marvel to us. At one place was a ledge of rocks almost perpendicular, about four feet high, down which it plunged as if it would turn over and crush the mules, while we involuntarily held our breath as we looked on. In the pass, two Indians on horseback met us as we were walking, and were loud in their demands for money, till some of the gentlemen allowed their arms to be seen, when their tone was moderated considerably. Had my companions been unarmed, it was evident they would have had no scruples about enforcing their wishes.

After passing the hills, our course for twenty-two miles was over a level plain, at the termination of which we entered, what was stated to be the most dangerous part of our journey,—a cañon, or winding defile through the mountains, about seventeen miles long. It is a narrow pass, hemmed in on both sides by the high mountains, often allowing scarcely room for the wagon to pass. A small stream flows through it, which is crossed by the road more than eighty times in the space of the seventeen miles. In addition to its being the resort of grizzlies, its fastnesses are the hiding places of the American or Mexican desperadoes who are such a scourge to this part of the country.

We stopped just at the entrance of it, near the only house there is for twenty miles in any direction, to take lunch and rest our mules. We had to choose this spot on account of a spring there. A short time before, this house had become so notorious a resort of robbers, that a party came out from Los Angeles, captured its inmates,—two Americans and four Mexicans,—and hanged them on the spot. As the spring by which we halted was only a few hundred yards distant, we noticed that the house had a new set of occupants, but did not learn whether its character had improved.

It was about noon when we entered the defile, the branches of trees on both sides often sweeping against our wagon, and long before sunset involving us in twilight. Many parts of it reminded me of our ride through the mountains on the Isthmus, from Cruces to Panama. So, on our mules dragged the heavy wagon over the rocks and through the streams, while most of the way we walked. Through the whole day we met no human beings and did not wish to, as they probably would not be of the class we would like to encounter.

It is strange to travel thus through a country with the feeling that every one you meet is supposed to be an enemy, and is to be treated accordingly. Mr. Calhoun has had occasion sometimes to ride about in this region by himself, and I asked him how he managed when he met anyone. He said—"When I see a Mexican approaching, I cock my rifle and cover him with it, at the same time calling to him to raise his hand away from his lasso which hangs at his saddle-bow. In this way I keep my rifle on him until he has passed and got beyond lasso distance, ready to pull the trigger the instant I see him touch it."

We had intended to extricate ourselves from the cañon before daylight ended, so as to encamp on the open plain beyond. But when night closed about us, we were still five miles from the end, our mules were tired out, and it was rapidly becoming too dark to thread our way through the ravines. We therefore turned aside on reaching a level spot, with the little stream on one side and high rocks behind us. A fallen tree furnished an abundance of wood for our fire, which was supplied with large logs to last through the night. Here our basket of provisions was opened, tea boiled, and reclining about the fire we had our evening meal. Willie and I slept in the wagon, the boards of which we found hard enough, while the rest lay round the fire wrapped in their blankets. Rifles were fresh capped, revolvers examined, and each slept with his arms within reach. No regular watch was kept, as some one was up every hour to replenish the fire, and the mules picketed around would prove the best sentinels. On the first approach of men or wild beasts, in such cases, they exhibit an uneasiness which cannot but rouse up at once the whole party.

Wednesday, Oct. 10th. We were up before daybreak, and on our way as soon as it was light enough to see the path. We were obliged to walk the greater part of the five miles through the ravine. At last, we emerged into an open valley, covered here and there with oaks. In this we found a company of Californians camping with several hundred cattle, which were scattered over some miles, and which they were driving to the upper country to sell.

Where the valley expands into the wide plains, Elizabeth Lake was pointed out to us at a distance. It is about half a mile long, and lay glittering in the sunlight, exactly like snow of the most dazzling whiteness. On coming near, we found it was without a drop of water but filled with a deposit of saleratus. Not far off was the canvas hut of a settler, the only house we were to pass in our day's journey, near which lay the remains of three bears he had lassoed and killed.

The plains here are about fifteen miles in width. As the day advanced it became intensely hot; yet we were obliged to push on until we could reach some water to prepare our breakfast and refresh our mules. About half past ten o'clock, after traveling five hours, we reached a little spring, at which we stopped, as there is no water for the next fourteen miles. By damming it up we obtained enough for our wants. There was, however, no shade, and no tree within miles of us. We all scattered, therefore, about the plain to collect sticks, and the wagon was arranged so as to get as much shade as possible on one side of it. Into this we crowded, and our fire was built to prepare for breakfast. Some of our party were almost exhausted, but we found that hot tea equally with sleep merited the praise of being

" Tired nature's sweet restorer."

We had a long, hot drive all day over the plains. There was no timber, except in one place, where the plain was covered with a kind of palm for a space of two miles. We saw numerous bands of antelopes, but, frightened by the ambulance, they kept at a distance. There was a dreary uniformity in our prospect,—the same flat, scorched prairie. Descending a few feet, we passed for half a mile over the dry sandy bed of what was once a wide river. We saw no one, except a train of four or five wagons, containing a party of Mormons going from Salt Lake to their settlement of San Bernardino in the southern part of the State.

In the middle of the afternoon we reached the only water to be found for many miles, and, of course, had to remain till next morning. It is a small spring, of which an Irishman has taken possession. He has a canvas house of one room, and supports himself by his gun, and by furnishing provisions to parties passing over the plains. A pile of antelope skins lying near the house, gave an intimation of what our fare was to be, and we soon had a dinner of the meat, cooked for us out in the open air. Towards evening, some of our party went to the neighboring hills to try to shoot an antelope for themselves, but came back unsuccessful. At night, we camped out near the house.

In the evening a man arrived on horseback, leading another horse. He proved to be a Mormon belonging to a party, camped twelve miles distant in the hills, by whom he had been sent down for provisions. He was a perfect specimen of the wild, reckless, swearing class of men who infest this country, utterly careless of his own life and regardless of that of every one else. Late at night, to our relief, he took his departure, and we heard him shouting and singing, as he went up through the hills, "making night hideous" with his ribaldry.

Thursday, Oct. 11th. The stars were shining when we arose, and as there is no dressing to be done, it does not take us long to prepare for our journey. Before we set out, "Irish John" cooked breakfast for us. In a few miles the plains ended and we reached the hills, and then wound through valleys dotted with old oak trees. Occasionally we saw a little lake, and, as on the day before, frequent bands of antelopes. About noon we reached Tejon Pass, a valley hemmed in by mountains. At its entrance a large dry lake of saleratus glittered in the sun. The loose powder wafted up by the wind hung over it like a white cloud. The valley here is several miles wide, and as we drove through it we saw on the soft earth, the whole length of our way, the tracks of two large grizzlies which had shortly preceded us. As we approached the military post, Bell cracked his whip vigorously, and the tired mules, urged to a spasmodic effort, dashed up to the officers' quarters where we found Captain Gardiner ready to receive us.

The post at the Tejon is on a little plain, entirely surrounded by high mountains, which give it a confined appearance. It is, however, beautifully situated in a grove of old oaks. Under one of these, which stands on the parade ground, in 1837, Peter Le Bec, an old hunter, was killed by a bear, and his companions buried him at its foot. They then stripped the bark, for some three feet, from the trunk of the tree; and carved on it an inscription, surmounted by a cross, which remains to this day, though the bark is beginning to grow over it on all sides.

The barracks,—handsome *adobe* buildings,—were being erected around the sides of the parade ground. None of them were yet finished, and the soldiers were living in tents. The officers, too, were living under canvas, except Captain Gardiner, who had a small temporary *adobe* building, which is soon to be demolished. Willie and I stayed with him, while the rest of the party were distributed among the other officers. There are ordinarily about six officers and one hundred and twenty dragoons stationed here, besides the numerous civilians who are storekeepers and employées of the post. A squad of dragoons is kept seventeen miles off, on the reservation, to watch the Indians.

Friday, Oct. 12th. To-day Major Townsend attended to his official duties. The soldiers were all paraded for him to inspect. As their horses are pasturing four miles off, they were inspected as infantry. Most of the horses have lately come over the plains with Colonel Steptoe's command, by the way of Salt Lake, and will need some time to recruit from the fatigues of the march, where both water and forage were often exceedingly scarce. The Major afterwards inspected every department of the post. The officers were all invited to meet us at dinner at Captain Gardiner's.

Saturday, Oct. 13th. We all dined to-day at Captain Kirkham's. He had one canvas tent in front for his family, and another, a few feet back of it, for his kitchen. Between them was a large oak tree, and under it was stretched an awning connecting the two tents. This was the dining-room. Beside the table rose the rough trunk of the old tree, so that we had (as one of the party remarked), "oak carvings about us."

In the afternoon we rode out about four miles, through the passes of the mountains, to where the dragoons' horses were pasturing, and in the evening, in company with Captain Gardiner, I visited the widow of Lieut. Castor, who had died about a month before.

Sunday, Oct. 14th. There is no service of the Church within two hundred and fifty miles of this place, nor a religious service of any kind nearer than Los Angeles. It happens, however, (not an unusual circumstance in the army,) that all the officers at this post are Churchmen—several are communicants—and Captains Gardiner and Kirkham have their families residing here. The former was, therefore, some months ago, licensed to act as lay reader, and one service has been regularly performed. My object in spending the Sunday here, was, by myself holding service, to give in the minds of the men a sanction to that of the lay reader—to administer the Holy Communion, which some of them have had no opportunity of receiving since they left the Atlantic States—and also to baptize several children, whose families may remain for years at this secluded post, without the opportunity of seeing a clergyman.

We had service in a large room of the unfinished barracks. All the officers and quite a number o the men attended. At the Holy Communion there were seven recipients besides the members of our own party. At noon, at Captain Kirkham's quarters, I baptized his infant, only one week old, and after the Second Lesson in the afternoon, baptized the child of Captain Gardiner. In the evening I visited the family of a soldier who had died that day. He was buried early the next morning, his comrades firing their volleys over his grave, after I had read the burial service.

Thus ended my visit at this dragoon station, made so pleasant by the warm hospitality of the officers. I was fully compensated for all the fatigue of the journey by the opportunity afforded me to administer the solemn Sacraments of the Church where they had never before been witnessed, and to those who otherwise might not receive them for many years.

III. *The Plains and Fort Miller.*

Monday, Oct. 15. About eleven o'clock we took leave of our hosts, several of the officers accompanying us on horseback for our first day's ride. We had the same driver and heavy ambulance as before, with six mules, a dragoon on horseback to act as guide, and two saddle horses, so that we could in turn have the relief of a ride and also lighten the wagon of our weight.

In the first few miles through the pass of the mountains the scenery was exceedingly wild, and the descent so great that we had to walk most of the way. The road descends twenty-four hundred feet in five miles. From the mountian side we had a view of the plain stretching as far as the eye could reach, and in the distance, glancing in the sunlight, the waters of Kern Lake. Just as we entered on the plain, we passed a small Indian village of about forty persons,

After skirting the mountain for some twelve miles, we arrived at the Indian Reservation. Here we were obliged to stop for the rest of the day, as Major Townsend was ordered to investigate its condition. There is here a tract of thirty thousand acres set apart by Government for the Indians, but at present there are not three hundred residing on it. At this season, however the wild Indians from the mountains have come down to unite with them in holding their annual Dog Feast, so that there are about one.

thousand present. We passed several groups of them, almost in a state of nudity, washing their clothes by the little stream which flows through the Reserve; and on reaching their grand encampment, stopped and walked through it. Their lodges were arranged in a circle, all opening inwardly. The Indians were lounging in the shade, roasting dogs and eating them, while the greater part of those not thus employed, were gambling. The women seemed even more engrossed in this than the men, most of them so intensely interested that they would scarcely look up at us. They sat in circles on the ground, and the favorite game was one in which sticks a foot long were thrown about like jack-straws.

We drove on about four miles to the residence of the Indian agent. He has a plain house, with one room on each side of the hall, where he lives with eight or ten employées. A short distance from the house, on a little knoll, is the grave of one of his men who was killed a month before by a grizzly.

The agent entertained us to the best of his ability, giving one room in which there was a bed, to myself and son, and the only other room to the rest of our party, who slept on the floor wrapped in their blankets. We had for dinner, some tough meat, and hot bread as heavy as lead, coffee sweetened with a kind of maple sugar made on the premises, but no milk.

After attempting this dinner it was thought advisable to have a gallop on horseback before we endeavored to sleep. In the latter part of the afternoon, therefore, Mr. Stanly and Willie rode down to the Indian camp, while the rest of our party waited till dark to go with the Indian agent, who was to provide us with horses and act as guide. There was just moon enough to show the trail as we galloped over the prairie, and long before we reached the camp we heard the sound of the Indian drums. We found them all very busy, and fires lighted in every direction. Some of the party tried dog's meat, but I was contented to take their report on the matter. This feast was in honor of the dead of the past year, and on one day during its continuance they bury all the effects of the departed.

There was to be a war dance late in the evening by some of the wild Indians, which was to take place outside of the camp. A large fire was made, and we waited for an hour, during which some of the Indians, who had been at one time at the old Missions, were singing songs in a nasal tone very much like the intoning of the service by the old Padres, from whom they had undoubtedly acquired it. Tired out with waiting, I went into an unoccupied Indian lodge near by, and threw myself down to rest. As I lay there, looking up to the roof above me made of tule reeds, through which the occasional glimmering of the stars was seen, the only light being the glare of the fires before the opening of the lodge, and listening to the discordant singing of the Indians without, I thought how strange it was to find myself in such a situation in this wild country on the Pacific coast.

Hearing at last that the war party had finished painting and were nearly ready, we walked out in search of them. We found them grouped around the dim embers of a fire, singing in a low, droning tone, as if preparing their spirits for the task. After a time they rose, and repairing to where the large fire had been built, ranged themselves before it. The musicians, seated on the ground on the other side, began playing a rude chant,—in which the dancers joined,—

accompanied by the noise of sticks struck together. The dancers were entirely naked, except that each had a slight girdle round the loins, a necklace of bears' claws, and a tiara of feathers. Their bodies were painted all over, while their leader had a horizontal line drawn across his face just below the nose, the upper half of the face being daubed with a white pigment, and the lower half with black, through which his teeth gleamed like those of a wolf.

Then commenced the dance, which was so violent in its character that the perspiration rolled off them in streams. It was a commemoration of the dead, and as those who died in battle were mentioned in succession, the leader went through the representation of their deaths, throwing himself down on the ground and acting the last scene with its struggles and exhaustion. Sometimes he assumed the precise attitude of the antique statue, "the Dying Gladiator." As the dance went on, they seemed to work themselves up into an intense excitement, and would continue it, we were told, till morning. It was a wild scene as the glare of the fire fell upon the dancers and a thousand Indians gathered in a circle round them, and when I looked around on our little party in this dense throng of excited savages, I felt some apprehension as to what the rising war spirit might lead to. I confess, I was somewhat relieved when late at night the signal was made to disengage ourselves from the crowd of Indians and get without the camp, preparatory to our return. It was clear star-light and there was something exhilarating in our ride, as for about an hour we followed the guidance of the agent over what seemed to us the pathless prairi.e

Can anything be done for the spiritual benefit of these

Indians? It is difficult to tell, as they are so migratory in their habits, seldom remaining together in large bodies for any length of time. The old Padres succeeded with them because there was no outside influence to oppose their plans. There is every variety of Indian tribe in this region, from the warlike Indians at the north and on the borders of Mexico, down to the Digger Indians, who seem to live a mere animal life. Still, the experiment might be tried on one of the Northern Reservations, where a better class of Indians is collected. Intellectually these Indians seem to be exceedingly bright, and children taken into families as servants learn the English language with great facility.

I copy the above paragraph from my journal kept at that time. Several years have since passed, and no steps have yet been taken to improve the condition of the Indians. In fact, they are subjected to outrages from our wild frontier settlers which must soon end in their extermination. When, years hence, this narrative is first submitted to the eye of a reader, I believe there will not be an Indian living within the bounds of this State; but then, looking back upon the time that has passed, and ⸢the tribes which have melted like the snow-drift, leaving no trace behind, we fear the record in regard to them will be.—" no man cared for their souls."

Tuesday, Oct. 16th. We were up by daylight, and after washing at a little stream near the house, had breakfast at the agent's. After driving about six miles, we came to some springs called "the sinks," where we found two men who had camped during the night. This was the last water we were to see for more than thirty miles, and here, too, we took leave of all evidences of human life for the rest of the day. Before us stretched a plain, scorched, dry, and apparently boundless, without a tree for miles. At a distance, during the earlier part of the day, we saw a lake, the borders of which seemed lined with bands of antelopes. The gentlemen estimated there must be at least a thousand. Major Townsend and Mr. Calhoun rode off in pursuit of some which came within a few miles of us, but the nature of the ground allowing no concealment, they could not get near enough for a shot at them.

By mid-day the sun was burning hot, and we had dragged over wastes of sand till our animals drooped and we ourselves were almost exhausted. At noon, we halted for a few minutes to rest, though in the glare of the sun; and without leaving the ambulance, took such lunch as our stores afforded. Then on—on we toiled for the rest of the day. We met but one person—a Mexican on horseback. During the afternoon the ground became rolling, and as we dragged up each knoll, we hoped to see some traces of the promised river, but before us was only a new succession of the same barren mounds. Our driver and the guide began an animated discussion about the direction of the different trails, and we feared that they had mistaken their way. At length Major Townsend, riding forward to the crown of one of the mounds, announced that he saw the river below. We found that it was in a deep valley with a line of trees through it, showing the presence of water. We left the ambulance to let it drive down the precipitate bank, and walked half a mile to the Kern River, having travelled thirty-three miles without water.

Kern River is about one hundred feet broad, and at

this season of the year from two to six feet deep, flowing with a beautifully clear stream. On the bank we found a canvas shanty belonging to a man who had settled himself here and constructed a scow, with which, in the rainy season, when the river is high, he ferries over any chance passengers. He warned us to be on our guard, as the Mexicans, having been driven out by the inhabitants some fifty miles above, were dispersed over the country and had committed a number of murders.

We crossed the river and encamped in a grove of cottonwoods and willows, perfectly tired out. Never was the sight of water so grateful to us, and we now could realize the meaning of the Oriental description,—" a barren and dry land, where no water is." A good bath in the river, however, refreshed us, and after building our fire and having supper, we spent a pleasant evening reclining on our blankets about the burning logs.

Wednesday, Oct. 17th. We were awakened before dawn by the howling of the coyotes about us, and, after a few hurried mouthfuls, were off before six o'clock. Late at night we had seen on the opposite side of the river a fire, showing that some travellers had camped there. At daylight they crossed, and we found they were two men from the Upper Mines who were going on horseback to the Kern River mines. On the plains they had taken the wrong trail and wandered about all day, almost dying of exhaustion. As one of them expressed it—" starved to death for want of water." Providentially, late at night, they struck the Kern River.

After leaving the grove by the river, we entered at once among the most desolate hills. Not a sign of herbage was seen on them—not enough to attract a bee. We met with no animal life through the whole morning, except a large gray wolf which was stealing away between the hills. As one of our party said, it was "Sahara in mountains." The road (if such it could be called) was an old Indian trail winding through the defiles between these barren hills, and so little worn that most of the time we were obliged to walk, to avoid the steep pitches. As the day advanced the heat became almost suffocating, for the hills excluded all air, while the reflection of the sun from their sandy sides made an intolerable glare.

Our guide informed us that at noon we should reach a camping ground where there was water. At that time we saw indeed a line of green trees in one of the valleys, showing a water course, but on reaching it, we found it almost entirely dry. There were two springs near it, but they were strongly impregnated with sulphur, so that we " could not drink of the waters for they were bitter." We had to content ourselves, therefore, with the hope of reaching White River in the evening. We saw, however, numerous places around where stakes had been driven into the ground for picketing animals, showing that it had been frequently used as a camping ground.

The journey of the afternoon was as oppressive as that of the morning. We were constantly passing through deep gulches and over hills where we had to get out and walk. Often, when we had taken refuge behind some rock, against the heat of the sun, did we realize the force of that Scripture imagery—" Like the shadow of a great rock in a weary land!" Towards evening a large grizzly was seen about a mile from us among the hills. Mr. Stanly and Major Townsend, who were on horseback, together with

Mr. Calhoun (who mounted the guide's horse), went off with their rifles to attack him, advancing from three points so as to distract his attention, as he would probably make a rush at the first who fired. But the bear, perhaps alarmed by seeing so many approaching, galloped over the hill and took refuge in a ravine where he was lost to them.

At sunset, we saw at a distance in the valley, the line of green trees which marked the course of White River. At the sight, our exhausted animals seemed to toil on with new vigor; but our disappointment cannot easily be described when we found that it was entirely dry, nothing but a bed of shining sand. We had travelled thirty-three miles, equal to fifty-three miles of ordinary travel. We crossed on the dry bed, and after ranging up and down the bank for some miles, came to the canvas house of a squatter, near which we camped, in a grove of oaks. He had dug a shallow well, which was not a spring, but the water oozed up through the earth, and was as muddy, therefore, as the usual water of our gutters. We procured enough, however, to make some tea, though there was none for our poor animals after their hot day's work, and after a hasty meal we were soon asleep around our fire.

Thursday, Oct. 18th. We were stirring long before dawn, and off as soon as it was light enough to harness, it being necessary to push on as fast as possible to find water. The country was of the same character as yesterday, sandy and desolate. When going up a hill, we discovered that one of the hind wheels was just coming off. The lynch-pin was gone, and we were detained while our guide rode back some miles to look for it. His search, however, was vain, and as a last resource he cut off the end of his hickory whip and made one of wood, a poor substitute for the iron pin, and needing constant watching. At about ten o'clock we found a spring among the hills, surrounded by a clump of willows, where, by building a dam across the little trickling stream, we procured enough for our breakfast and to refresh our wearied animals. After leaving this spot we had a striking view of the Great Tulare Valley. It stretched as far as the horizon, one unbroken, scorched and yellow waste, with what seemed a single thread of green running through it, showing the course of Deep Creek. Yet as soon as the dry season is over and the rains come, so that vegetation revives, this view must present a perfect sea of green.

A few miles further on we met a wretched looking man traveling on foot on his way to the mines. He seemed almost exhausted. We relieved his wants as far as we could, by giving him something to eat and drink, and directed him where he could find the spring we had left. He is one of the many who, in traversing these wastes alone, sink down and die. Their remains are not seen by any traveller for months; and their friends at home never know the manner of their end.

Two hours after this we met the sheriff with his posse, who informed us he had been breaking up a band of robbers, some of whom had been taken, while others were still lurking in the thickets on Tulare River, where we expected to encamp.

At noon we reached Three Creeks, but found it dry. A squatter by the river had, however, dug some pits, from which we procured a small supply of water. We passed through the same kind of country till the middle of the afternoon, when we saw at a distance the trees on the banks of Tulare River. We crossed and camped in a grove of oaks. Just afterwards, the Fort Miller ambulance which had been despatched to meet us, drove up ; but as it was small, (they only expected Major Townsend and myself,) the Major determined to keep the Fort Tejon wagon to Fort Miller, and to use the last arrival to carry our baggage.

After a refreshing bath in the beautiful clear water of the river, we had a visit from a settler who had stationed himself near our camping ground. As the officers were accustomed to go back and forth by this trail, he had formed an acquaintance with many of them, and now came to ask us to tea at his cabin. We were most happy to accept his invitation and shall long remember the hospitality of these good people. Their cabin was but a single room, with beds in the corners, but they gave us a capital tea, at which they presided with a dignity not often seen in " the States." We spent an hour after tea with our host, during which time he entertained us with accounts of his manner of life in this secluded spot, with adventures in the wilderness, and stories of grizzlies attacking parties in the thickets by the river where we had camped. That night we were a little more careful than usual in keeping our fire replenished.

Friday, Oct. 19th. On our way by daybreak. I awoke with a feeling of illness which increased during our drive of nineteen miles over a scorched plain. We at length entered an oak forest of the most splendid trees, having in it, here and there, small settlements of Indians who were busily engaged in collecting their winter store of acorns. After going through this for nine miles we came to a stream called " Four Creeks," which we crossed, and camped beyond among the oaks. It was but little past noon, but the next water being eighteen miles away, it was too far for our mules to go that day. The woods here seemed to be swarming with Indians, so that we were obliged to keep a strict watch on our wagon.

My illness having increased, I lay down on the hard boards of the wagon, where I remained till sundown, wondering, in case I was to be really ill, what I should do— two days' journey from any physician or settlement. Towards evening, feeling better, probably from rest and abstinence, I crossed the river to a shell of a house which a squatter had erected on the opposite side, where we got some tea. The woman who prepared it for us was suffering from fever and ague, which is common on all these river bottoms. Her wretched appearance did not make the prospect of our night's rest in the open air very agreeable.

Saturday, Oct. 19. We were up before light, and drove about nine miles through the oaks to a solitary house where we breakfasted. The house consisted of but one room, three of its corners occupied by beds. The next eighteen miles were over the hot plains,—then about seven miles through the forests again, crossing several dry river beds filled with cobble-stones, till late in the afternoon we reached King's River, a bright stream about two hundred feet wide. We forded it and found on the opposite side a beautiful plateau covered with oaks. Two teamsters who had camped there with their mules, told us they were obliged to cross the plains we had been over, in the night, to avoid the excessive heat. There were large bodies of Indians on the banks, whom we visited after our camping was arranged. They were living in the open air, without even any lodges, and employed themselves in fishing and hunting, being exceedingly skillful with the bow and arrow.

Being out of provisions, we purchased some fish of the Indians, while Major Townsend and our guide forded the river on their horses, and riding up some distance came to a settler's shanty, where they bought some chickens and eggs. Fallen trees furnished us an abundant supply of fuel for our cooking and for fires through the night.

We had expected to have reached Fort Miller this evening, but found ourselves thirty miles distant. We had lost time, owing to the necessity of arranging our journey each day with regard to the supply of water. Stay where we were, however, over Sunday, we could not. We had no provisions, and the air was so malarious, that we found the Indians about us, though born on the spot, rapidly decreasing in numbers through the effects of the fever and ague. Nothing remained for us, therefore, but to push on next morning and reach Fort Miller as early as possible, that at least a portion of the day might be devoted to its proper object.

Sunday, Oct. 21st. We were up this morning by four o'clock, long before the faintest streak of dawn appeared in the east. After a hasty breakfast of sea biscuit and hard boiled eggs, we set off while it was so dark that we could not see the trail through the open woods, but were obliged for some miles to trust to the sagacity of the mules, leaving them to walk and find the path for themselves. After a few miles we emerged from the oak openings, when the rest of our way was, as usual, over the dusty, scorched plains. Between ten and eleven o'clock, we reached the hills overlooking Fort Miller; but missing the road, we had to dismount, while the heavy ambulance went plunging down the side of the hill. We passed through the little town of Millerton on the San Joaquin River, about half a mile from the Fort. It was composed of some twenty houses, most of them of canvas, two or three being shops, and the majority of the rest drinking saloons and billiard rooms. The population was Mexican or the lowest class of whites, and on this day they seemed to be given up entirely to dissipation.

As the formidable cavalcade of two ambulances, three horsemen, and a party on foot, wound round the hills towards the post, the officers, (as we afterwards learned,) turned out with their glasses to see who could be coming, as they had only expected Major Townsend and myself. The post is situated on a plateau overlooking the town and river. There are only about seventy men of the Third Artillery stationed here. The officers met us as we arrived, and we had a warm welcome. Major Townsend went with Lieut. Loeser and the rest of us to Dr. Murray's quarters.

The service of our Church had never been held here, nor, when Sunday came, had there been anything to mark the day. Arrangements were soon made, after our arrival, for service in the evening, and a broad hall in one of the buildings devoted to the officers was cleared for that purpose. The officers with their families, and many of the soldiers attended, and after the Second Lesson I baptized the child of one of the privates. A beginning having thus been made, before I left the post, I licensed Dr. Murray, the surgeon, a communicant of the Church, to act as lay reader, and arrangements were made for having the service every Sunday.

We remained at the post for two days, resting from the fatigue of our journey and enjoying the open hospitality of the officers. Of these two days there is little to tell. On Monday, Major Townsend had his inspection of the troops and visited all the buildings of the post. We dined and took tea with the officers, rode, and passed our time quite pleasantly. Tuesday, the Major had a grand pow-wow with the tribe of Digger Indians near the post, and presented their head man with a gay flannel shirt, with which he was hugely delighted,—thus, as the Major expressed it,—" transforming the Indian Chief into a red shirt miner." As he was obliged to wait till the end of the week and then to stop at the Indian Reservation on his way down, we determined to leave him, and to return in the little stage which runs from this place to Snelling's. It had made but two trips, and before it commenced to run, travellers were obliged to pass those seventy miles on horseback. When we reach Snelling's, we are in the region of the regular stage routes.

Wednesday, Oct. 24th. Long before daylight, we were up and our little stage with two horses was ready. After taking leave of our kind entertainers, we commenced our journey on the banks of the San Joaquin. At about nine o'clock we stopped at a solitary house intended for teamsters, where, for one dollar each, we had a breakfast; but everything was so filthy that we could hardly eat even after our long morning ride. The drive, for the whole day—was over the same kind of country as during the preceding week—desolate plains varied with an occasional hill and river, and then a cattle ranch. At noon we reached a place similar to the one at which we had breakfasted, where they wished us to dine, but we declined, and preferred waiting till we reached Snelling's at evening.

As we stopped at a solitary ranch to change horses, the owner got in and went on with us. I had noticed two very fine looking young Indians, about eighteen years of age, standing before the door, and remarked to him that they were the best specimens of Indians I had seen.

"Yes," said he, " I was offered twelve hundred dollars for one of those boys."

"But how," I asked, "could you sell him ? "

"Why, just as I could anything else—my horse or my cow. I got him some years ago and trained him up. He's mine."

"But suppose," I continued, "he should leave you and refuse to work any more."

"Then, I should do just as I have done before,—catch him and put him right down to his work."

"If you were nearer San Francisco," remarked Mr. Stanly, "there might be such a thing as a *habeas corpus,* to find out what you were doing with these Indians."

"That might do, sir, in San Francisco, but let me tell you that here in the mountains, might makes right."

The next topic was the story of a gambler who came and "squatted" on his ranch to levy blackmail on him and his brother. After narrating his grievances and annoyances, Mr. Stanly asked—

" What became of him ? "

"Oh, my brother shot him with a derringer. The ball went in here," (touching one temple,) "and came out here," (touching the other temple). And all this was said just as coolly as if he were describing the shooting of a coyote.

Then came a description of the killing of Joaquin, a noted bandit, for whose head the government had offered a reward of five hundred dollars. Our travelling companion was one of the party which hunted him down, and he described the whole affair with great gusto, as if it had been a most agreeable sporting expedition ; which, in fact, it was to him.

I have given these conversations to illustrate the character of the men, wild and lawless, generally from the frontier of the West, who have formed so much of the emigration to this country.

Just before dark we reached Snelling's, a small settlement with fine trees about it. The hotel here is large and seemed full, this being a central point from which stages go up through Mariposa County. There is probably no place in California which collects so many outlaws as this tavern, or which is so marked for deeds of bloodshed. After supper we retired early to prepare for our last day's travel.

Thursday, Oct. 25th. Off in the stage by bright moonlight, which fortunately lasted till daylight. We had six passengers, including a Chinaman. After fording the Stanislaus River, we ate breakfast at a tavern on the bank. The country we passed through is much richer and more thickly settled. Oak trees are scattered park-like through it, and we passed cultivated farms, increasing in frequency as we approached Stockton. We reached there at four in the afternoon, just in time for the boat. Here, for the first time in several days, we had an opportunity to dress, and the next morning awoke at the wharf in San Francisco, after having been absent about a month.

Thanks to kind Providence, we reached home without a single accident. I believe but one of our party suffered any ill effects from the journey. More than a year afterwards, Mr. Calhoun told me that he had not recovered from the effects of the cold and chills which resulted from his camping out. I was able to accomplish all that I designed. I learned the state of things at Los Angeles, and the nature of the country in the eastern half of the State. It is a section which evidently cannot be settled for many years, and I shall probably, therefore, never again be obliged to travel the route we did on this occasion.

XXII.

THERE are several places in California, where the Church has been founded, the story of each of which is short, and yet the annals of this diocese would not be complete if it were omitted. I shall group them together therefore in a single chapter, taking them in succession.

At the close of my first year's residence here—in 1854—I received an urgent appeal from a young man at Coloma, to pay it a visit. He described it as a thriving town—the county seat—and yet, without any place of religious worship. I determined therefore in the following month to go there.

January 21st, 1855, I was officiating at Marysville, where Mr. Hager had recently begun his labors. The following day, Monday, I left Marysville, to return to Sacramento, in the little, high pressure steamer, *Pearl.* Another steamer started at the same time, so that we raced down at the top of our speed, reaching Sacramento at two P. M. Five mornings afterwards, the *Pearl*, in repeating the race, was blown to pieces, every officer and about seventy passengers killed, leaving only twelve unwounded out of one hundred and twenty-two individuals who were known to be on board.

242

On Tuesday, I took the stage at daylight for Coloma in the mountains of El Dorado County. It was a long and wearisome ride. The distance is about fifty-five miles, but it was the rainy season—the roads had been cut up—and there were occasional showers through the day. After about twenty miles, the road turns aside into the mountain mining district. We passed through several little mining settlements, such as Negro Hill, and Mormon Island; and in the gulches and ravines saw the miners, by twos and threes, at their hard tasks. The country, too, is traversed in various directions, by ditches and flumes constructed to carry water to the "diggings." We reached our destination at about four in the afternoon, where my correspondent met me; and I found a place had been provided for me at the hotel.

The town proper of Coloma contains only between six and seven hundred inhabitants, but a numerous mining population is scattered around it. Although ranked among the mining towns it has beautiful gardens which are famous for their fruit, and extensive vineyards are being planted in the vicinity.

It is a beautifully situated place, surrounded by high mountains on which the lights and shadows play; and the effects, particularly at sunset, are sometimes exceedingly fine. Through the mountains, flows a little stream, on which is a mill that has become historical as the spot where gold was first discovered in California. Some men were digging a mill race for General Sutter, when their attention was attracted by the glittering ore. This led to further explorations, the riches of California were disclosed, and as soon as the news reached the world, the rush of immigration began. While here, I saw the first piece of gold that was discovered, which is still in the possession of the wife of the finder. They are poor people; and the State of California should procure the specimen, which may have in it about five dollars worth of gold, and place it in security with the archives of the State.

In the evening I met some members of the Church who were arranging a choir for their first service. Wednesday was spent with Mr. Searle in visiting all those in the town whose tendencies were in favor of the Church. In the evening, the Court House was crowded, and I held service and preached, baptizing an infant after the Second Lesson. The next day I returned to Sacramento, reaching there in time for the noon boat for San Francisco.

I found, as they had told me, there was not a religious service of any denomination held in Coloma. Now and then, some wandering Methodists came, but they were generally so illiterate that the congregation could not listen to them with patience. While I was there measures were taken to erect a Church—a subscription was commenced—and they soon after wrote me, that a plan had been adopted and the building commenced.

During the following May, I once more visited Coloma, arriving there on the evening of the 11th. The first object which greeted my sight as we entered the town, was the little Church which had been built since my last visit.

On the next day—Saturday—I drove over to Placerville, eleven miles distant, in company with Judge Robinson of Coloma, who kindly volunteered to be my guide. My object was to inquire into the feasibility of establishing the Church in that place, and if possible, to become acquainted with some of those who were Churchmen at home. While there I met a State Senator whom I knew, and upon inquiring with regard to several persons, as to whether or not they were Churchmen, he at last gave me in a single sentence the Californian practice on this subject: "I don't know," said the honorable gentleman—(poor man! the next year he was in his grave)—" when a stranger comes here, we inquire into his political creed and financial ability, but never ask any questions about his religious belief."

Sunday, May 13th. The Court House was well filled for our services both morning and evening, when I read service and preached.

I remained over the next day for the purpose of visiting the different members of the Church; and to give some advice with regard to the interior and chancel arrangements of the new building.

During the following January, 1856, the Rev. James W. Capen arrived and entered on his duties as Rector. The health of his wife, however, in a few months, obliged him to remove to Oakland for sea air. Then the Rev. D. F. Macdonald came, who remained for more than a year. During their residence I visited the parish several times, and on one Sunday evening officiated at Placerville in the Presbyterian house of worship, which was crowded. About this time, however, Coloma began to decline. The "diggings" in the neighborhood proved less rich, and the removal of the county seat to Placerville took away some of the best people. Mr. Macdonald went to Stockton; and while I write this the church is without a pastor. If possible, I will send some one to Placerville, who will hold occasional services at Coloma.

Oakland is another rural parish. It is situated directly

across the bay from San Francisco, and is the residence of many who are engaged in business in the city. My first visit was on Wednesday, Nov. 15th, 1854. I went over in the afternoon, expecting to hold a service in the evening; but owing to some mistake, notice had not been given, as was expected. I therefore spent the evening with Mr. Compton, an English gentleman residing there; and did what I could by personal conference with the members of the Church to induce them to begin its services among them.

The result was, that a commodious room was arranged for service, with altar, chancel, pulpit, vestry-room, etc. I spent Sunday, Dec. 17th there, and held the first service, reading prayers and preaching, morning and afternoon. Then, Rev. Mr. Syle, who had gone to China as a missionary, but being unable to accomplish anything there had settled down in Oakland, took the parish. In a few months, however, it died on his hands and he returned to China. Then Mr. Capen removed thither from Coloma on account of his wife's health. In a few months, however, he returned to the East. Then the room used for a chapel was burned down, and for two years nothing further was done.

Then Rev. Benj. Akerly entered on his duties as missionary, and by his untiring energy the congregation was collected and the present Church erected, which was consecrated March, 1860.

Among my most pleasant recollections is that of my first service at Petaluma. Mr. Wickersham, one of the congregation, had called on me, and I made an appointment for Tuesday, March 10th, 1857. I found Petaluma, a flourishing town which had sprung up in the last two years, and as it is at the outlet of some of the richest valleys in the State, the prosperity is likely to continue.

It was a soft and beautiful moonlight night. In accordance with notice given, I had Evening Service and preached in the Methodist house of worship, which had been offered for our use. The building was crowded, very many not being able to obtain admission. Immediately after service I baptized two children, and the next day returned to San Francisco.

Napa is a similar agricultural community. My first visit there was on July 31, 1858. I officiated in the morning in the Presbyterian house of worship, and again in the evening in the Methodist meeting house. These were our first services in Napa.

XXIII.

WITH this chapter I conclude the history of my early labors in this Diocese. On April 20th, 1857, I returned to the Atlantic States, with my family. Our voyage down the coast was in the *Golden Age*, over an unrippled sea, and with every attending circumstance to make it pleasant. On the other side, our steamer was the *Central America*, Capt. Herndon, U. S. N. Some three months after, on her return voyage, she went down with three hundred passengers on board, including the gallant Herndon.

During this summer my election as Diocesan was ratified by the Bishops and Standing Committees; and in the autumn I prepared to return to California. It was not, however, until November 20th that I was able to set out. Of my own family, I had only my wife with me. My eldest son Lawrence, (a Lieutenant in the Third Artillery,) I left stationed at Governor's Island, and my other son, Willie, was a student at Yale College. I had, however, the wife and daughters of the Hon. William Duer under my charge.

A more disagreeable voyage than this proved to be, is seldom made. I copy the record of it from my letter to Rev. Dr. Van Kleeck, as published in the *Spirit of Missions.*

243

I.

My dear Brother: It was with no pleasant feelings that I parted from you, as well as my other friends, on the deck of the *Star of the West,* on the 20th of November. It seemed as if the pain of leaving was even greater than it was four years since ; and yet, I know not why it should have been so, for then I was going to a strange land, " not knowing the things which should befall me there ; " but at this time I was only returning to my new home, where I knew many earnest friends were prepared to welcome me.

Shall I give you an account of our voyage? It has little of adventure, but it may be interesting to some of your readers, who have friends in this land, merely as showing what a voyage to California sometimes is.

Friday, Nov. 20th. If was at three P. M that we cast loose from the wharf—our signal gun was fired—the cheers of the crowd, watching our departure, were given, and soon we could see no longer even the waving handkerchiefs of those who, with tearful eyes, were thus striving to keep, to the last moment, their connection with some whom they should not see again for years.

It was evident enough, before we cleared the Narrows, that our steamer was crowded to excess and greatly overloaded. She is but eleven hundred burthen, (little more than one third that of the steamer which is to receive us on the Pacific,) and carries probably more than a thousand passengers. The officers acknowledge seven hundred and sixty passengers, while she might comfortably accommodate half that number. The first night out of New York, in winter, is always dismal. The severe cold—the single stove in he cabin, blocked up by hundreds trying to reach it—and the desolate air of everything, to those who have come from comfortable homes—effectually remove all the poetry from " life on the mountain wave." To add to our discomforts, a gale began before midnight, a most unfortunate time of the voyage, as most of the passengers had not yet settled into their places or become accustomed to the sea. It was with many of them a night long to be remembered.

Saturday, 21st. Unable to leave our berths, we passed the day in half-unconscious, dreamy misery. The rough weather continued, and the only thing of which we were thoroughly sensible was the steady pitch—pitch—of our vessel.

To gain places for more passengers, two rows of state-rooms have been built on the deck of the *Star of the West*— the only steamer in which I have sailed on the Atlantic which has such upper works. The *San Francisco* was built in this way, and during the storm in which she was wrecked, this upper cabin was swept entirely clear from the deck, with almost every passenger it contained. Our state-room was selected in this place for the sake of air, in anticipation of tropic heat—but in this rough weather a deck state-room is the least desirable location on the steamer. Our own room, too, happens to be the one nearest the stern, where, of course, the motion of the vessel is more felt than in any other part. In the evening we had a renewal of the gale, followed by another night of sickness and discomfort.

Sunday, 22nd. No Sabbath-day of rest and quiet; but our vessel still pitching, we remained in our berths through the morning. At noon, I was up for the first time since we left New York, and managed to get Mrs. Kip to the

Captain's state-room, midships, where the motion is less felt.
There she lay on the sofa through the day, while we thought
and talked of those who were in peace at home, and whose
prayers we knew at that hour were ascending, that we
might safely reach "the haven where we would be."

At night, a renewal of the gale. We have in our state-
room not only more motion than in any other part of the
ship, but we hear more of the force of the waves. Below us,
at the stern, the parted waters meet again, and seethe and
dash together, and we cannot escape the ceaseless sound.
Every few moments a wave would strike the bows, and our
vessel would seem to stop as though a giant had struck
her, and quiver for a moment in every plank, and then
again dart forward on her way. As our upper cabin creaked,
and seemed to sway in the wind as we rolled, the fears
of my wife reached their height, and most earnest were
her entreaties to me to take her down into the lower cabin.
Knowing, however, that it was perfectly suffocating there,
where every table and seat, and even the floor, had its
occupants, I was obliged to insist on our running the risk
of the upper cabin.

In the night we were opposite Cape Hatteras, and probably near the spot where the ill-fated *Central America* went
down. The thought recalled melancholy remembrances of
pleasant hours with Herndon and Van Rensselaer, when I
went home in her in the early summer. Now, the Gulf
Stream, over which we are passing, is sweeping on her
wreck to where it pours its treasures into the Arctic Seas.

Monday, 23rd. Sea still high. We have lately been making, against this head wind and sea, but one hundred and
fifty miles in twenty-four hours. Our steamer, though

naturally a good sea boat, labors terribly, and shows how she has been overloaded, with the most culpable reckless-ness of life.   Were any accident to happen to our machin-ery, with this dense mass of human beings on board, it would probably involve the loss of all ; for she has not boats for one fifth of the passengers.

When able to leave our berths we took refuge in the Captain's room, where we remained till late in the evening. The other ladies under my charge I have not seen for two days. They are in the dining room cabin, where I have not dared to venture ; and I suppose, like myself, they are *hors du combat.*

The night was the worst we have yet had; not only very rough, and with a strong head sea striking our bows, but at midnight a rain storm commenced, and it poured in tor-rents.   In the last few days and nights the crowded steer-age passengers must have suffered terribly.   We have been frequently shipping seas, from which it was impossible to protect those forward.

Tuesday, 24th.   Day dawned with a dull leaden sky, the horizon in mist, the sea running high, and every prospect of bad weather.   I found, however, that the barometer was rising, and at ten it commenced clearing.   The sunshine dried our decks, and though the sea is still heavy and we are making little progress, everything wears a more cheerful aspect.

During the next few days, though never calm, it was suffi-ciently smooth to bring out the passengers, some of whom had not been seen since we left New York.   We have the strange medley to be seen nowhere but in a California steamer—army and navy officers ; Spaniards, Mexicans,

Costa Ricans, (whom Walker had dislodged,, returning
home; ladies going to join their husbands in California ;
two Presbyterian missionaries returning to the Sandwich
Islands ; six Sisters of Charity; and over one hundred
children. We have the usual developments of evil, which
mark those who have broken away from the restraints
of home, and who, by their conduct, falsify the old maxim
—" *Coelum, non animum mutant, qui trans mare current.*"
But there are also the good and true—who are to be the
leaven of all that is pure in that distant land, and whose
prayers are the incense which rises up before the Throne of
the Highest. Some of them are members of our Church,
and when Sunday comes, they welcome the services which
remind them of holy scenes at home.

Among our passengers is the celebrated German traveller, Wagner, who, twenty years ago, won a world-wide reputation by his explorations in Africa and afterwards in the
East. He is now sent out by the King of Bavaria as head
of an exploring party, to spend a couple of years in
examining the Equatorial Regions of South America, on
the western coast. They go from the Isthmus to Peru.
With him is a distinguished artist, and also a German Bar-
oness who has joined the party to pursue certain botanical
researches. On her card, which she gave me, her name is
La Baronne de Hermayr Hortenburg, née Baronne de Sternburg.
She was perfectly familiar with the cities of Southern Europe, and it was a pleasant relief, in this distant sea, thus
to revive my recollections of the galleries of Italy.

26th. In the evening made our first land, the light on
Salt Keys, one hundred and twenty-three miles from Ha-
vanna.

27th. At eight A. M. when I came on deck, found we were coasting along the shores of Cuba. The "Gem of the Antilles" was before us, and in the distance was seen Moro Castle, at the entrance of the harbor of Havana. In an hour more we had come to anchor. A narrow passage, strongly fortified on both sides, is the only entrance.

We were soon surrounded by boats from the city, and after the proper officials had made their visit, were permitted to go on shore. The first thing at landing was to go to an officer on the wharf, where passports were furnished us, for which we paid one dollar each. We walked up to the public square on which the palace fronts. It is filled with tropical trees—the palm, the cocoa, and the banana—presenting a strangely beautiful view to one from a colder clime. Soldiers meet us at every turn, and it is said that thirty thousand can be collected in this city in a few hours. The streets are narrow, to secure shade and coolness, and the high, substantial houses and shops remind one of cities in the South of Europe. Ladies, in their light summer dresses with the *rebozo* over their heads, were shopping; but in all cases remained in their carriage, and the goods were brought out to them by the clerks.

The usual vehicle is the *volante*, a kind of gig holding two, with very long shafts, so that the horse is at a distance from the carriage, and is ridden by the driver postilion fashion. We hired several of these for our party, and set off to see the city and its environs. Driving through the large open square where the fashion of Havana assembles in the cool of the evening, and through the parade ground, we reached the open country beyond. In every part of the city are marble fountains, generally surmounted by a statue of one of

the royal family of Spain. Beyond the city, we passed through
long lines of elegant villas. Most of them are built low,
painted with gay colors, a species of China tiling being
much used. The house is buried in tropical foliage, and
the avenue which leads to it is entirely overarched with the
meeting boughs.

We drove out to a deserted villa, about four miles from
the city. We heard that it had been for years in chancery,
and had thus been suffered to fall to decay. The house
itself was rapidly crumbling to pieces, its frescoes peeling
off, and its gay colors fading. Around it, stretched long
walks, lined with statues, now mutilated, but showing that
it had once possessed every convenience for comfort and
pleasure. We saw the out-houses, where the proprietor
must once have kept an extensive aviary and zoological collection. All the departments were untenanted but one, through
which a stream of water flowed, where a solitary alligator
was yet imprisoned. The air was like June, and as we
walked around the grounds, we saw on every side evidence
of the luxury of this climate.

We returned to the city by a different road, affording
similar scenes. Our next visit was to the Cathedral, a fine,
extensive building, the exterior presenting a venerable appearance, and the chancel within being rich with varied
marbles. Beneath this was buried the remains of Columbus—" the worthy and adventurous general of the seas "—
as the old Spanish chronicles call him. He died at Valla-
dolid, in 1506, and in 1536 his remains were transported to
St. Domingo, that he might rest in the new world which he
had discovered. When that island was ceded to France in
1796, they were once more removed and interred in the

Cathedral of Havana, that they might be in Spanish soil. They were brought with great parade on the man-of-war called the *Discoverer*, the full account of which is given in the appendix to his life by Irving.

Against the wall, on one side of the chancel, is the monument, the upper part of which contains the portrait of Columbus, in bold relief, while on the lower part, surrounded by nautical instruments, is the Spanish inscription, of which this is the translation:

> Oh, remains and image of the great Columbus!
> May ye last a thousand ages, preserved in the urn
> And in the remembrance of our nation !

It was blowing very fresh when we left the wharf in a little sail-boat manned by native boatmen. It danced over the waves, to the great terror of the ladies, and it required a series of tacks to bring us up to the steamer. At three o'clock we were again under way, having taken in about seventy passengers, who came from New Orleans.

28th. Another rough day. We had, too, this morning, an alarm of the most fearful kind that can occur at sea. We were just leaving the breakfast table, when below in the second cabin there was a rush, and the shriek of women, and the cry of fire. It took but a few steps to bring the Captain to the spot. One of the women, in a room below containing three berths on each side with a narrow passage between them, had undertaken to cook with an alcohol lamp. After lighting it, she left the room, when a roll of the ship upset it, and in an instant the burning alcohol was all over the floor. The children shrieked, when a man in

the cabin rushed in, and providentially, had presence
of mind enough to tear off the bedding and commence
smothering the flames. This he had partially succeeded
in doing, when the Captain came to his aid. In an instant
more the flames would have been beyond all human control, and in this crowded vessel, out of sight of land,
with not boats enough for one-fifth of the passengers,
there would have been but few left to tell the story of our
fate.

Sunday, 29th. The sea too rough, and I myself too ill to
attempt the service in the morning. In the afternoon, the
weather being more pleasant, arrangements were made
upon deck, and the greater part of the cabin passengers
were present. I read the service and preached a brief
sermon.

We are now beginning to have a new firmament about
us. The old familiar constellations which shine upon our
own land have some of them sunk below the horizon, and
in place of them we have the Southern Cross.

30th. The sea smooth, but we have the excessive heat
of the tropics. For some days there has been a whispered
report of sickness aboard. It has gradually deepened into
certainty, and to-day the officers acknowledged that yellow
fever is prevailing. It is fearful to be crowded together
thus, in this stifling heat, with an infectious disease gradually increasing, and no way of escape.

Tuesday, Dec. 1st. To-day the deaths began. The
steamer has been stopped three times in seven hours to
enable me to read the Burial Service. In the morning, a
man died,—at noon, his daughter,—and in the afternoon,

a young man, a cabin passenger.   There is something inex-
pressibly solemn in a burial at sea.   The body, swathed in
canvas, like a mummy, and covered with the American flag,
with a heavy weight at its feet, is placed upon a board at
the gangway.   As I begin the service, the wheels of the
steamer gradually grow slower, until they stop for an instant, when I reach the words—"We commit his body to
the deep."   As I utter this sentence, the flag is withdrawn,
the board is tilted up, the body glides down into the sea,
and our vessel once more quickens its speed, leaving the
waves of the Caribbean Sea to sweep over him who was
lately our fellow passenger.

To show the crowded state of the steamer and the impos-
sibility of separating the sick and dying from the well, I
will mention one fact.   There was but one saloon, out of
which the state-rooms opened (except the few on deck), and
where we were obliged to take our meals.   On the cushions
of this saloon, during the last few days, two ladies, a mother
and daughter, have been dying of the black vomit, in full
sight of our dinner table.   The mother died as we entered
Aspinwall, and the daughter, it was known, could not sur-
vive till night.

This night many of the passengers passed on deck, rather
than risk the pestilential air of the cabin.

Wednesday, Dec. 2nd.   Near Aspinwall; and well for us
it is so.   A few days' longer crowding together, would have
infected half our passengers.   We heard another death reported early in the morning, and with great thankfulness
took our last breakfast on this vessel.   But never can we
forget that Capt. Gray has done everything in the power of
man under these difficult circumstances.   He has been un-

tiring as a navigator and in his attentions to his passengers. He is worthy of a better vessel, and we took leave of him with regret.

II.

We came in sight of Aspinwall at about nine o'clock. It is my third visit to it, yet there seems but little improvement. A few wooden hotels, and shops whose only harvest is reaped from the steamer passengers, are the abodes of those who choose to live on this pestiferous spot. The palm trees wave above it and around is all the luxuriance of tropical vegetation. Two miles from shore, the U. S. steam frigate, *Wabash*, was lying, to some of whose officers we were indebted for kind attentions during our brief stay.

We landed at ten o'clock, and as the train did not leave till three P. M., remained at one of the hotels. There are but few Americans here, the inhabitants being principally Mexicans or natives. The sick were now selected from the passengers, and left behind in a hospital belonging to the Company.

It was a pleasant afternoon, unusually cool, when we set off for Panama. I made the journey four years since, by boat, up Chagres River for one day, and then another day from Cruces on mules, through the mountain passes. Now, by the railroad, the fifty-five miles are travelled over in about four hours.

Just beyond Aspinwall, is the cottage in which John L. Stephens died. After all his experience in Egypt and the East, he yielded on this spot to the deadly malaria. Our train went but slowly, for the heavy rains had, in some places, undermined the road; yet every moment opened prospects through the ravines of the mountains, or amid the dense tropical foliage of the forests, with an occasional glimpse of Chagres River, which charmed the eye. Every few miles we passed a little native settlement, the light walls of the houses made of cane and the roof thatched with leaves. The children were playing around, generally in a state of nudity.

We reached Panama just before dark. Since the massacre by the natives, two years ago, the passengers have not been permitted to enter the city. The depot is without the walls, and we were conveyed at once to the steam-tug. Here we were all crowded on board, while the steerage passengers were towed behind in barges; and in about an hour we reached the *Golden Gate*. We have a magnificent steamer, three times the size of the *Star of the West*, and there is a prospect of as much comfort as is usual at sea.

A fortnight's voyage is before us, yet the Pacific is not liable to storms, and we dread it less than we did our thirteen days on the other side. We have reason to be thankful for our preservation from the dangers through which we have already passed, and may well say, in the words of Dr. Wm. Croswell's Traveller's Hymn—slightly altered,

> Lord, go with us, and we go
>   Safely, through the weariest length,
> Travelling, if Thou will'st it so,
>   In the greatness of Thy strength;
> Through the day, and through the dark,
>   O'er the deep and pathless sea,
> Speed the progress of our bark,
>   Bring us where we fain would be.

But I must curtail the rest of this narrative, particularly as I have already given, four years ago, my experience on the Pacific. For the first week we were speeding on over a scarcely rippled sea. With a splendid steamer and cloudless weather, there was nothing we could wish altered. As we crossed the Gulf of Tehuantepec, and again in passing the Gulf of California, we had rough weather, as is usual, for the wind sweeps down over these bodies of water. On the morning of the 8th, we stopped at Acapulco, Mexico, to coal. The entrance to the harbor is by a winding passage, and the inner basin is so enclosed that you are surrounded by the hills and cannot see where you were admitted.

We remained here through the day, anchored a short distance from shore, so that the passengers had an opportunity of landing. Acapulco is a mere Mexican town, commanded by a fort, and picturesque from the palm trees which line the shore. Amid the political troubles of Mexico it has been rather famous for its turbulence, and at the present time some two hundred of its political prisoners are confined on a desolate island a few miles from shore. As our steamer passed in the evening we saw their fires at the water's edge. The canoes, rowed by he half naked natives, soon surrounded our steamer, bringing a plentiful supply of all tropical fruits. I did not go on shore, as it was my third visit to this place, but our stopping formed a pleasant episode in the voyage.

The following evening we ran into Manzanillo, another Mexican port, to land some passengers. It is an obscure town, but the place at which the steamers, on their downward trip, generally receive a large amount of silver from the interior, to be sent to the United States and England.

We spent two Sundays on board. On the first, I read service and preached in the saloon. On the second, as the Rev. Dr. Armstrong, from the Sandwich Islands, was to preach, I went forward, and held service among the steerage passengers. A small cask was covered with the American flag, for my desk, while the congregation sat down on the deck in circles around me. There were probably no Church-men among them, for I saw no Prayer Book. I therefore read a few appropriate Collects and a Lesson, and preached a short extemporaneous sermon. In the hymns, however, which I gave out two lines at a time, they joined most heartily.

Wednesday morning, 16th. We crossed the bar at about four o'clock, and in an hour more were at the wharf. Our two guns rang over the hill-sides, and shortly we were greeted with a warm welcome, and the announcement that kind friends had put our house in order and that the fires were now lighted and breakfast preparing. So we drove home and sat down to our morning meal as quietly as if we had never left the house.

XXIV.

CONCLUSION.

I now lay down my pen. During the past year I have at leisure moments—sometimes with intervals of weeks—noted down my early experience in this Diocese. When our successors read this volume, I trust it will furnish them with some interesting facts with regard to the early Church on the Pacific.

How will this narrative seem to them? When they are worshipping in splendid buildings and members of powerful parishes, how will they regard our early struggles? With us the contest is a hard one, as we strive in an unsettled state of society to inculcate a regard for the things which are "unseen and eternal" on a people given up to the greed of gold.

Children of the next generation! to you we bequeath this contest. Living over our dust and inheriting the fruit of our labors, we pray you worthily to wage this warfare till you resign your weapons to others and join us in the land of spirits.

March 16th, 1860.

THE BEAUTIFUL LAND:
PALESTINE,
HISTORICAL, GEOGRAPHICAL AND PICTORIAL:

DESCRIBED AND ILLUSTRATED AS IT WAS AND AS IT NOW IS, ALONG THE LINES OF

OUR SAVIOUR'S JOURNEYS.

BY

JOHN FULTON, D.D., LL.D.

Introduction by the Rt. Rev. HENRY C. POTTER, D.D.

ILLUSTRATED BY FIFTEEN MAPS AND CHARTS, OVER THREE HUNDRED ENGRAVINGS, AND A GRAND PANORAMA OF JERUSALEM.

THREE IMPORTANT WORKS IN CHURCH HISTORY.

I.

History of the American Episcopal Church. From the Planting of the Colonies to the End of the Civil War. By Rev. S. D. McCONNELL, D.D. Third Edition. 8vo, cloth, $2.00.

"Among the most notable and valuable of the books that appeared during the past year—in the closing period of the book season—was, 'The History of the American Episcopal Church' from the planting of the colonies to the end of the Civil War. The author, the Rev. Dr. McConnell, is one of the most vigorous, clear-minded, progressive and valuable men enlisted in the ranks of the Protestant Episcopal clergy. He has given us a book of rare merit and great interest, one marked feature of which is its fairness, its determination to tell the true story of the Church without desire to give her more credit than she deserves, or withhold from her any of the praise to which she is entitled. . . . Not only do the literary execution of the work and the pervasive spirit of candor and impartiality deserve peculiar commendation, but one is struck with the patient and vigilant scholarship which, in depicting the relation of the Episcopal Church to the colonial communities, has sought out the original authorities."—*Buffalo Commercial.*

II.

The Church in Nova Scotia, and The Tory Clergy of the Revolution. By Rev. ARTHUR WENTWORTH EATON, B.A. 12mo, cloth, $1.50 *net.*

"This is a book of historical value and interest, not merely to Anglican and Episcopalian Churchmen, but to all students of early American history. Nova Scotia ought to have a great deal of interest for Americans, for it was to that Province that thousands of New York and New England tories went at the time of the American Revolution. As might naturally be expected these tories were nearly all staunch and devoted Anglican Churchmen, so that while on one hand their withdrawal seriously weakened the Episcopal Church in this country, it made Nova Scotia, the oldest Colonial diocese of the Church of England, the most important centre of Anglicanism on this continent. That alone would make a chronicle of Anglicanism in Nova Scotia well worth reading even if it were not for the circumstance that it is also necessarily and inferentially a history of the society and political life of the Province.

"Mr. Eaton, who is himself a Nova Scotian, already distinguished in the world of letters, has done his work well. His study of the old archives of Nova Scotia has been thorough and painstaking. He is not only imbued with that genuine respect for facts which distinguishes the true historian, but he is also gifted with that sympathetic imagination which is so essential for a comprehensive and lucid presentation of facts."—*N. Y. Tribune.*

III.

The Constitution of the American Church: Its History and Rationale. The Bohlen Lectures for 1890. By Rt. Rev. WILLIAM STEVENS PERRY, D.D. 12mo, cloth, $1.50.

"Bishop Perry could scarcely have rendered a more acceptable service to this generation than he has done by writing this book. . . . We wish that our Bishops and all examining chaplains would insist upon the study of this book by candidates as a necessary qualification for ordination."—*The Standard of the Cross.*

THOMAS WHITTAKER, 2 AND 3 BIBLE HOUSE, NEW YORK.

THE CYCLOPÆDIA OF

NATURE TEACHINGS.

WITH AN INTRODUCTION BY REV.

HUGH MACMILLAN, LL.D., F.R.S.E.,

AUTHOR OF "BIBLE TEACHINGS IN NATURE," ETC.

8vo, Cloth Extra.   Price, $2.50.   Just Out.

One of the most characteristic features of modern culture is the attention given to the facts, moods and suggestions of " Nature."

Teachers and preachers are feeling the need for illustrations from Nature in their pulpit, platform and class work, and as the scientific knowledge and the love of Nature increase in schools and in congregations, there must be an increasing demand for illustrations taken from the spheres in which audiences are becoming daily more interested.

The Cyclopædia of Nature Teachings is a collection of remarkable passages from the writings and utterances of the leading authors, preachers and orators, which embody suggestive or curious information concerning Nature.   Each passage contains some important or noteworthy fact or statement which may serve to illustrate religious truth or moral principles, the extracts being gleaned from the widest and most varied sources.

The passages are arranged alphabetically under subjects, and subdivided so as to elucidate the topic treated of and illustrate it in every possible way. Thus under the head of THE AIR, we find on this subject passages are given on THE BEAUTY OF CLOUDS, THE MYSTERIES OF THE CLOUDS, CHANGES IN THE SKY, MISTS AND SUNSHINE, THE MESSAGE OF THE HEAVENS, SKY INFLUENCES, AUTUMN, SUNSHINE, PLANTS, THE ATMOSPHERE, etc., etc.

That the Cyclopædia is a work of true value and reliable information will be seen by the names of the following authors, from whose writings, among many others, some of the extracts are taken, viz., RUSKIN, JEFFERIES, MACLAREN, McCOOK, HUGH MACMILLAN, BEECHER, SMILEY, WILSON, PULSFORD, GUTHRIE, FROUDE, LYTTON, ROBERTSON, ARTHUR, ARNOT, HERSCHEL, PROCTER, FABER, TAYLOR, DAWSON, HELPS, EMERSON, DICKENS, AGASSIZ, PARKER, CONDER, CHALMERS, BALDWIN, BROWN, CUVIER, RICHTER, GŒTHE, etc.

The volume forms a most valuable work of reference, and by its orderly arrangement puts its wealth of information and suggestion at the disposition of the student or teacher ; but the varied character of the selections, the freshness of the subjects treated, and the literary grace of many of the paragraphs will also make the work welcome to general readers.

The Cyclopædia of Nature Teachings is furnished with a very copious index of subjects, and also one of Bible texts.

NEW YORK : THOMAS WHITTAKER, 2 AND 3 BIBLE HOUSE.

THE RIGHT ROAD.

A Hand-Book for Parents and Teachers.

BY THE

Rev. JOHN W. KRAMER.

12mo, cloth binding, - - *Price, $1.25.*

" There is not a dull page in it. Even the bad boy who dislikes moral lectures will like pleasant chats : he will take the moral pills for the sake of their sugar coating, if for nothing else. Parents will find this excellent book helpful in getting their children on the right road and keeping them there."—*The Home Journal.*

" 'The Right Road' presents John W. Kramer's plan of giving instruction to children, and of arousing their personal interest in the principles and practice of Christian morality. By means of simply worded observations, and a great variety of short stories, he undertakes to teach a child something about personal responsibility, right and duty. Under duty, instruction and illustrations are given concerning duties to one's self—such as cleanliness, temperance, truthfulness, courage, self-control, order, thrift, culture and purity, duties to others—honor of parents, patriotism, honesty, justice, mercy, philanthropy, courtesy, gratitude and kindness to animals, duties to God—embracing reverence, worship and service."—*The Interior.*

" As a treatise on practical ethics the book has decided merits. It treats of nearly all aspects of morality, setting forth the nature and the obligation of the various kinds of duty in a clear and simple style and in a manner likely to interest the young. The different virtues and vices are illustrated by numerous examples in the story form, some of them historical, other fictitious, and many of them are fitted not only to illustrate the habits of good conduct, but to inspire the reader with a love for them. The book is more manly than such books usually are, the strong and positive virtues being given the importance that justly belongs to them. The last section of the book and duty to God is excellent, and is by no means uncalled for in times like these."—*Critic.*

THOMAS WHITTAKER, 2 AND 3 BIBLE HOUSE, NEW YORK.

AUBREY L. MOORE'S WRITINGS.

"With preachers like Phillips Brooks and M. Bersier the late Rev. Aubrey L. Moore was not unworthy to take rank, though his strength lay, perhaps, in delicacy of spiritual perception rather than in the more ordinary and popular forms of pulpit eloquence."—*The London Times.*

I.

Sermons Preached in the Chapel Royal, Whitehall. By the late Rev. AUBREY L. MOORE. 12mo, cloth, $1.50.

Just Out.

II.

The Message of the Gospel. By the late Rev. AUBREY L. MOORE. 12mo, cloth, 75 cents.

This volume contains three addresses on the Message of the Gospel; two on Vocation; and six sermons before the University of Oxford on the following topics: "The Veil of Moses," "The God of Philosophy and the God of Religion," "The Claim to Authority," "The Power of Christ on Moral Life," "The Presence of God in the Christian and the Church," "Decision for God."

"In bulk this is a small book, but like a jewel casket, small itself, its contents are of great price."—*The Churchman.*

III.

Some Aspects of Sin: Three Courses of Lent Sermons. By the late Rev. AUBREY L. MOORE. 12mo, cloth, 75 cents.

IV.

Science and the Faith. Essays of Apologetic Subjects. With an Introduction. Second Edition. 12mo, cloth, $1.50.

THOMAS WHITTAKER, Publisher,

2 and 3 Bible House, New York.

CANON FARRAR'S SERMONS.

I.
EVERY-DAY CHRISTIAN LIFE;

Or, Sermons by the Way.

By FREDERICK W. FARRAR, D.D.   12mo, cloth, $1.25.

"These sermons by Canon Farrar are the ordinary discourses of a parish priest to a customary congregation. They are upon subjects of every-day life. There is no wide-ranging speculation among them; nothing to gratify the seeker after suggested heresies, or at least the novelties of modern rationalism. But they are very delightful sermons to read—full of tender thought and happy suggestion, and written in a style which when the English clergy do attain it is one of the happiest known to the pulpit. As the other extreme of English preaching, the dead-and-alive manner of mere perfunctory talk is hateful to the last degree, so is this, its opposite, peculiarly pleasant."—*The Churchman.*

II.
TRUTHS TO LIVE BY:

A Companion to "Every-Day Christian Life."
By the same author.   12mo, cloth, $1.25.

"This is a volume of practical sermons written in a style free from mere technical language. The discourses are just what Dr. Farrar claims them to be—simple pastoral sermons. They deal mainly with doctrinal and fundamental subjects as they represent an attempt "to make clear some of the most essential truth of Christian faith."—*The Observer.*

CONTEMPORARY PULPIT LIBRARY.

New Sermons by the leading Anglican Preachers.   Square 12mo, cloth, gilt top, $1.00 each.

No. 1.   **FIFTEEN SERMONS.** By CANON LIDDON.
No. 2.   **SIXTEEN SERMONS.** By BISHOP MAGEE.
No. 3.   **TWENTY SERMONS.** By ARCHDEACON FARRAR.
No. 4.   **FOURTEEN SERMONS.** By CANON LIDDON.
No. 5.   **FIFTEEN SERMONS.** By BISHOP LIGHTFOOT.

THOMAS WHITTAKER,
2 AND 3 BIBLE HOUSE, NEW YORK.

THE DIVINE LITURGY.

Being the order for Holy Communion historically, doc-
trinally, and devotionally set forth in fifty portions. By
the Rev. HERBERT MORTIMER LUCKOCK, D.D., Canon
of Ely. 414 pp. 12mo, cloth, $2.00.

"We can heartily recommend this as one of the best things of the
kind yet published for the general reader. It treats of the history of all
parts of the service, rubrics, the text itself, technical and liturgical terms
and expressions, and also the ritual acts in rendering the service, giving
brief expositions of the meaning and teaching, with practical suggestions
of a devotional character. The author's position is that of a positive
but conservative Churchman, in the best sense Catholic. His style is
clear and simple."—*Pacific Churchman.*

"We gladly give our recommendation of "The Divine Liturgy"
in its historical aspect, and add that we can think of nothing equal to it
in trustworthiness and wide array of facts."—*The Christian Union.*

"The Catholic mindedness, historical accuracy, and wise caution,
of Canon Luckock is nowhere more apparent than in this important
work. It will prove a most valuable help to the parochial clergy in the
regular instruction of communicant classes, a design which he had in
view in its preparation. The book is in fifty portions, so that in the
case of monthly instruction, it would extend as a manual of aid for a
period of four years."—*Living Church.*

BY THE SAME AUTHOR.

AFTER DEATH. An Examination of the Testimony of the
Primitive Times respecting the state of the Faithful Departed and
their Relationship to the Living. Fifth edition, revised. 12mo,
cloth. $1.50.

STUDIES IN THE HISTORY OF THE PRAYER BOOK.
With Appendices. Second edition. 12mo, cloth, $1.50.

FOOTPRINTS OF THE SON OF MAN, as traced by
St. Mark. Being eighty portions for private study, family reading
and instruction in Church. With an Introduction by the Lord
Bishop of Ely. New and cheaper edition, complete in one volume.
12mo, cloth, $1.75.

THE BISHOPS IN THE TOWER. A Record of Stirring
Events affecting the Church and Non-conformists from the Restoration to the Rebellion. 12mo, cloth, $1.50.

THOMAS WHITTAKER,

2 AND 3 BIBLE HOUSE, NEW YORK.

CANON ROW'S NEW BOOK.

CHRISTIAN THEISM.

A Brief and Popular Survey of the Evidences upon which it rests, and the Objections urged against it considered and refuted. By C. A. Row, M.A. Small 8vo, cloth, $1.75.

"Prebendary Row has attained high repute by his previous publications, but we doubt if he has written anything more likely to be useful than the present volume, in which he sets forth in a popular form and with clearness and force of style the chief reasons on which Christian theistic belief is founded. It is avowedly a popular argument, adapted to the needs of the multitude of people who justly complain that many excellent treatises dealing with the subject are 'over their heads.' It also claims to be a comprehensive survey of the whole question as it is now debated, and grapples with current difficulties and objections which, if they do not subvert the faith of many, do nevertheless prevail with some, and cause widespread disquiet and perplexity."
— *The Standard of the Cross.*

"Among all the works of Prebendary Row in the general line of Apologetics of Christian belief, and they are many, this will be the most prominent in the list, the most thoroughly and lastingly useful."
— *The Living Church.*

BY THE SAME AUTHOR.

REASONS FOR BELIEVING IN CHRISTIANITY. Addressed to busy people. 12mo, cloth, gilt top, 75 cents.

CHRISTIAN EVIDENCE VIEWED IN RELATION TO MODERN THOUGHT. Bampton Lectures for 1877. Fourth Edition. 8vo, cloth, $3.75.

A MANUAL OF CHRISTIAN EVIDENCES. 16mo, cloth, 75 cents.

FUTURE RETRIBUTION, VIEWED IN THE LIGHT OF REASON AND REVELATION. 8vo, cloth, $2.50.

THOMAS WHITTAKER,

2 AND 3 BIBLE HOUSE, NEW YORK.

REASON AND AUTHORITY IN RELIGION.

By J. MACBRIDE STERRETT, D.D., Professor of Ethics and Apologetics in Seabury Divinity School. Author of " Studies in Hegel's Philosophy of Religion." 12mo, cloth, $1.00.

Press Notices :

"A philosophical, keen and clever mind has given us in brief form, one of the most satisfactory studies upon these important topics that we ever tried."—*The Living Church.*

"A thoughtful and prudent balancing of the arguments and considerations that are apt to be uppermost in the speculations of open and inquiring minds in these times."—*The Independent.*

" I have never seen so much thought put into so narrow limits or so clearly and concisely stated."—*Rev. E. A. Warriner.*

" This book is a vigorous essay on the burning question regarding the seat of authority in religion. It is marked throughout by candor, vigor and incisiveness of thought and will repay a careful reading."—*The New Englander and Yale Review.*

" The author of this volume has already become favorably known to all thinkers upon such themes by his 'Studies in Hegel's Philosophy of Religion.' His honesty and fairness, his clearness of statement, and the vigor of his style unite to form a model in this method of discussion. It is a book compelling close thought, and filled with stimulating, healthful, interesting work for good thinkers or those who would become such."—*Public Opinion.*

" He writes as a scholar and a philosopher, and his discussion in the present work is timely and fitted to restrain adventurous minds from dangerous extremes."—*The Interior.*

THOMAS WHITTAKER,

PUBLISHER,

2 & 3 BIBLE HOUSE, NEW YORK.

CHRIST IN THE NEW TESTAMENT.

By THOMAS A. TIDBALL, D.D., Rector of St. Paul's
Church, Camden, N. J. With an Introduction by
S. D. McConnell, D.D. 12mo, cloth, $1.25.

"We notice on nearly every page the extensive reading of its
author and the judicial mind, which not only attempts but proves the
authenticity of the New Testament Books and their drift and purpose.
The first lecture is to us the most striking ; but all show learning and
the Christian spirit. We know of no work which in like compass in-
troduces so well the various books of the New Testament."—*The
Southern Churchman.*

"The volume is scholarly, reverent, gracefully written, spiritual in
tone ; a really good book that makes one better as it clears his mind
and lifts his heart."—*Every Thursday.*

"Dr. Tidball's style is felicitous for the lecture room, exact in ex-
pression, careful in the right presentation and due rounding of his facts,
and agreeably free from any pedantries of learning."—*Living Church.*

"It can stand on its own merits as a popular presentation of a subject of perennial freshness."—*The Critic.*

"While there is little that is directly polemic in these pages, this
purpose is largely attained, and that in the best possible manner. To
each of the writers of the New Testament the question is virtually addressed, ' What think ye of Christ ? ' and the answer is of great apologetic value. Through all the obvious differences of style and treatment
can be seen the one Lord and Saviour, and these apparent variations
serve only to give a clearer outline of the life and work of the Great
Exemplar."—*Churchman.*

"The introductory chapter to this volume, consisting of thirty
pages, is in substance very similar to the ' Introduction to the New
Testament ' as commonly found in good commentaries. It treats of the
origin and formation of the several books of their authors, of their
general scope, and of recent criticism. It also gives an excellent
definition of inspiration—the manner and measure of it. Then follow
nine other chapters in which the author gives a study of the whole New
Testament, in groups of books—the Synoptic Gospels, St. John's
Gospel, The Acts, the Pauline Epistles, etc., the main object being to
bring out their testimony to Christ as the Son of God and Saviour of
the World."—*Pacific Churchman.*

THOMAS WHITTAKER,
PUBLISHER,

2 & 3 BIBLE HOUSE HOUSE, - *NEW YORK.*

The Prayer=Book Reason Why.

A Book of Questions and Answers on the Doctrines, Usages, and History of the Church as suggested by the Liturgy. For Parochial and Sunday-school uses. By Rev. NELSON R. Boss, M.A. 16mo, paper covers, 20 cents, net.

The design of this book is three-fold. (1). To familiarize the reader with the Doctrines, History and Ritual of the Church, as they are suggested by the Offices ; (2). To bring out clearly and concisely those principles of Historic Christianity which distinguish the Episcopal Church from all other religious bodies ; (3). To furnish clear and concise answers to the popular objections so commonly raised against the Church by those not familiar with her ways.

Bishop Seymour says:

Whoever reads " The Prayer-Book Reason Why" will find it a treasury of useful information. I welcome it heartily. I believe its publication will be eminently useful and beneficial. It covers a great deal of ground and instructs as it goes forward.

The Rev. Dr. Samuel Buel, Emeritus Professor of Systematic Divinity in the General Theological Seminary, says :

The book is a desideratum which I wonder has not been disclosed before. That it is eminently fitted to do great good I cannot doubt, and that it will be a most useful book in the hands of the pastors of the Church I firmly believe. Throughout the work the Church herself has spoken for the benefit of her children.

Bishop Littlejohn says :

To thousands of adult members of the Church, if the book could only be placed in their hands, it would be a valuable help to clear and sound thinking on the very important subjects of which it treats.

Mr. Whittaker, the Publisher, says :

In almost every case where I send out a sample copy of " The Prayer-Book Reason Why," more copies are immediately ordered.

PUBLISHED BY

THOS. WHITTAKER, 2 and 3 Bible House New York,

And For Sale by all Church Booksellers.

THE CHIEF THINGS;
OR, CHURCH DOCTRINE FOR THE PEOPLE.
By REV. A. W. SNYDER.

12mo, *Cloth binding*, $1.00. *Paper covers.* 50 Cents.

THOMAS WHITTAKER,
2 and 3 Bible House, **NEW YORK.**

www.ingramcontent.com/pod-product-compliance
Lightning Source LLC
Chambersburg PA
CBHW030627030726
47497CB00006B/1663